"Has anyo ... **that you** ta ... **too much.**

D0790522

Meg swallowed. "Of course not."

"Well, then no one has been honest with you. You talk entirely too much."

Boldly she took a step toward Gareth and pointed one dainty finger in his direction. "That was rather boorish of you. No one has ever told me that because everyone finds me, and what I have to say, pleasant and interesting. What gives you the right to stand there and accuse me . . ." She felt herself sputtering for words. "Can you not be kind?"

"Madam, so far this evening you have called me unfriendly, insufferable, and boorish, and you want to question my kindness? I'm trying my damnedest to get us out of here so that you might lay your pretty head on a nice pillow tonight. But I find that I simply cannot concentrate while you are talking. All I want is some peace and quiet. Peace and quiet," he repeated with a flash of resignation. Then he closed the distance between them and grabbed her by the shoulders. Without another word, he leaned in and kissed her.

Other AVON ROMANCES

BE MINE TONIGHT *by Kathryn Smith*
FROM LONDON WITH LOVE *by Jenna Petersen*
NO MAN'S BRIDE *by Shana Galen*
ONCE UPON A WEDDING NIGHT *by Sophie Jordan*
THE PERFECT SEDUCTION *by Margo Maguire*
SINS OF MIDNIGHT *by Kimberly Logan*
TAKEN BY STORM *by Donna Fletcher*

Coming Soon

THE EARL OF HER DREAMS *by Anne Mallory*
TOO GREAT A TEMPTATION *by Alexandra Benedict*

And Don't Miss These
ROMANTIC TREASURES
from Avon Books

HIS MISTRESS BY MORNING *by Elizabeth Boyle*
HOW TO SEDUCE A DUKE *by Kathryn Caskie*
TEMPTING THE WOLF *by Lois Greiman*

ATTENTION: ORGANIZATIONS AND CORPORATIONS
Most Avon Books paperbacks are available at special quantity discounts for bulk purchases for sales promotions, premiums, or fund-raising. For information, please call or write:

Special Markets Department, HarperCollins Publishers, Inc., 10 East 53rd Street, New York, N.Y. 10022–5299.
Telephone: (212) 207–7528.   Fax: (212) 207-7222.

ROBYN DeHart

Deliciously Wicked

AVON BOOKS

An Imprint of HarperCollinsPublishers

This is a work of fiction. Names, characters, places, and incidents are products of the author's imagination or are used fictitiously and are not to be construed as real. Any resemblance to actual events, locales, organizations, or persons, living or dead, is entirely coincidental.

AVON BOOKS
An Imprint of HarperCollins*Publishers*
10 East 53rd Street
New York, New York 10022-5299

Copyright © 2006 by Robyn DeHart
ISBN-13: 978-0-06-112752-6
ISBN-10: 0-06-112752-3
www.avonromance.com

All rights reserved. No part of this book may be used or reproduced in any manner whatsoever without written permission, except in the case of brief quotations embodied in critical articles and reviews. For information address Avon Books, an Imprint of HarperCollins Publishers.

First Avon Books paperback printing: October 2006

Avon Trademark Reg. U.S. Pat. Off. and in Other Countries, Marca Registrada, Hecho en U.S.A.
HarperCollins® is a registered trademark of HarperCollins Publishers Inc.

Printed in the U.S.A.

10 9 8 7 6 5 4 3 2 1

If you purchased this book without a cover, you should be aware that this book is stolen property. It was reported as "unsold and destroyed" to the publisher, and neither the author nor the publisher has received any payment for this "stripped book."

Emily, my partner-in-crime and favorite lunch buddy. I don't know how I'd write without you, especially this book. But above and beyond that, you are the most giving person I've ever known. Words simply can't express my gratitude. Give that baby-bug a kiss for me.

And to my husband, Paul, you are my true hero and I love you.

Chapter 1

Piddington Confectionery
Outside London, 1892

Meg Piddington tried the heavy door one more time, to no avail. "It's locked." She leaned against the barrier and eyed her fellow captive.

"I told you that already," he said, the slight hint of an Irish brogue tickling at her ears. He leaned against a table stacked with small boxes.

"Well, how are we to open it?" she asked.

"I'm thinking." He pinched the bridge of his nose. "If you would but keep your mouth shut, I might think of something useful."

She shot him an exasperated look, which he didn't even notice.

Shut her mouth, indeed.

She took the opportunity of silence to study him as

he propelled himself away from the table and began to
move about the room. Gareth Mandeville had been in
her father's employ for only a handful of weeks. And
he'd been in London only a few weeks longer than that,
or so she'd been told. At the moment he crouched and
leaned and moved things about, presumably trying to
locate a way out of the locked storeroom.

Tall and undeniably handsome, he had attracted
Meg's notice the moment she'd seen him in her father's
confectionery. Something about him looked as if he'd
feel more comfortable in a ballroom than in a factory.
The way he carried himself, or perhaps it was the refinement of his well-sculpted features.

Light from an oil lamp flickered across his face as
he turned to examine a shelf. He had the sort of eyes,
thickly lashed and intense, that could see into a
person—into the tiny, hidden places that housed
dreams. She'd never stood so close as to determine
their exact shade, but she pegged them for an intoxicating brown.

He turned and examined another stack of boxes.
No matter what time of day she'd seen him, he always
had a shadow of stubble outlining his mouth and along
his chin. She knew it would feel devilishly prickly to
the touch. His mouth, even though set in a frown, was
enticing. Full-lipped and perfectly crafted, it was
nearly mesmerizing to look at.

Oh, good heavens, she was becoming quite dramatic.

"How the bloody hell did you get locked up in here
with me in the first place?" he muttered.

Attractive, but surly. Some women might find that

mixture appealing, but Meg suspected that after a while it would begin to lose its effect. She frowned at him. "What is that supposed to mean?" she asked.

His glance trailed across her, taking his sweet time as his eyes slid down her body. She shivered in response.

"It means, what are you doing here?" he asked. "It's well past dark. What are you doing out at night all alone? Do you not require a chaperone or something?"

She thought she detected a slight smile. He was baiting her. "I do not need a keeper, if that is what you're implying. I can very well take care of myself, thank you very much." Perhaps he didn't know who she was. "My father owns this factory; I have every right to be here."

"I know who you are."

Then again, perhaps he did. "Well, what are *you* doing here this time of night?" She planted her feet and crossed her arms over her chest. She wasn't certain, but she believed that it wasn't customary for employees to be here after hours.

He shrugged. "I was working late," he said, then turned away from her to examine a tower of boxes stacked on the floor.

Evidently she was wrong. Not only did she not know if it was legitimate for employees to work late, she still hadn't figured out all the different rooms. This part of the factory housed the main divisions; her father's office overlooked the grinding and mixing floor. There was still much to learn.

A voice inside her insisted that she should probably be alarmed. It was late. Not the middle of the night, but still past dark, and she was alone in a factory with a strange man. Well, not precisely strange in the odd or peculiar sense, but more so in the never-spoken-to-him-until-today sense. For all she knew, Gareth was a ravager of innocents. She barely suppressed a shiver.

Then she sighed with resignation. No, her father would never have sent her out if he believed she might be in danger, she reminded herself. She was being silly and allowing her imagination to wander to one of the many adventure stories she'd read in the past. Where ladies wound up in all sorts of trouble.

Since her papa had broken his leg, he'd had to do business from Piddington Hall. Tonight he'd sent her to the factory to retrieve last quarter's ledger book for a meeting with his factory director the following morning. But before she made it into her father's office, she heard a noise and came in to investigate. Then the door had shut behind her. And locked.

She'd found the source of the noise. It was Gareth digging through his locker. And here they were, half an hour later, locked in with no discernible route of escape. She surveyed the room. Lockers neatly lined one side of the room. These were used by the employees to store any belongings they brought with them to work, as the men were using this storeroom until their dressing room was completed. The other side of the room housed supplies: shelves and tables piled with smaller boxes, and larger boxes stacked into towers on the floor.

She walked closer to him and peeked over his shoulder to better view what he was examining.

"What did you find?" she asked without moving away from him.

He straightened, causing his back to brush against

her arm. Stepping away, he turned to face her. "Boxes," he said flatly.

"I can see that." She frowned. "You're not terribly friendly, are you?"

A slight grin slid onto his face. "No, I don't suppose I am."

He was peevish, rude, and uncivilized. There was simply no reason for him to be irritated with her. It was not her fault they were locked in here together. Meg knew that the life of factory workers was rough. It was why her father's employees were so loyal and why everyone in London wanted to work for him. They were treated kindly, paid well, and even provided with affordable living quarters on the factory grounds. The factory was outside London, where the air was cleaner. Purer air resulted in more refined cocoa. Fewer health complaints from the employees as well. But perhaps Gareth's past employment had not been so pleasant. Perhaps that was why he was so surly.

Because it couldn't possibly have anything to do with her. She'd always gotten on well with everyone. There was no discernible reason that this man should be any different. She didn't like to consider that she might not be quite so put out by his poor humor if he wasn't so handsome.

Still, she desperately wanted to see if she could make him smile or even laugh. Even those with poorly developed humor laughed on occasion. And she wanted to get close enough so she could decipher the precise shade of his eyes. Shameful as it was to admit, she wanted to brush her lips against his just to see if they would be as soft as they looked.

Gracious, what was the matter with her? She'd never been accused of being level-headed, quite the contrary, most thought her impulsive, but she'd never wanted to kiss a man she scarcely knew.

Hoping to distract herself from the temptation, she opened her mouth to ask him a question, but he held up his hand.

"Now is not the time for idle chitchat. We need to find a way out of here. We cannot stay in here locked together all night long. So if you're not going to help, find somewhere to sit. And be quiet." He waved his hand in front of him. "You rattle my concentration with all of that chatter."

She stood back for a moment and watched him return to his investigation of the boxes. "I don't believe you're going to find anything useful back there." She resisted the urge to mock his irritated tone.

He pinched the bridge of his nose. "I suppose you're going to tell me that you've grown up in this factory and you know where everything is."

"Actually no, we only moved to this location last year." If they were keeping score in this verbal battle they were engaged in, that would have earned her a point. "What precisely are you looking for beneath those boxes? A trap door? Because I don't think you'll find one." There, she was being helpful. Two more points.

"It's not the floor I'm trying to get to. It's the opposite wall. There could be a door."

He had her there. Perhaps there *was* a door. She actually hadn't been in this particular storeroom very often. And every time she'd been in here, that side of the room had been laden with boxes. You could scarcely see the opposite wall. Either shelves or boxes climbed all the way up to the ceiling. For all she knew there was a circus hiding behind all the supplies.

Gareth did not wait for any additional commentary from her. He turned back to the boxes and began shifting some of them aside.

He made it impossible for her to be even remotely flirtatious, not that she was giving it great effort. Nor should that have been her goal for this evening. Nonetheless, he had not looked at her long enough for her to offer him a coy glance beneath her lashes. No, he simply took all the fun out of the situation with his surly mood. She nudged a box with her toe. "What is in all of these?" she asked.

He looked behind him to the one she'd just moved. "Boxes," he muttered.

She frowned. "Pardon?"

"That group there beside you are all filled with decorative chocolate boxes. Those were a special order."

"Oh yes, Lady Glenworthy's order."

He raised his eyebrows.

"I keep abreast of the goings-on at the factory. But why are they in this storeroom?" One more point; she might be winning this imaginary competition.

"I don't know. Best I can tell, they're using this room for a little of everything right now."

"The rest of the enlargement should be completed soon," she said. She peeked into the container to see the decorative chocolate boxes. "Such a lovely idea. Don't you agree?"

He ignored her.

He was trying her hospitality. He went beyond simply not being friendly. He was completely insufferable, if she was honest.

Perhaps no one had ever told him. "You are an insufferable man," she said. There, she'd done her duty and notified him.

But rather than turn to her and apologize, he kept his back to her and chuckled.

That was not how she'd intended to make him laugh. "I was not being funny," she said.

"Yes, you were." He turned to face her then. Walking toward her, he wiped his hands on his pants leg, drawing her attention to his long legs. "Has anyone ever told you that you talk too much?"

She swallowed. "Of course not."

"Well, then no one has been honest with you. You talk entirely too much." He inched closer still. "So much so that someone ought to bind your mouth simply to give the world some peace and quiet for a few hours a day."

Boldly she took a step toward him and pointed one dainty finger in his direction. "That was rather boorish of you. No one has ever told me that because everyone finds me, and what I have to say, pleasant and interesting. What gives you the right to stand there and accuse me . . ." She felt herself sputtering for words. "Can you not be kind?"

"Madam, so far this evening you have called me unfriendly, insufferable, and boorish, and you want to question my kindness? I'm trying my damnedest to get us out of here so that you might lay your pretty head on a nice pillow tonight. But I find that I simply cannot concentrate while you are talking. All I want is some peace and quiet. Peace and quiet," he repeated with a flash of resignation. Then he closed the distance between them and grabbed her by the shoulders. Without another word, he leaned in and kissed her.

She'd been forming a saucy retort, but the thoughts flew out of Meg's head as Gareth's soft lips slanted across hers. His kiss, unlike his words, was gentle and teasing. His tongue made no great assault of her mouth, but rather coaxed her lips and teeth. And then, as abruptly as the kiss began, it ended.

She stood there staring at him, not completely certain if, when he released her, she would slide to the floor. He stepped away from her and went back to moving the boxes. Luckily the kiss hadn't affected her balance as much as she anticipated, because she was still standing.

With one kiss he'd won their little competition, because there was nothing she could do to recover from that. But how could he walk away and say nothing of the kiss? Continue working as if nothing at all had occurred? As if their lips had not created sparks and tiny explosions within his flesh as they had her own.

She frowned. Of all the audacious things to do. She marched over to him and prepared to tell him precisely how she felt. If she had been unkind it was most definitely his fault. He seemed to spur her to unkindness.

"There. This is it," he declared.

She swallowed her words. "What is *it*?" she asked.

"A window. Up there." He pointed to a spot above one pile of boxes.

She peered up and did, in fact, spot the window. But it was terribly small. "It's tiny."

He nodded. "True."

"Well, what good will it do us?"

He leveled his gaze on her. "You are going to have to climb through that window and walk around to the door and let me out."

She eyed the window a second time. He was delusional. "How do you suppose I do that? The window is far too narrow."

"No, it is big enough for you to fit through. With a few adjustments." He looked from her to the window. "Take off your dress," he said simply.

She felt her eyes go round and her cheeks warm. "Are you mad? I cannot take off my dress."

"It's either that, or we're locked in here all night. I am too large to fit through that window, else I'd crawl up there myself. But you are the perfect size." He motioned to her. "Without all that fluff attached to you. I don't know about you, but I'm hungry."

Her stomach betrayed her and growled in agreement. He smirked. He was right; they could not stay in here all evening. But it was immensely annoying that he was right.

Meg didn't know if she was angrier because he wanted her to save them or because he hadn't acknowledged their kiss. It was ridiculous. And now he wanted her to remove her dress. Not so that he might ravish her, she couldn't help but notice, but so he could be relieved of her company. Clearly she did not actually wish to be ravished.

The window was far too narrow for the breadth of her dress with her puffed sleeves and bustle. She could clearly see that. And she could also see that without the excess material, she would be able to squeeze through. If they were to escape before morning, she would need to climb out of the window. Only one problem. She could not get out of the dress on her own. The buttons went from her neck to her waist. Earlier today, it had taken her maid a good five minutes to button them. She'd have to be some sort of contortionist to reach them all. Narrowing her eyes at him, she asked, "Can you behave as a gentleman would?"

"That all depends."

"Either you be a gentleman and assist me, or we shall stay in here all night. I'm certain I can make myself quite comfortable." A complete fabrication. In an hour or less, she'd be longing for her bed.

"What do you need help with?" he asked.

"I cannot get out of my dress without assistance." She turned her back to him, but looked over her shoulder to see him. "Too many buttons. You'll need to unbutton them quickly, then turn the other way."

He took a step toward her and smiled.

The white of his teeth looked even more so against his tanned skin. Warnings should have sounded in her head. When a man looked at a woman in such a manner, the woman should be concerned for the security of her virtue. But Meg felt no concern, only curiosity and perhaps a tad of hopefulness as to whether he would kiss her again.

Her body reacted to the memory of his lips. She swallowed.

"I've never had a lady ask me to undress her quickly," he said.

She put her hand to her throat. "Well, this isn't that sort of request." Her voice was weak.

He chuckled.

The sound caressed her ears, and she found herself eager to hear it again regardless of the current situation.

She closed her eyes because, while she might have enjoyed the stolen kiss and might fancy a harmless threat to her virtue, she wasn't actually prepared for him to steal anything else. She felt his warm breath behind her, and shivers scattered across her body. While she did not feel his fingers, she knew he was working the buttons as her dress was loosening.

Gracious. She felt her face flame. She'd never before had anyone, save her maid, undress her. It was intensely intimate, and she didn't know what to feel or think about the matter. She suspected she should be horrified, but she knew that was not the feeling coursing through her at the moment.

"There," he said. He stepped away from her. Without his body standing that close to her, she could now feel a slight breeze brush over her neck and across her back.

She faced him, then twirled her finger around to tell him to turn away, but he did not catch her hint. "Do you mind?"

He crossed his arms over his chest and smiled. "Not at all. I might fancy a show, actually."

Her face burned. She'd heard of such shows, and she certainly would not perform one now. "That's not what I meant," she said hotly. "Please avert your eyes."

He turned away from her, but clearly found the situation far more amusing than was necessary.

"I'll have you know that I do not find any humor in this situation."

He angled to look at her from over his shoulder. "Duly noted."

She quickly slipped the dress from her shoulders and then held it up in front of her to block his view. "I'm finished," she said.

He turned, then cleared his throat. He stood a moment longer simply watching her before closing the distance between them. Perhaps he would kiss her again. She should move away from him. Instead of a second kiss, Gareth reached over and snatched the dress from her hands. "To ensure you come back and let me out."

She swallowed a scream. No need to be overly dramatic. Standing in front of him in nothing more than her combination garment and petticoat was enough to cover her body in the heat of a blush. More than likely it already had, but she dared not look down to see if pink shaded her skin. Meg took a deep breath and tried to relax. Aside from the lack of sleeves and the fabric difference, it was not too different from a swimming costume. He could not see all that much flesh. She was a grown woman; she could take this situation in stride. To prove that to him, and to herself, she tilted her chin up a notch, then walked over to stand beneath the window.

"Shall I fly up to that window, or are you going to give me a boost?" She gave him a mocking smile.

He dropped her dress on a table, then came to stand behind her. Without a word, he wrapped his hands around her waist and hoisted her up. She grabbed onto the windowsill, then with a great amount of effort popped the window open. He moved his hands to her bottom and gave her a shove enabling her to climb through. She scarcely had time to feel embarrassed by the touch, as the encounter had been so brief that she had not even been able to tell if his fingers were warm.

From the window, she jumped into a bush, tearing

her petticoat and scraping her arm and face. *Brilliant.* When she finally made it home tonight, everyone would assume she'd been assaulted.

She took a quick look around the grounds to ensure no one was around, then made her way back into the factory and opened up the storage room door.

Gareth strolled out and dropped her dress at her feet. He gave her a once-over and then walked off.

"Where is my thank-you?" she called out to his back.

But he didn't stop walking.

She grabbed her dress, then rushed to meet him. "Very well," she said loudly. "I'm certain, I'll make it home alone, in the dark, completely unharmed."

He stopped, and his shoulders sagged. He turned slowly. "Don't you live right over there?" He pointed to the manor up on the hill.

"Yes."

He walked back to her. "Let us be off then. I have delayed my supper so long now, I'll skip it for sleep." He passed her and started for the slope that led up to Piddington Hall.

She quickly locked the factory door, then tossed her dress over her head, leaving the fabric to gape open. It took considerable effort on her part to match his pace as she had significantly shorter legs. At this rate, she'd be panting like a horse before they crested the hill.

"Could you slow down a little," she asked.

Surprisingly enough, he did.

"Tell me, Miss Piddington, are you always this much trouble?"

She smiled. "Yes, I believe I am."

They spent the remainder of the walk in silence. The

occasional hoot of an owl and their shoes treading upon the grass were the only sounds. Then the noise changed to crunching rocks as they stepped onto the driveway.

"In the future," he said, "if you continue to go out at night, and you find yourself in questionable situations, you might want to consider a chaperone." And with that he left her on the stairs to her house and headed toward the employee boarding rooms.

The man was an absolute cad.

Chapter 2

Meg was still frowning when she crept into her bedroom. Ordinarily she would awaken her maid, Ellen, to help her out of her dress, but seeing as she didn't need her services tonight she would let the woman sleep. Thankfully no one had awoken upon her entrance, so she hadn't had to come up with a story for her state of undress. She shrugged out of her dress and dumped it on the floor. Standing in front of the mirror, she took a good look at herself. Her petticoat was torn, and the scratches on her face and arm stung, but there was no permanent damage to anything. But neither the tears nor the scratches was the source of her irritability.

No, that came in the form of a tall, arrogant Irishman who, for all intents and purposes, seemed to hate her for no good reason at all. But the most annoying part of the entire ordeal was that, despite his ill temper, she was rather intrigued by him. She sat at her dressing table and swiftly unbraided her hair.

Why would a man be nasty to her, kiss her, and then offer advice about her safety? For that matter, why had he kissed her at all? He was a complete paradox. There was something about him, though. Something she couldn't quite put her finger on, but nonetheless she couldn't *not* explore it. She was too curious by nature to ignore a man with such contradictions.

Samson, her great black tom, jumped onto her dressing table demanding attention. Meg ran her hand over his lush fur, and his rhythmic purr filled the room.

He watched her through sleepy green eyes, then decided he'd had enough caressing. He moved to the bed and curled up with the already sleeping Bandit. Evidently they were not overly concerned that their mistress had come home late. Traitors.

The fact that Mr. Mandeville could get her riled into a less than pleasant mood was intriguing as well. Meg took great pride in the fact that she was nearly always agreeable, if not cheerful. In a world where people walked around looking as if they smelled something rotten, she had always tried to see the sunnier side. But tonight she was feeling almost ill-tempered.

He hadn't liked her, but he had kissed her. And then he had seen her practically nude. The kiss wasn't merely a friendly sort of kiss, but rather the sort that devilish men stole from maidens in the dark of the night. She ran the brush through her hair. Try as she might, she could not deny the simple fact that she'd enjoyed it. Immensely.

She was being foolish. The fellow might be intriguing, but there was no sane reason she should set her cap for him. Not only did he work for her father, but she knew nothing about him.

Meg finished undressing and examined the damage done to the silk petticoat. No doubt her friend Charlotte, who was rather skilled with a needle and thread, could fix it. Longing for a hot bath to soothe muscles and calm her nerves, Meg resigned herself to the basin so she wouldn't wake the servants at this hour.

Then it occurred to her that after the evening's trying ordeal, she had not even retrieved the ledger book that her father had sent her after. She would have to return to the factory tomorrow. Her poor papa was nearly losing his mind being laid up. The riding accident had happened a few weeks earlier, and he'd been confined to his bed ever since. The good thing was, the doctor didn't believe it was a bad break and expected it to heal rather quickly.

When it became clear he couldn't return to work immediately, she had assured him she would tend to the factory in his absence. He'd humored her and said yes, but she knew he wasn't expecting her to actually do work. This could be the perfect opportunity for her to prove to him she has the necessary skills to care for the factory when he passed on. As it stood now, upon his death the factory would no longer be a personal business and instead would become a public company. Her father pretended not to be bothered by such a thing, but Meg knew different. He didn't want Piddington Confectionery to belong to anyone else.

It wasn't that he'd prefer her to be a male, but having a daughter as his only heir weighed on him. Meg couldn't ask for a more doting father, but that was part of the problem. He still saw her as a little girl and didn't want to burden her with the strain of a growing business.

She'd purchased new dresses befitting a woman of business and she'd eagerly agreed to assist in any way. Regrettably she had not been successful with the one task he'd sent her on, but she would not dwell on the evening's failure. Tomorrow she would retrieve all that was necessary.

The great concern was how to handle the situation with Mr. Mandeville. Inevitably she'd run into him on a few more occasions. If they happened to interact, she could persuade him to be civil. Perhaps he was shy, and it merely took him a bit longer to warm up to people than it did with her.

She doubted that was true, but everyone could learn to be pleasant. And to prove it, she would endeavor to be kind to him, regardless of how he baited her.

What the hell had he been thinking? Gareth flopped onto his bed and stared at the ceiling. The moonlight cast shadows against the wall that resembled fleshless fingers more than the branches from the ash tree outside the window.

He wouldn't have gotten himself into this mess had he not been doing twice the workload today, which caused his shift to run over. But Jamie, the man who worked at the next station, had looked so defeated when he'd come to work that morning. A man should get to be by his wife's side while she gave birth, so Gareth had volunteered to work Jamie's load that day and let the man go back home.

His mind was too active to fall asleep. Too many

thoughts about the fair Miss Piddington. Other men might have been able to avoid provoking her. Avoid speaking to her, let alone teasing her.

Apparently he was not other men. Not only had he been unable to avoid those behaviors, he'd kissed her. He still couldn't believe it. He wasn't in the habit of kissing women he did not know. Hell, he wasn't in the habit of kissing women he did know. But he'd thought that if he could kiss her once, the desire to do so would wane and he'd be able to concentrate on freeing them from their storeroom prison.

She wouldn't stop talking, and her sweet voice had been distracting. Her beauty hadn't helped matters. She was all inquisitive green eyes and blazing red curls. All feminine curves and clean lace. Then when he'd gotten close to her, she smelled so clean and fresh and feminine that one look at her mouth and he couldn't resist the temptation.

Blast it, how tempting it had been. He still could feel her soft, wet mouth. He groaned and rolled onto his side, ignoring the hint of arousal building. Clearly that one kiss hadn't sated his appetite.

The last thing he needed was to allow himself indulgences that would distract him from his main purpose. He'd finally found a factory where he felt he could move up the ranks. Shortly after he'd been hired, it had been announced that in the months to come they'd be opening some staff positions. These would be managerial, administrative duties, something he felt he could excel at. He needed to make a good impression at the factory so that when they began hiring for the staff positions, he would make his intentions known.

Precisely the reason Gareth didn't need a woman

diverting him from his plan, especially the daughter of the factory's owner. In the future, he would ignore Meg Piddington and hope fate would be kind to keep them apart.

The following morning, Meg knocked on her father's door.

"Come in," he said loudly.

She stepped inside. "Father, I apologize, I completely forgot to retrieve that ledger you wanted, but I will stop by the factory after my meeting today."

Her father lay propped on a pile of pillows, his silk dressing gown covering his tall, lean frame. She'd never seen him so helpless before; usually he was the pinnacle of health. His valet was taking good care of him, though, as his soft white hair looked newly washed and combed.

It was then that she saw Mr. Sanders, her father's factory director. "Many apologies, I didn't realize you were already having your own meeting," she said.

"Not to worry dear, this is your house too," her father said. "Sanders here was about to give me a rundown of the financials."

She winced. "And you don't have your ledger. I am really sorry, Papa. I can go fetch it now."

"No, no, we'll manage with the information we have, Meggie." Her father nodded.

She sighed. He would always see her as a child.

"Do not fret, Miss Piddington, I have other information we can discuss today." Henry Sanders wasn't an overly tall man and his thin stature always left Meg wondering if the man ever ate. He had a kind face with warm eyes and a ready smile. "We'll look at last quarter's earnings once you have delivered the ledger to him," Mr. Sanders said with a smile.

"He's absolutely right," her father said. "You run along and tell those girls I bid them hello."

She nodded in agreement. "Thank you, as always, Mr. Sanders, for being so well prepared. We are quite fortunate to have you." She made a mental note to keep Mr. Sanders employed when she retained control of the factory. He would be invaluable.

"If I might be so bold, he is quite lucky to have you for a daughter. And I must say you look lovely this morning," he said, although his voice sounded far from bold.

"Thank you, sir, you are too kind." She ran over and placed a kiss on her father's cheek. "I must be off to my meeting."

"Stay out of trouble, dear girl," her father said with an indulgent twinkle in his eyes, as if he neither expected nor wished her to comply.

He knew her only too well.

Perhaps her propensity for trouble was part of the problem.

Yes, staying out of trouble is precisely what she ought to do. It was perhaps years of her foolish antics that prevented her father from seeing her in a different light. Well, she would remedy that today. No more trouble.

Despite her best efforts, Meg was late. Not an unusual occurrence for her, but she always strove to be prompt. Especially to her Ladies' Amateur Sleuth Society meetings. Amelia, the creator of the society, preferred to start the meetings on time.

Meg supposed it really did not matter all that much

since they were not an official society, merely four friends who had a fancy for mystery stories. Amelia had actually solved a real mystery not too long ago, and it was how she'd met her husband, Inspector Brindley. For the most part they looked for mysteries where they could, but because they were ladies of good breeding, it was a challenge. Yet still they met weekly to discuss potential cases.

Meg made her way into Amelia's town home, the usual location for their meetings, yet a different home now. Amelia and Colin had married, and shortly after that Amelia's father had remarried and moved in with his new wife, leaving the town home to his daughter and her husband.

She entered the parlor. It looked different as of late. Less blue and ornate. An improvement, in Meg's opinion. Now it was more welcoming.

"Ah, there you are," Charlotte Reed said. Charlotte was Meg's closest friend, and Meg longed to have a private conversation with her. She wanted to tell her about getting locked up in the storeroom and the kiss. And she wanted to let Charlotte know she was swearing off trouble for the time being. Since Charlotte was her usual partner in such activities, she deserved to know.

"Many apologies on my poor timing," Meg said. "I was assisting my father." She claimed her favorite seat.

"How is he faring?" Willow Mabson asked. "Mr. Piddington has always been so strong."

Meg shrugged. "He's doing as well as can be expected. His spirits are high, and he's alert and ornery as ever, but quite tired of lying about."

"Well, of course he is," Amelia said. "He's always been so energetic."

"He shall overcome this obstacle as he has all the others," Meg proclaimed.

"Indeed," Willow said.

"And you are taking marvelous care of the factory, are you not?" Charlotte asked.

"Papa and Mr. Sanders still manage most of the work from my father's room at the manor, but I am doing what I can," Meg said. "I did run into a bit of trouble last night, however." She never had been a great liar—even if the lie was more of a withholding than a blatant fib.

"What did you do this time?" Willow asked.

Quite like Willow to ask such a question. She didn't mean it in a nasty way, she was merely concerned, and they all had been friends for so long that no one ever got offended by Willow's zeal for propriety. She had always been so aware of the proper conduct, or lack thereof, in any situation. Whereas Meg had always sorely been remiss in that area.

Meg surveyed the room. Her friends sat with eager faces waiting to hear the details of her plight. Willow would be scandalized by Meg's brazen behavior. Charlotte seemed to thrive on anything daring, so she would find the events of last night enthralling. Amelia, ever the fair-minded, was a genuine friend to all and would manage to see the situation from every angle, but would secretly feel a catch in her chest from the adventure.

Her friends, all so different, but she needed each of them. Those differences, however, would demand she temper the details she would share.

"It was not my fault," she said cautiously, then gave a sheepish grin. "Well, not *entirely* my fault. My father wanted me to go and retrieve a ledger for him. So I went for the book. It was rather late, and I inadvertently got locked in a storeroom for a bit."

"Good heavens, are you all right?" Amelia asked.

"Certainly. Mr. Mandeville was able to locate a window, eventually, and he gave me a lift up. I crawled out and went around to unlock the door."

"You were locked in a storeroom with someone named Mr. Mandeville. At night?" Willow asked, clearly concerned.

Charlotte sat up. "Oh, not simply someone. This is Mr. Mandeville, the new employee she finds so devilishly handsome," she said with a big grin.

"Do you ever forget anything?" Meg asked. "I briefly mentioned him weeks ago and I don't believe I said anything other than he was handsome."

"Devilishly handsome, your words, Meg, not mine," Charlotte said with a smile.

"Oh, Meg," Willow said. She steepled her fingers, then placed her hands in her lap. "I know I do not need to tell you how irresponsible that was. Now you'll be ruined."

"I realize the implications, but it's not as if I intended to become locked in with him. It just happened," Meg said.

"She's not necessarily ruined," Amelia offered. "Does anyone know you were there?"

Meg shook her head. "I don't believe so."

"There you are, Willow, her secret is safe," Amelia said brightly.

"Ah." Charlotte held up one finger. "But is your virtue still intact?"

Willow frowned. "You don't have to look quite so

thrilled at the prospect, Charlotte. This is quite serious."

Meg glared at Charlotte, who was enjoying this far too much. She shouldn't tell them, but she really wanted to. A woman could die from the weight of such a secret. Irresponsible or not, it was a memorable kiss, and to not be able to share it was more than she could bear. Willow would be horrified, but the others would understand. But to be on the safe side, she'd leave out the part about her having to remove her dress.

"The majority of my virtue is well intact," Meg said.

"The majority? What, precisely, does that mean?" Charlotte asked.

"It means that I most certainly was not compromised." Perhaps that would provide her with a cushion. "But he did steal a kiss." She suppressed a giggle.

Charlotte came and sat next to her. "Honestly? I was only jesting with my question."

Meg nodded. She might have vowed to stay out of trouble in the future, but she could enjoy bits of it from the past.

"And?" Charlotte said, her tone rather impatient.

"And!" Willow shrieked. "He kissed you! Meg, this is dreadful."

"No, actually it was rather pleasant." Meg frowned. "Yet it was short, and he seemed rather annoyed afterward." She heard Amelia sigh. "Although he was bothered the entire time we were trapped. So I don't believe it was the kiss that had him in his foul mood. It was more than pleasant. It was sinful."

Charlotte fanned herself with her hand.

"His foul mood has absolutely nothing to do with the current crisis," Willow said. "What of your reputation?"

"If no one saw the two of them together and we are the only ones who know of the kiss, then Meg should be safe. With her reputation intact," Amelia said.

"What if he boasts of his conquest to his friends?" Willow asked.

"He doesn't have any friends," Meg said.

"He must have friends," Charlotte said.

"Not necessarily," Amelia said. "Colin only recently acquired friends."

"No, Colin had friends, he simply chose to ignore them," Charlotte argued.

"Well, that is true," Amelia acknowledged. "He and James Sterling have had a few visits lately. James is attempting to convince Colin to return to Scotland Yard."

"Must we speak of Detective Sterling?" Willow asked.

"You aren't still writing him letters, are you?" Meg asked. Willow had been sending anonymous letters to Detective Sterling for months. She saw great deficits in his methods of pursuing criminals and proceeded to notify him of those deficits at every opportunity.

"I have restrained myself from pointing out his incompetence for the past three weeks, I'll have you know." Willow pursed her lips. "But it has not been easy."

"Poor detective," Charlotte cooed.

Willow huffed and crossed her arms over her chest. "A bodger is what he is."

"If you met him, Willow, perhaps you would think better of him," Meg suggested. "Amelia should be able to arrange such an encounter."

"I'm not so certain about that," Amelia said. "He is much as she believes him to be. Arrogant and prefers to be in charge. That being said, he's a delightful man. Kind and thoughtful in his own way. And he's quite dashing."

"I care not a whit how dashing the detective is." But Willow's protests sounded a little too firm. As a blush tinged her cheeks, she hastily turned the direction of the conversation. "Let us get back to Meg's predicament with Mr. Mandeville," she said. She turned in Meg's direction. "Will you at least admit that he is the wrong sort of fellow with whom to associate?"

Society would agree with Willow. He was poor and she was wealthy, but to Meg that was inconsequential. Meg thought on that a moment before answering. "You're probably right, he is rather suspicious. Why, for instance, is he so annoyed? It is perplexing, and I admit, somewhat of an intrigue."

"You are hopeless," Willow said.

"Ah, but you still love me," Meg offered.

"That is debatable today." Willow turned her head, but Meg detected a slight hint of a smile creeping up.

"Perhaps he is unhappy," Amelia said.

"I beg your pardon?" Meg asked.

"Your fellow of intrigue," Amelia said. "Perhaps he is unhappy and that is why he is in a perpetual state of annoyance."

"Or perhaps you"—Charlotte poked her in the side—"are a dreadful kisser," she offered with a smile.

"No, that can't be it," Amelia shook her head. "He was annoyed before that, isn't that what you said, Meg?"

Meg nudged Charlotte in return. "Yes, that is what I said. I think he's hiding something. A dark secret."

"You read too many of those novels," Charlotte said.

Meg shrugged. "They're entertaining."

"Yes, but now you believe everyone to have a dark secret," Willow said.

"And many do. You cannot argue with that." Meg tucked a curl behind her ear.

Charlotte chuckled and Amelia nodded.

"What are you going to do about him taking liberties with you?" Willow asked.

If he were the sort to take liberties, he would have done so while her dress was off. The kiss had been a mistake, and likely not one Gareth was eager to repeat. Meg frowned. "I don't believe there is anything I can do now. Perhaps I should have boxed his ears, but I admit that did not occur to me at the time. It is not as if under normal circumstances I'm alone with men, giving them opportunity to steal kisses. In any case, it is unlikely that it will happen again."

"Take care that you aren't," her well-meaning friend advised. "He obviously cannot be trusted."

"Willow's right," Amelia said. "He sounds unpredictable. Unpredictable men can be trouble."

"I shall heed your warning." She wanted to move the meeting along, for all this advice and attention was getting tiresome. Her father still needed her to retrieve that ledger. There was a distinct possibility she would see Mr. Mandeville while she was there.

Would he say anything about their kiss or seeing her in her undergarments? Would he apologize? Probably not, on all accounts.

"Shall we move on to something that pertains a bit more to our meeting?" Amelia suggested.

Meg smiled in gratitude.

"The Jack of Hearts?" Charlotte asked.

The jewel thief was quickly becoming notorious. The Ladies' Amateur Sleuth Society had been following the articles in the newspapers about his escapades. Most recently, he walked directly into a Society event and blatantly stole from the guests, then disappeared before anyone could call for the authorities. His clever name was due to the jack of hearts playing card he left at every scene of the crime. They had investigated some shops that sold playing cards, but learned that most did not keep records of who made purchases. Meg had seen the latest mention of him in the *Times*, but had not yet read it.

"You saw the article as well?" Willow asked.

"Indeed," Amelia said. "His boldness never ceases to amaze me. Weren't you attending that soiree, Charlotte?"

Charlotte released a great breath. "Yes. But I saw nothing. Nothing." She tossed her arms up. "This is really trying my patience. What are the odds that I would be tending to some personal matters at the precise moment he snuck into the parlor and robbed every woman there? It's grossly unfair."

"I suppose you wish you were robbed as well," Willow asked, her voice shrill.

"Not robbed, necessarily, but I should have welcomed

the opportunity to catch a glimpse of him." Charlotte pouted.

"So we still have nothing new on him?" Meg asked.

"Only that Society is as enamored of him as Charlotte seems to be," Willow said, her voice laced with disdain. "Victims have even gone so far as to claim he's charming."

Charlotte huffed. "This is the fourth time he and I have crossed paths." She made an unpleasant face. "Or rather not crossed paths when we well should have."

"Some would argue you have rather good luck," Amelia said.

Charlotte snorted. "It is not as though I want to be robbed of my personal belongings; I merely want to meet him. I shall keep trying, but it is increasingly frustrating that I keep missing him. And to make matters worse, all of my recent activity in Society has given every clod the perfect opportunity to attempt to woo me."

"Marriage would be good for you," Willow said.

"Why is that?" Charlotte asked.

"Look how it has eased Amelia. She is far less reckless than she used to be. She is careful with her actions."

"That is because she nearly got killed," Charlotte said. "Twice." She held up two fingers to emphasize. "I have not had the slightest brush with danger." She signed dramatically. "Besides, I'm not ready to marry."

"There is nothing wrong with not wanting to marry," Meg said. "Many women feel that way, but sadly not all of us have the freedom to choose." She took a breath and squared her shoulders. "I don't want to marry either."

"I still think you'll change your mind. All of you," Amelia said. "If you remember correctly, there was a time I didn't want to marry."

"No, you always wanted to marry," Charlotte corrected. "You simply didn't believe you'd have any offers. And see, we were right."

"I do not have time for love," Meg said. "I want to pour all my energies into proving to my father that I can manage everything," Meg announced.

"He will see it," Amelia said. "Give him a little time."

Meg nodded. "So I will leave marriage to the rest of you. Charlotte obviously needs more help than I do."

Charlotte swatted Meg's arm. "Not funny."

Willow smiled. "It is, actually."

"Laugh all you like," Charlotte said. "Someday I shall not have to put up with pesky men."

"Are you are going to begin carrying a pistol?" Meg asked.

"Now that is a brilliant idea," Charlotte said with a smile. "No, I only meant that once I find him, the rest of the men will cease pestering me."

By "him" she meant her great love. Everyone knew Charlotte was waiting for a passionate love affair that would sweep her away.

Meg, on the other hand, was not looking for her great love. She'd seen firsthand the damage that could be brought about by something that powerful. So she was content to remain single and avoid loving at all costs.

Charlotte glanced at the mantel clock. "I'm afraid I must be leaving. I'm supposed to go shopping with Frannie this afternoon."

"I should be off as well," Meg said. A few hugs and

reminders to keep her distance from Mr. Mandeville, and she was on her way to the confectionery. Piddington's was only four miles outside town. During the short ride to the factory, Meg tried to think about the Jack of Hearts and how they might gather more clues to his identity, but in truth her heart wasn't in it.

Her attention was back at Piddington's. And try as she might, she could not guide her errant thoughts to ledgers, finances, or factory improvements. No, her mind kept creeping back to one surly, disreputable Irishman.

By the time Meg saw the red brick building rising in the distance, she was thoroughly fed up with herself. Obviously she would have to avoid Gareth at all costs. And he'd called her a distraction.

Chapter 3

       Gareth closed his eyes and bit down a curse.

"I asked you a question. Where are the boxes?"

Gareth leveled his eyes with the foreman's. "And I answered. I don't know," he said through his teeth.

Mr. Munden, the foreman in the grinding room, walked around him as if they stood in a boxing ring rather than a factory office. In the weeks since Mr. Piddington's accident, Munden had grown increasingly demanding. He now prowled around the office, with his ever-present cigar and his gravelly voice barking orders, as if he were the factory manager, not merely a foreman. "They were here last night, and this morning they are gone. And I know that you was here last night." His eyes narrowed. "Someone saw you. You just took it upon yourself that while you were in the factory alone, you'd just borrow something that don't belong to you."

Gareth shrugged, keeping his expression carefully

blank. Munden made no mention of Piddington's daughter being here with him, so perhaps he didn't know. That was a relief, because Gareth couldn't figure out how he was going to talk his way out of that. He hoped that whoever saw him last night had seen him on his way back from Piddington Hall and had not seen Miss Piddington walking next to him with her dress open in the back. No one would believe their story if they had to share all the details.

"This is a very serious matter. Lady Glenworthy is a shrew. If we have to go to her and tell her that her special chocolate boxes are missing, she'll have a fit. That will make me look bad. I can't allow that to happen."

"I don't know anything about the lady's boxes," Gareth said evenly. Not precisely the truth; he'd seen them last night. But in Gareth's experience, the less you pretended to know, the better off you'd be.

"I say you're lying," Munden snarled.

Gareth rolled his eyes. How did men such as this become foremen? He'd worked for a lot of half-wits in the years he'd been struggling to support himself. Munden was as bad as they came. Unscrupulous as well as incompetent. Gareth could do his job ten times over.

The situation was made only worse by the fact that they both knew Gareth could do Munden's job. And someday, if things went as planned, he'd be Munden's supervisor instead of the other way around. *If* this nonsense with the chocolate boxes was ever cleared up. And if he could avoid further encounters with Meg Piddington, especially those with passionate kisses.

"I say you know exactly where those boxes are." Munden glared at him through squinty eyes.

"I don't know what happened to them." He turned to leave. "Who do you want to see next?"

"What?" the man asked.

"The other workers. Who do you want to question next?"

The manager laughed. "There won't be no more questioning. I know you took them. You was the only one here last night. I'll find out. I'll find out what you did with them. And when that happens, I'll have you tossed in prison."

"Go to the devil," Gareth said and turned on his heels, nearly running straight into Miss Piddington. The day got better and better.

"Mr. Munden, what is going on in here?" she asked.

Munden's beady eyes rounded as much as possible. For a moment he seemed to flounder as he fumbled for a response. Then he puffed his chest out. "Mr. Mandeville here has stolen some property, and I was asking him questions about it." The foreman's voice dripped with disdain.

Gareth couldn't help but wonder if the fool knew who she was. Surely he wouldn't be so ignorant to be disrespectful to the owner's daughter.

She turned her gaze to Gareth. "Is this true?"

"The theft happened last night," he said evenly.

It took her a second before recognition lit her eyes. "Oh," she said brightly.

Bloody hell, but she was pretty. The blue confection she wore today magnified the contrast between her deep red hair and her fair skin. And the freckles splattered across her face formed the most intriguing patterns. Blast it, what was the matter with him? Now was not the time to notice her freckles. There was never a time to notice something so trivial.

"Did you ask Mr. Mandeville where he was last night?" she asked.

If possible, Munden's chest expanded even more. "I know he was here late last night. Someone saw him and reported it to me."

Meg's gaze darted to his in surprise, but she recovered quickly. "Well, then. I'm sure you must have inquired what he was doing at the factory so late." When Munden didn't answer immediately, she pressed him. "Surely you thought to ask such an important question."

The foreman shook his head and swallowed visibly. "No, Miss Piddington, I did not."

"Perhaps you should do so before you accuse him of stealing," she said, just a hint of smugness in her voice. Her eyes merely flickered in his direction.

Gareth listened to the exchange with building dread. As much as he enjoyed seeing Munden put in his place, especially by the impassioned Miss Piddington, Gareth could see where this was going. She fully intended to clear his name by providing him an alibi. She was going to compromise them.

Not in this lifetime, lass. Providing him with an alibi for last night would all but mandate that Gareth marry her. A fact she was obviously missing. Marrying her, or anyone else, was not an option because he was not the marrying sort.

"Very well," Munden said grudgingly. "Mr. Mandeville, what were you doing at the factory so late?" he said tightly.

Gareth looked straight at Meg and said, "I worked late, then after I retrieved my belongings from here, I went back to the boarding rooms. Alone." There was no reason to tell Munden that he'd worked late for Jamie. Having Munden on one person's back at a time was sufficient.

She opened her mouth to disagree, but he grabbed her arm. "I'm done with this discussion," Gareth said, then led Meg out of the office with him.

"Why did you lie to him?" she asked once they were out of earshot.

He glared at her. "Are you dense?"

She shook her head. "I don't believe so."

She was so literal. That was odd for women, who generally spoke in circles around their intentions. "Had I announced that we were locked alone together in a storeroom, it would have compromised your reputation."

Meg blinked in surprise. As if she hadn't expected someone like him to consider such a thing. "Well, I hardly think—"

"I am not looking for a wife, especially one obtained in such a manner. So I request you kindly keep last night to yourself." He turned to walk away from her.

She caught up with him. "I hadn't considered that," she admitted.

"Evidently." Proof that she was exactly the kind of trouble he thought she was. She was the kind of woman who acted and then considered later. Impetuous. Dangerous.

He kept walking, hoping Meg would let it go. However, she continued along beside him and he couldn't ignore the looks they garnered from the other workers.

Thankfully the grinding machines were noisy enough to mask their conversation.

"But what shall you do now? What was stolen?"

"Lady Glenworthy's chocolate boxes. And I shall do nothing save get back to work."

She grabbed his arm. Her brow crinkled. "Those boxes were still there when we left."

"I know that."

"But Mr. Munden believes you to be a thief."

"People have believed far worse of me. It is not my concern how people view me. I'm here to do my work, not make friends." Why did it annoy him that she seemed to believe the very best of him? He turned to walk away again, but stopped to tell her one more thing. "Miss Piddington, do not concern yourself with me or this situation."

"But I could have relieved you of this, had you allowed me to help."

"Well, we've discussed why that won't work."

"Because you do not wish to marry me." She puffed out her chest and tilted her chin. "Well, might I say that I have no desire to marry you either?"

Were he not already in a piss-poor mood, he would have smiled. "Duly noted. Now, if you don't have any further objections, I have not yet been dismissed from my position today, and I'd prefer to keep it that way."

Her sparkling green eyes narrowed. "You don't speak the same as the other factory workers."

He found her tiring, yet he could not dismiss her as easily as he dismissed other people. There was something about her, something he'd rather not spend the time discovering. His eyes fell to her mouth. Her lips were not overly round or full, but they arched perfectly. And he knew their softness. Knew their sweetness.

Tempting as they were, he certainly could not lean in to taste them again. Not here in front of everyone.

Oh, but he wanted to.

"You sound more cultured," she continued. "Educated," she added with a whisper.

His frustration with the situation, with wanting what he couldn't have, reached a boiling point. "Even poor people read books," he snarled with far more force than he intended.

She looked affronted. "I realize that. It's only that the majority of my father's employees do not speak with as much refinement as you."

Which was precisely why he needed to cease speaking to her before she suspected more of him than he was willing to reveal. Gareth shrugged, then added. "Good day to you, Miss Piddington."

"Good day," she said, defeat clearly lining her voice.

Her disappointment pricked at him, but he couldn't help it. The last thing he needed was for the rest of the workers here to think he received special treatment because of his relationship with the boss's daughter. He shook his head. He had no relationship with her, and he needed to ensure it stayed that way.

Gareth made his way to his machine and put on his apron. He'd just gotten everything started when she appeared at his side.

"I do apologize for interrupting you again, but I had one last question."

He nodded in response.

"What shall you do about that tiny accusation?" she whispered nodding toward the office.

"Not a damn thing. He has no proof, and it matters not to me whether he believes me."

"But he could dismiss you," she said.

"He hasn't yet."

She eyed him for a moment, suspiciously, then turned on her heel, leaving him to watch her pretty ruffled bustle walk away.

She had a nice backside.

Thoughts like that would be the death of him.

As he watched Meg Piddington leave the factory office trailing after that Irish riffraff, resentment boiled in his stomach. Things were not going as planned, and he hated that. He prided himself on meticulous and rather clever plans. But one idiot, and things had really gotten shaken up.

He took a deep breath. No need to panic just yet. There had to be another way. And sooner or later he would find it.

"What are you doing here, Mandeville?"

Gareth turned his head to find Mr. Munden standing behind him. Apparently a night's sleep hadn't cooled the foreman's temper.

"What the bloody hell does it look like I'm doing? Working." Gareth turned back to the machine. "Idiot," he murmured.

"I heard you. Don't think I didn't hear you."

Gareth ignored him and continued to work.

"Mandeville," Munden roared. "I'm talking to you."

He turned his machine off. "What?"

"We can't be having no thief work here. Mr. Piddington don't like people who steal from him."

"I worked yesterday, and you didn't say anything."

"That's because pretty Miss Piddington was here to save you. She ain't here today."

Perfect.

All he needed was to lose this job. Then what would he do? He supposed he could get another job, but Piddington's was the best factory to work for. Everyone wanted to work here. And aside from Munden's swollen head from his "more responsibilities" since Piddington's accident, it was the best place Gareth had ever worked.

But he would not beg this man. With Munden's half-chewed cigar hanging from his mouth, and sweat dripping between his eyes, he looked more the part of a dealer at a gaming hell than a foreman at a cocoa factory.

By this time the rest of the machines around him had been turned off and all eyes watched.

"What are you waiting for? An escort? Get your stuff and get out."

"You don't have the authority to dismiss me. I'm not leaving until Piddington himself asks me to do so," Gareth said.

"I beg your pardon, Mr. Munden. I thought we settled this little conflict with Mr. Mandeville yesterday."

At the sound of Meg's voice, it was all he could do not to squeeze his eyes closed in exasperation. However, under Munden's scrutiny, Gareth kept his expression carefully blank.

"Has something new arisen?" she asked.

Munden cranked his beefy body around to face the lovely Meg Piddington. Gareth gave in to the temptation to do the same. He couldn't ignore the green and pink striped dress. It hugged her body in all the right places; the bonnet atop her red curls and the matching umbrella swinging from her wrist gave her an innocent look.

"Miss Piddington?" Munden stammered. "We still have not found those boxes, so I was ridding your father's factory of a thief. I know he wouldn't take kindly to a man who steals from him."

Her delicate eyebrows arched. "Indeed. Nor would he take kindly to you dismissing someone without appropriate proof."

At that, snickers scattered around the factory floor.

She glanced around, then took a deep breath. "Might I have a word with you, sir? In my father's office," she added tartly. With that she turned on her heel and walked off, clearly expecting the manager to follow her.

Which he did. Rather quickly.

The spectacle did not end at that moment, however, as Edward Piddington's office overlooked the factory floor with a wall of windows. The old man enjoyed keeping an eye on things and ensuring he maintained a presence within his company.

So no one returned to work. With the unison of an army brigade, they all turned and looked up to the windows above them. The door shut behind Mr. Munden, and while no words were heard, it was quite evident who was in charge.

It gave Gareth the perfect opportunity to study Meg without any questions about his motive. Aside from the obvious gender difference, she was the very picture of his opposite.

He could practically hear the coins rubbing together as they jingled in her purse. Petite and fair with fiery red hair, while he was tall and dark from far too much sun. Every last inch of her was sparkling clean, from her button-up boots to that tiny bonnet perched on her head. He, on the other hand, was covered in cocoa powder. His fingernails looked as if he worked as a chimney sweep, rather than in a confectionery.

She held her dainty gloved hand out to Munden. They shook, and Munden nodded his big head. Gareth couldn't help but wonder if she'd just made a deal with the devil.

And then as quickly as she blew into the office, she was walking down the stairs. And looking straight at him.

"Please return to your duties, gentlemen," she said with a smile. "There is nothing of interest occurring. Now then," she said as she reached Gareth's side.

"What was that all about?" he asked.

She gave him a toothy grin. "I saved your job," she said, clearly pleased with herself. Machines around him started up, and soon the familiar noise surrounded them.

He wished he could tell her that it wasn't necessary, that he could take care of himself, but the truth of the matter was he needed this job, and he'd had no idea how he was going to convince Munden to let him stay on. You couldn't really ally yourself with someone while they believed you to be a thief.

It was kind of her to stand up for him. Especially to a man such as Munden. She was plucky, he'd give her that. It had been a damn long time since someone had defended him, and part of him wanted to thank her.

So long since someone didn't make assumptions about him based on what they saw or thought they knew.

But there was a reason for her generous intervention. She'd only defended him because she knew he was innocent. That, and because Meg clearly took pleasure from being in the middle of the action. He could tell that about her from the very beginning. She enjoyed attention. And he was her newest undertaking.

So he refused to feel guilty for not thanking her, as her motives had not been genuine. So he merely nodded.

"You're quite welcome," she said brightly.

"I could have managed fine without you, Miss Piddington," he lied, then cranked his machine and started the grinding to put some noise between them.

"Of course," she said.

But something told him she knew different. She knew he'd needed saving, and that irritated him to the bottom of his scuffed boots. She was irritating, with her matching clothes and her sunny outlook. She was everything he couldn't have and shouldn't even want. And yet want her he did. For that reason alone, her very presence prickled his skin with annoyance. He frowned simply to spite her.

Yet he had the sudden urge to pull her to him and kiss her senseless. More than likely that was only a reaction to prevent her from talking.

She leaned over and stilled his arms. "I realize you are working now, but I do have something we need to discuss. Might you meet me later today?"

Did he have a choice? She'd saved his hide, and he owed her at least this much. Not to mention his skin was boiling beneath the heat of her touch. He nodded. "Where?"

"Here is fine. In my father's office. I shall return this afternoon at the conclusion of your shift. I have some other appointments right now."

"Very well."

"Excellent. Until then," She tapped her umbrella on the floor once, then turned to leave.

He refused to watch her retreat. As it was, the rest of the men had been eyeing them carefully. He did not need any additional attention at the moment.

"Don't think I won't be watching you," a voice snarled from behind him.

Munden. What a bastard.

"Making friends with Piddington's daughter won't save you forever," the foreman said.

"I have no doubt. Now, if you don't mind," he said, then turned his machine on, relieved finally to be able to concentrate on his work.

And concentrate on it he would, as soon as he could get the image of kissing Meg out of his mind. He should never have touched her the other night. Hell, he didn't even know why he'd done it in the first place. He wasn't generally in the habit of seducing wealthy virgins.

Which meant keeping his mind, mouth, and hands off Meg.

"Munden's got it in for you," Jamie said from across his machine.

Gareth nodded. He didn't want to tell his friend that he would likely not be in this trouble had it not been for Jamie.

"He's a fool," Gareth said.

"Aye. But the lass, she's a pretty one."

Gareth didn't reply to that one.

"I know you think so too. I've seen the way you look at her. That red hair must flame up your Irish blood." Jamie wiggled his thick eyebrows.

Gareth chuckled. "If you spent less time worrying about flaming blood, Jamie, you might not have so many children."

"Och. Seven's not so many. As soon as Mary is healed up, we might go for number eight." The Scot laughed heartily at his own jest. "Thank you. For the other night. She gets right cranky if I'm not there when the wee ones come."

Gareth nodded. If he had a wife who was birthing, he'd certainly want to be there.

"So what does Munden want with you? And why is the lass involved?" Jamie asked.

"He thinks I stole something. Miss Piddington is handling things while her father is out and she saved my job," Gareth said.

Jamie grinned broadly. "She's a good one, then, like her father." Jamie nodded. "Good for her. Munden will get his someday. Men like him always do."

Chapter 4

Meg waited in the phaeton outside the factory. Ordinarily she would walk over to the factory, but the slight mist in the air felt too damp. She didn't want to go inside until the rest of the men filed out. But more so, she wanted more time. More time to breathe deeply and gather her wits.

Something about Gareth rattled her senses, an occurrence she'd never before experienced. She generally knew precisely what to say at precisely the moment it needed to be said. Or at least she always had something to say. Most of the time everything fell into place, and it made sense. But with him, she felt the utter fool. As if her stomach were tied in knots, and her tongue equally so.

It was those skills she had—her communication with people—that she'd planned to use to impress her father. Prove to him that she was ready to take on responsibility at the factory. But she'd bumbled it by losing her ability to verbalize coherently while Mr. Mandeville was about. There was still time to recover, though. It was only the kiss that had thrown off her mental acuity; she could reclaim it. Forge forward.

She'd made her first decision that would put her on the road to leading this factory. Earlier today she'd played the boss's daughter and retained Gareth's job. If she spoke to her father, she could secure his job indefinitely, but Meg didn't want to handle it that way. That wouldn't prove she could manage things on her own, and that she didn't always need her papa's guidance. She'd told him she would take care of things, and that was precisely what she would do.

Then there was the case of the missing chocolate boxes. There was a thief in their midst and she could not allow that. No one would steal from the factory and get away with it, not on her watch.

Aside from her own concerns, there was Gareth's part in the situation. She wanted to help him in some fashion, since this whole mess was her fault; this would put her in a better position to do so. It seemed wrong that a simple admission that they had been alone together would expose a great scandal when there really hadn't been. Granted, there had been that one tiny, passionate, breath-stealing kiss, but there was no need to make that known to anyone. It was incredibly frustrating, and frankly she couldn't abide standing by and doing nothing.

So she'd played the actress and convinced Munden she was just as concerned as he, but that dismissing someone without proof was not a viable practice.

Instead she'd offered two solutions. Now she had to convince Gareth to play along with her scheme.

Earlier when she told him she had appointments, she'd lied to Gareth. She only had to bring her father the ledger book, then she had absolutely nothing else to do. She wasn't in the habit of lying to others, but she'd wanted to give herself a bit more time. Not to mention make herself appear more authoritative than she felt.

She'd gone home and tried on no fewer than seven dresses attempting to find the perfect one. For what, she was not certain. It was not as if she were going to the park with a suitor. Besides, she'd never been one to pay much attention to her clothing, but today she'd felt as if she'd needed some additional assistance. If she were to play this role, she needed the right costume. Something that spoke clearly: confident, controlled, clever.

She looked down at her tailored brown dress. The cut was excellent for her stature. The square neckline boosted her small bosom to reveal hidden curves and a chest dusted with freckles. She'd heard once that men liked freckles. Not that it mattered one bit if Gareth liked this dress or not. She was helping him, and in turn, it seemed, she was helping herself. She smoothed the front of her dress, freely admitting she felt smart in the concoction. She especially fancied the matching boots that clicked nicely when she walked.

She was dawdling, and she knew it. It was time now. Time to go in and face Gareth Mandeville. What was she afraid of in the first place?

That he'd kiss her again?

Or that he wouldn't?

Sitting in the carriage would not decide for her. Grabbing her reticule, she made her way into the factory. She did not stop to look for Gareth. Instead she marched herself straight up the stairs and into her father's office. It had been quite a while since she'd been up in his private office, and he'd made some changes.

Behind the desk sat the first chocolate-making machine he'd purchased; it wasn't even really a machine, more of a hand-held grinder. But it was a reminder of how far the industry had come. The armoire in the corner housed his personal belongings, a box of employee files, and extra pieces of clothing in case he needed to change. Hanging up her cloak, she noticed that the bookshelf on the left looked the same as it had since the day he moved into this office, and housed mostly books from his personal library.

She straightened the two red leather chairs that sat on the visitor side of the desk. The windows overlooking the factory floor provided the office with some light, but it wasn't much, as the day was progressing to dusk. So she lit the desk lamp, then sat, glancing around for something to inspect. Something that would make her appear busy.

She'd barely located a new order form when there came a knock on the door.

She straightened in the chair, then looked down at the order form. "Come in," she said.

Gareth entered but did not walk toward her. Instead he stayed near the door.

"Why don't you sit?" she offered.

"I'd prefer to stand."

Well, that would never work. She'd sit here and he'd tower over her from the doorway. It would be just as awkward for her to stand on the stairs and holler at him down at his machine.

"Then I shall stand as well." She set the paper down, then stood. Coming around the desk, she leaned against it for effect. On more than one occasion, she'd seen her father stand precisely this way, so perhaps it would help her appear more official.

"What did you want to discuss with me?" he asked.

"Yes, well, earlier when I spoke with Mr. Munden, I had to do a bit of negotiating. I felt it would be better if he believed I was as concerned with the theft as he." Gareth's eyebrows rose a fraction of an inch. "Not to imply I'm not concerned. There is a thief at the factory and that cannot be allowed. But I also know you're innocent. So I insisted that you retain your job until we have absolute proof . . . In short, I made a bargain on your behalf."

"On my behalf?" He swaggered forward and stood behind the chairs, placing a barrier between them. "That was rather bold of you, Miss Piddington. Precisely what did you agree to, on my behalf?"

Meg released a little giggle that sounded supremely false. This was not going well. She shook her hands out, hoping to release the excess nerves that had settled in her body. It was most annoying.

"It's a tiny thing, really. Mr. Munden was quite insistent that you stole those chocolate boxes. And since you will not allow me to give you an alibi, I cannot convince him of your innocence. But proof or not, the boxes are still missing and we have an order to fill before Lady Glenworthy discovers the truth and goes elsewhere for her chocolates. So I agreed that you would put a new batch together."

"Put those fancy boxes together?" he asked.

"Yes."

"How the devil am I supposed to do that? I work a grinding machine. There is an entire packing block designated for this."

"I realize that. But we've received six more similar orders and so the packing department is already behind." She hoped her father would be pleased by her administrative decisions.

Gareth pinched the bridge of his nose. "How many boxes are we talking about?"

"Seventeen. One for each year her lovely daughter has graced the earth," she said in a melodious voice that perfectly mimicked Lady Glenworthy's.

Gareth smiled.

"Don't concern yourself about the boxes. I've already seen to it that the supplies will be brought over. And I'll personally see to it that you're paid for the extra time. I know they are detailed work and am told they take a while to produce, so I shall help you with that as well."

"No more help from you," he argued. "I do not need help with the boxes."

"There is one tiny problem with that," she said. She used her thumb and first finger to illustrate her words. It was, in fact, a tiny problem. Gareth, however, might not see it that way.

"I'm almost afraid to ask. What would that tiny problem be?"

"You are not to be alone in the factory. So either Mr. Munden shall supervise you, or I shall. Your choice." She crossed her arms over her chest. She knew he would not select Munden; he detested the man.

He came around the chair. "Miss Piddington, you

seem to enjoy playing the part of the factory manager while your father is gone. You're meddling in the business and fiddling with the paperwork."

He gestured to the desk behind her and the order form she'd been pretending to read when he came in. She felt her cheeks begin to burn, partly from the truth in his accusations, partly from the heat of his gaze.

She wanted to quip a response, but her mind was blank, and she was fairly certain that her knees no longer functioned.

"Do not think to use me as some pawn in your game with Papa's factory. I don't take kindly to games."

He now stood right in front of her. She straightened to her full height, which frankly wasn't all that much, and was rather difficult considering how wobbly her legs felt. She didn't even come to his chin. But that didn't stop her from tilting her head back and meeting his eyes.

Hazel. Luscious, rich mixture of brown and green. And they nearly stole the words right from her mouth, but she caught herself.

"Do not be so arrogant as to think I should use you for anything, Mr. Mandeville," she said tartly. "I do not play games with my father's factory. I am merely aiding you with a sticky situation, since I am not able to give you your alibi." His eyes were watching her lips, and she nearly forgot what she was saying. She frowned. "Consider it a favor."

Her heart was pounding so hard in her chest, she was certain he could see it thumping through the fabric in her dress. And her hands were shaking fiercely, which made it convenient that she was holding on to the desk behind her.

He grabbed her by the waist with one arm and pulled her to him. With one swift movement, he planted his lips to hers in a quick but passionate kiss. How was he able to keep penetrating her barriers? She thought she'd done an admirable job of feigning control and disinterest. No sooner had she melted into his lips than he abruptly let her go.

"Nor do I play games, Miss Piddington." And with that he turned, and left her to slump against the desk with nary a thought in her head.

Gareth slammed his head into his hands. He really had to stop kissing her in such a fashion. He really ought to stop kissing her in any fashion at all. Teaching her a lesson was only an excuse to taste her sweet lips, and he'd be a fool not to admit that.

Touching her lips a second time had not fettered his desire. He wanted her. Her kisses were an intoxicating mixture of passion and innocence, and they left him wanting more. Which was why he needed to tighten the reins on his lust.

He would work with Meg, because he had no other options, but he would not give in to temptation to touch her in any fashion. He could play the gentleman long enough for the winds to change and this minor accusation to blow away. He laughed. The irony of that was too much to ignore.

Play the gentleman. He'd been playing the poor Irishman for so long, he wondered if he even remembered how. But surely the last vestiges of the gentleman he truly was lingered somewhere deep inside. Somewhere very deep.

Wouldn't everyone here love to know the truth about him?

How would Meg react? Would his kisses thrill her even more if she knew he was a viscount? It mattered not. She would never know. No one would.

Meg was quite relieved that, as circumstances would have it, today was the weekly meeting of the Ladies' Amateur Sleuth Society. She had no doubt at all that they would be able to help her discover the identity of the true thief.

Given Gareth's reaction to her plan for him to make the replacement boxes, she'd been reluctant to tell him the rest of her scheme. That she herself would uncover the identity of the true thief.

Though, of course, like any good sleuth, she would use all the resources at her disposal. In this case, the Ladies' Amateur Sleuth Society.

So she had considerable eagerness as she entered the parlor.

"Good morning, my dear friends," she said joyfully.

Charlotte narrowed her gaze but smiled knowingly.

"Good morning yourself," Amelia said.

"Technically it is not morning," Willow added. "It is nearly midafternoon."

"Very well," Meg said. "Good afternoon."

"You seem quite pleased to see us," Charlotte said.

"Indeed I am. I have a task for us. A task for the Ladies' Amateur Sleuth Society."

Amelia raised her eyebrows. "Do you indeed?"

Meg nodded. "But we can certainly go along with business as usual and then proceed to my business when it is more appropriate."

"Oh no, I think now is most appropriate. Do you not agree, Amelia?" Charlotte asked.

"I suppose we can break from standard protocol for an immediate case in need. What say you, Willow?"

Willow nodded. "I must admit, I'm rather intrigued at the possibility."

"Very well," Meg said. "Let us get seated and I shall fill you in on all the details."

It took less than five minutes for them to take their seats and help themselves to the tea and cakes offered on the occasional table.

"Now then," Amelia said. "Do tell us this official task you have for us. I'm most eager."

Meg took a quick sip of her tea and allowed the warm liquid to soothe her throat before she began. "Apparently the evening Mr. Mandeville and I were locked into that storeroom, some special-ordered chocolate boxes were stolen from the factory, and now he has been falsely accused of the crime."

"Somehow I knew this would involve the handsome Mr. Mandeville," Charlotte said.

"Let her finish," Willow said.

"It appears that Mr. Munden, the foreman in charge of Mr. Mandeville's block, is quite convinced of Mr. Mandeville's guilt. For obvious reasons, I cannot offer him an alibi without severely damaging my reputation." She gave a courtesy nod to Willow. There was no reason to tell them she'd come very close to compromising them without a single thought of her reputation. "So I feel it is only right that I offer my skills, our skills if you're willing, to help clear his name. I've done what I can to secure his position at the factory, but I feel as if I must do more. Not only Mr. Mandeville's innocence is in question, though. More importantly, there is a thief working at my father's factory. He must be brought to justice. Will you help me?"

"Of course we will," Amelia said.

"What does your father have to say about this situation?" Willow asked.

"I haven't told him. He does not need to worry about this. I want his recuperation to go as smoothly and quickly as possible." Meg popped a bite of cake into her mouth.

"What is it that you would have us do, Meg, to help with Mr. Mandeville's situation?" Amelia asked.

"I suppose we can start with determining whether whoever did steal those boxes sold them anywhere," Meg said.

"How will we do that?" Charlotte said.

"We should start with our servants; they often hear about these sorts of activities," Willow said. "But Meg, you should inquire from the other workers if anyone saw anything. Then we can speak with some pawn-brokers, see if any of them have made a similar purchase."

"I'll speak to Colin tonight to see if he has any ideas," Amelia said.

"Brilliant!" Meg said. "I knew you would help."

"What of Mr. Mandeville?" Amelia asked. "Does he mind us assisting you?"

"He's not doing any investigation on his own," Meg said.

"Why on earth not?" Charlotte asked.

Meg relayed his feelings to them, about not needing to prove himself. "Perhaps once we're making progress, he'll be more inclined to join in."

"We've all been falsely accused of something at some point in our lives," Willow said. "Perhaps not of the criminal nature, but nonetheless it is most disturbing, and everyone reacts quite differently in those situations."

"I do believe Willow is feeling sympathetic toward Mr. Mandeville," Charlotte said playfully.

Willow crossed her legs. "I was only trying to present an explanation for his reluctance. Give him the benefit of the doubt, so to speak."

"It was an excellent point to make," Amelia said.

"It is exciting to have an actual case to work on," Charlotte said. "Something besides the exceedingly frustrating Jack of Hearts case, that is."

"Perhaps next time we meet, we will have uncovered something," Willow said.

"And if, in the meantime, we discover anything pertinent, we can call a special meeting by messenger," Charlotte suggested.

"Agreed," Meg said.

It was settled. Now that the Ladies' Amateur Sleuth Society was working on the mystery of the missing boxes, revealing the truth shouldn't be too far off.

Chapter 5

Today they would start the work on the decorative boxes. Yesterday Meg had gone over to the packing department to see the boxes herself. She needed a better image of what she and Gareth were to create. Her father had told her all about them when he'd first developed the concept and she'd thought it was a brilliant idea.

Keepsake boxes filled with fancy chocolates. Once all the delights were eaten, the velvet-lined drawers and spaces could be used to hold jewelry and other trinkets. Some were simple boxes with a hinged lid, but others were more like tiny chests with drawers and doors.

She and Gareth were to seal in the velvet and then paste the prints on the outside, and add tiny mirrors for decoration. It would be slow and detailed work.

It took a good thirty-minute carriage ride to get from Amelia's house back to Piddington Hall due to the wet and muddy roads. Meg's insides felt jostled, and she wasn't certain if it was from the bumpy ride or her nerves. It was the right thing to do to help Gareth. Not only that, but it was giving her another look at the inner workings of the factory.

She had to stop by and pick up Ellen, her maid, so that they might have a chaperone during their evening time at the factory. Far be it from her to be criticized for the same thing twice, so she wanted to ensure that she was prepared in case Gareth accused her again. Not to mention, Willow would be awfully proud of her attempt to protect herself.

So with Ellen seated in the carriage next to her, she rolled down the hill to the factory. Meg had already made a decision about tonight; she would not allow Gareth to rattle her or irritate her. Simply because he had a tendency to be surly, that did not mean that she would return his foul mood with one of her own. No, she would be sweet and charming. Witty, if she could manage.

Tonight could be considered an official task at the factory, so she took a moment to straighten her dress, taking careful consideration with the tie at the neckline. Then she opened the factory doors. As she had done before, she did not look to her left where the machinery sat and the workers toiled the hours away; no, she kept her attention straight ahead as she made her way to the stairs. If she were to prove she could manage the factory, then she should act the part. Which meant spending considerable time in her father's office.

Mr. Munden stepped into her path. She stopped before she ran into him.

"Good day, Mr. Munden," she replied. She tried to

keep her voice civil, yet laced with an air of authority. She'd rather not involve him in the situation any further.

He nodded and eyed Ellen, who stood beside her. He almost allowed them to pass, but spoke up before Meg took a step. "Might I ask why you're here, Miss Piddington?"

"My father has asked me to look in on things while he's at home healing."

Munden's gaze narrowed in either annoyance or offense. "You think we're not running things without him?"

"Oh no." She did her best to placate him, though it grated her nerves to do so. She wasn't quite ready to take her work at the factory so far as to goad a foreman into quitting. "Indeed, I'm certain you and the other foremen are doing a fine job managing the factory, Mr. Munden, but my father is eager for me to begin learning the business."

That wasn't precisely the way the conversation with her father had gone. Before he could question her further, she began moving toward the office. "I shall be here on a regular basis." She pointed upstairs. "In my father's office, should anyone need me." And with that she stepped away from him and started up the stairs.

She nearly giggled as she closed the door behind her, but minding the windows lining the office wall that overlooked the factory floor, she restrained herself.

"He is the vilest of men, Ellen," she said.

"He seemed as much," her maid agreed.

It felt good though to take control of matters. If she were any sort of daughter at all, she would have done this years ago and learned this business at her father's side.

Although it was quite likely that her father would have had none of that. He loved her dearly, but like all fathers, he wanted her to make a good match, marry, and produce children. But she couldn't afford to do that. Marriage was not for her. Not that she didn't want it. She wasn't foolish enough to pretend she did not desire a husband and children.

Loving involved too much of a risk. A risk of heartache, a risk of loss, and she simply wasn't strong enough. That had become all too clear to her when her mother had died. The pain had been so great, it had nearly consumed her. She'd learned quickly to swallow her pain and put on a smile for those around her. Especially for her papa.

So she squelched those desires, and on most days she managed just fine. On occasion, though, they'd creep out and threaten to choke her with their intensity. Today, however, was a good day, and the needs she couldn't permanently forget were nicely hidden away.

Meg unpinned her hat and hung it on the coat tree by the office door, then took a seat behind her father's large mahogany desk. It would be an hour or so before Gareth completed his shift. In the meantime, she would tidy her father's desk and read a few things to better acquaint herself with any new business. As she took in her surroundings, an overwhelming sense of pride welled in her chest. Her father had come from modest beginnings and had built this factory to what it was today, the third largest confectionery in England. She would never be so accomplished or so determined, but she would strive to carry on his legacy.

* * *

Gareth had watched Meg walk into the factory and straight up to her father's office. Again in one of those dresses that fit her body divinely. The cut of the jacket flaunted her tiny waist, and the bustle accentuated her rounded bottom. The fact that he actually knew her waist was tiny and her bottom rounded did not flee from his mind. Although he had only touched her a brief moment, while he hoisted her up to that window, neither his hands nor mind had forgotten.

It was enough to drive a man to Bedlam.

In a short time, he'd be alone with her. Caught in a situation he was still unsure how he'd wound up in. Rotten luck. Or maybe it was a family curse. His father had certainly had a lifetime of bad luck. Perhaps it made more sense to question how Gareth had managed to survive in London this long, even if he was slightly outside the bustling city, without encountering an even larger disaster.

So the fact that out of all the men working in this factory, he'd be the one accused shouldn't have surprised him in the least.

He was tired of it. He'd be a bloody liar to say he wasn't. People would believe what they wanted about a person regardless of the truth; he'd learned that long ago. Better to simply live life as quietly as possible in hopes of not being noticed at all.

Sometimes that plan even succeeded. Yet other times, as was the case with Mr. Munden, the plan failed miserably. It failed with Meg too. She had certainly noticed him, no thanks to his reckless behavior that initiated kisses.

He had not yet decided if it was a blessing or a curse

to be caught in Meg's attentions. A man would be a fool not to want attention from such a woman. Fool or not, he couldn't afford the risk.

Meg's attentions could lead to only one result. Marriage.

He'd long ago given up the accoutrements of a gentleman, but he still had a gentleman's honor. Being a selfish bastard might come as first nature with him, but he need not given in. Surely he could be stronger—stronger than his damn father had been. He would not toy with her affections or her reputation, any more than he already had.

He would end that tonight. There would be no more kisses, or thoughts of kisses. Meg was an innocent, and if he wasn't careful, he could hurt her in ways he didn't know where to begin to salvage. He wouldn't allow that to happen. She was helping him and he appreciated it. It was a gesture made from kindness, though, and he ought to remember that.

Gareth watched the men around him closing down for the day. They were working longer hours these last few weeks, trying to keep up with all the orders. The store in London was selling the goods as quickly as they opened their doors. It was good for all of them. There had even been whispers about a raise in the wage. But Gareth wouldn't hold his breath on that one. He'd worked long enough to know that the Piddington employees had it good. Damn good. And they'd do well to keep their mouths shut and be thankful for their current pay and all the other benefits of their positions.

"You working late again tonight?" Jamie asked.

"I have to replace those stolen boxes."

Jamie made a face. "Do you want me to stay and help you? I don't know how, mind you, but I can learn anything."

Gareth smiled at his unlikely friend. "No. You go home to your family." Jamie smiled, and Gareth was struck by the youthfulness in his face. He was a good ten years Gareth's senior, but he was the most contented, happy man that Gareth had ever seen. "Mary will have your hide if you're late for supper."

Jamie narrowed his eyes jokingly. "Are you certain you've never met my Mary?"

Gareth laughed. "No, I've never met her."

"Is the lass helping you tonight? I saw her come in earlier."

"Yes."

"It will make the time move by quicker to have someone to chat with. If you get bored, you need only look up and see her smile."

If only his friend knew that Meg's smile could be his undoing. "You're the worst sort of romantic, Jamie. Go home."

Jamie pounded Gareth on the back. "See you tomorrow then." He gave him a wink, then turned to go.

Gareth leaned against the far wall, partially hidden behind the shadow of a door. There was no reason for him to advertise the fact that he was staying behind. Especially since everyone else had seen Meg enter the factory. Surely everyone knew she had not yet left. It took only a few minutes longer for the rest of the men to file out of the factory, leaving Gareth alone.

With newfound determination to keep as much distance between himself and the beauty as he could, he made his way to the makeshift packaging room to begin work on the boxes. He saw no reason to go and retrieve her.

The room they were working in was going to be the office of the incoming staff. Men in cravats who wouldn't have to get their hands and clothes dirty. Gareth wanted one of those positions, but so far he'd done a rotten job showing that.

If his father hadn't wasted all their money, Gareth wouldn't need a job. He'd be wealthy and living comfortably in the country or in a luxurious town home in the best part of London. But life hadn't worked out for him that way, so he had to work, which was why he couldn't let anyone know the truth about him.

The long, narrow room had only one table to fill the space. He made his way to it and sat. Atop the wooden table sat the seventeen boxes, all different sizes and styles, and the rest of the materials they would need to complete their task. Plush velvet material, small cut mirrors, prints of kittens and maidens and floral landscapes, and glue all laid out for their use.

He grabbed one of the smaller boxes, figuring it was better to start with a minimal amount of work and build up to the larger, more elaborate boxes. He'd never even held one of the finished boxes before, but he had seen them. He hoped his memory would serve him well tonight.

It only took ten minutes for her to appear in the doorway.

"What are you doing?" she asked.

"What do I appear to be doing?" he asked. Then he added, "Working on the boxes."

"But you don't know how yet," she said. "I went and spoke to the women in the packaging room and they gave me instructions on how to proceed."

He caught her frown before he looked down at his current project. "I've seen them before. I decided that was enough information to get started."

"I am supposed to help you with these," she said firmly.

"Be my guest." He motioned to the chair on the opposite side of the table.

"I'll have you know that my maid is right outside the door. That should give me sufficient protection," she said.

He had half a mind to tell her she didn't need protection from him, but it would have been a lie. He was glad she'd brought her maid, glad to have a buffer between them so he might control himself and not give in to the temptation of her lips.

She sat across from him. "It appears that all of the supplies are here."

He knew she was not satisfied. That he had irritated her, and if he were half a gentleman, he would apologize for his rudeness. Instead he found great pleasure in her irritability. Not because he was cruel, but rather because she was so easy to rile. It didn't hurt that she looked so damn sensual when she got mad. She had this habit of chewing her lip, and it nearly drove him insane.

She leaned forward to eye his progress. "You're doing a nice job."

How he wanted to say something sardonic, but there was no reason to make her completely dislike him. Quite soon she sat working quickly, no longer pursing her lips, but rather grinning. And humming. It was as if he had invited little Snow White to work beside him. He nearly expected to see woodland animals gather at her feet.

She looked up and caught him staring. A wide smile spread across her face.

He scowled and looked back down to his box.

She laughed heartily, and the sound of it warmed his insides.

"You like me," she said.

That caught him off guard, and he found himself struggling to suppress a smile. "Do I?"

"Oh yes." She met his glance. "You don't want to admit it. But you simply can't help yourself. Rest assured, though, that it is a normal reaction."

That earned her a hearty laugh of his own. "Is that so?"

"Indeed. Everyone likes me." She nodded, and her red curls bobbed. "I'm a likable sort."

He found himself caught in a quandary. He wanted neither to confirm her audacious remark, nor to deny it. So he ignored her and returned to his work.

"It is all right though. You can pretend to dislike me and scowl. In our previous encounters it has made me scowl as well, but no more. I am a cheerful person, and I decided not to allow you to annoy me. It shall not hurt my feelings for you to pretend to find me annoying because I know that you do, in fact, find me utterly charming."

He could listen to her spout her attributes no longer. "I hate to be the one to tell you, but I find you utterly bothersome. You talk too much; you're entirely too cheerful." He ticked each comment off on his fingers.

"And you really ought not wear such dresses around working men. Makes them think of things that would turn your face as red as your hair."

Her mouth opened wide. From shock or irritation, Gareth could not ascertain.

And then she frowned. Tiny creases indented her forehead, and her nose wrinkled ever so slightly. He did find her charming, but he was too stubborn to admit it. He knew that about himself, it was an error of his character, not hers. But apologizing was out of the question. It was probably for the best if she found him beastly.

"Precisely what is wrong with my dress?" she suddenly asked. "It is rather fashionable, I assure you. I only recently purchased a closet full of new clothes. Or rather my father did."

"Why did you need a closet full of new dresses? Didn't you already have some?"

"Yes, but I did not have any suitable for working," she said quietly.

"Working?"

"Yes, working. While my father heals, I told him I would assist at the factory."

"Your mother has no issues with her daughter working at a factory?"

She didn't look up from her work; instead she seemed to be more involved with it, holding the box closer to her face. "My mother died when I was a child. So I'm not quite certain how she would react to my working here. I suspect had she lived, they would have had more children, perhaps a boy, and I would have married years ago and would be living in the country with a house full of children while my brothers would work here. But I have no brothers," she added with a tight laugh.

He'd hit a tender area. She was trying to pretend he hadn't, but it was there, under the surface. Pain. It was palpable, and he knew that if he reached out he would be able to touch it briefly before she was able to tuck it away. "I didn't realize about your mother," he said.

"How could you?" She waved a hand in front of her. "I remember plenty of things about her. She had red hair like I do." Her voice took on a remote quality. "And she was short, but she was very mild-mannered. Although my father has told me on many occasions that I get my spirit from her." She smoothed a piece of blue velvet on the inside of a drawer. "What of your family?"

"What of them?" He didn't want to give her too much information. She was clever, and it wouldn't take her too long to figure out he had a secret. She'd already detected the difference in his speech.

"Tell me about them. It will give us some conversation and that will make the work move by swiftly." She smiled at him. "It's a simple question, Gareth."

"Without a simple answer," he said.

She frowned. "Do you have parents?"

"Of course. Everyone has parents. People don't simply appear."

"I meant, are they still living?"

"My mother is."

"Where is she?"

"Ireland."

"What about brothers and sisters?

He shrugged. "A handful." She had such patience, and showed no sign of irritation at his terse replies. So he would answer her questions, but he would not offer her more than that.

"A handful? Is that large?" she asked.

He shrugged. "I suppose. There are five of us."

"I always wanted a sister or brother. But it was not to be."

"And your father never remarried?" he found himself asking. He probably shouldn't, but he wanted to distract her from inquiring more about his family.

"Oh no, never even considered it. He loved my mother far too much. Losing her nearly killed him. They had a great love," she said.

A great love. He had once believed that his parents had such a love. It hadn't taken him long to learn the truth, though. It was a shallow love built on conditions and it hadn't survived. He didn't think his father had ever been unfaithful, at least not with another woman, but his vices had nonetheless taken him away from his family. His mother's love hadn't endured, and she'd left his father when he'd needed her most.

"Do you miss Ireland?" she asked.

"Sometimes."

"Are your siblings still there as well, or only your mother?"

"They're all still there. Fiona and Maggie are both married with children of their own. But the two youngest still live with my mother. Aileen is sixteen and Liam is thirteen."

"Why, then, did you come all the way to London?"

He hesitated for a moment over his response. The answer to that question was something he'd been unable to make even his own family understand. This young woman, with her tailored dresses and her fiery hair and her sweet nature, how could she possibly understand how he'd been driven to prove himself? To prove to everyone that he could live in this city. That he could live here and not succumb to the very things that destroyed his father. Or perhaps he needed only to prove those things to himself.

"To see if it was all I remembered it to be," he said.

"You have been here before?" she asked, clearly surprised.

"I was born here," he answered. He knew he was giving her more clues, but he felt compelled to answer her questions. Chances of her recognizing the Mandeville name were slim; she would have been a small child by the time his father died. By then his parents' activity in Society had diminished a great deal, his mother had been desperate to remove herself from the rumor mill. "I lived here until I was twelve. Enough about my family. They are not interesting." He'd already said far more than he ever intended.

She wanted to ask more; he could feel her questions in the air. But she asked none of them. Silently she went back to work.

Born in London? Meg was still reeling from that admission and she wanted to press him more, but she knew he'd given her more than he was accustomed to. She eyed him cautiously. He was busy pressing a print of three kittens sitting in a basket to the lid of the box he was working on.

He'd been rather reluctant to share with her, but he'd given her more than she had expected. Perhaps if she changed the subject he'd forget he'd been so open with her.

"I have three dear friends who might as well be my

sisters," she said abruptly. Now was as good a time as any to tell him that the Ladies' Amateur Sleuth Society had taken on his case. She leaned in. "Would you like to know a secret?"

"I suppose," he said warily.

"My friends and I have a secret society."

He looked up at her then, surprise etching his features. "A secret society," he repeated dumbly.

"Oh yes. Now, you cannot tell anyone as it would most certainly create talk."

He motioned to the empty room. "Who would I tell? Besides, it's not as if my would-be friends and your friends are in the same circle."

He had her there. She'd originally intended to tell him all this after they found their first lead, but he clearly had wanted to direct attention off his family. He did not want to discuss his life in any great detail. At least not yet.

But often people felt more inclined to share when others shared first. So for the time being, she'd do the talking and see if things eased with him.

"Yes, as I was saying. A secret society. We are called the Ladies' Amateur Sleuth Society."

He eyed her suspiciously, then shook his head. "What do you do?"

"As it sounds, we sleuth." She shrugged. "Or we attempt to do so. It is most difficult to solve crimes when we are not privy to all the details. As the authorities are."

"You sleuth?" he asked.

She watched him carefully, looking for signs of what he thought. Only one of them had told someone outside their families. Amelia had told Colin before they had married, well before they were in love. Colin had found it vastly amusing, but then he was an inspector for hire, and the thought of four ladies scavenging around London looking for clues to mysteries sounded ludicrous to him. He was far more favorable toward the group now.

Gareth, on the other hand, did not appear amused. At least Meg didn't think so; from his blank expression, it was difficult to determine precisely what he was feeling or thinking. More than likely he would think her a fool, but she'd started the conversation; she couldn't very well back out of it now.

His eyebrows raised and she realized she had not answered his question.

"Yes, we sleuth. We are rather good at it, I might add."

"What have you solved?"

She frowned. That was a bothersome question. "The case we are currently involved in is still active." She released a breath. That was the honest truth.

"What case are you working on?"

This was her fault. She'd brought it up. She had wanted to impress him before telling him they would solve his crime, but she'd always had a difficult time waiting to tell people things. And now that she was in the midst of the conversation she couldn't see a way that any of this would impart a lofty impression.

"Well, for one, your case. I met with the girls earlier today and they agreed. So the Ladies' Amateur Sleuth Society is officially working on finding the real culprit and proving your innocence."

"I see," he said tightly. "Did you also tell them that if word gets out about that, we will be compromised?"

She released a nervous laugh, then mentally chastised herself. "You know, they were worried about you telling people, bragging, if you will. But I told them you were intent on keeping it a secret. They'll never tell."

He eyed her a moment longer before silently nodding. "And for another?" he asked.

He didn't seem to have much of a reaction to the news. She hoped he'd be excited. But she supposed that was expecting a bit much.

"Another?" she asked.

"You said, 'For one.' That implies there are others."

Oh dear.

If nothing else she would make him laugh, and that was worth something indeed.

"Do you read the papers, Mr. Mandeville?"

He winced slightly. "If you must call me something, call me by my given name. And yes, I do read the papers when I find them lying about. I don't generally spend."

"Then you must have read about the Jack of Hearts."

He leaned back and crossed his arms over his chest. A tight smile played at his lips. "I have. You and your lady friends are thinking to catch the Jack of Hearts?"

Meg smiled broadly. "We are."

"What do you know so far?" he asked.

"Well, we know that he only steals from the wealthy," she said.

He shook his head. "That doesn't count. The only people you can steal from are wealthy. Poor people have nothing to take."

"Of course. I simply meant that he frequents events that are filled with the titled."

He nodded.

"We think that this means he's arrogant."

"In what way?" he asked.

He wasn't mocking her, she realized. He was listening, participating. Meg's chest swelled and she felt a surge of confidence. She'd never before been able to discuss her fascination with mysteries with anyone save the other girls. It was exhilarating. Especially when she'd expected mockery, and thus far, he'd reserved his reaction and only put forth questions. "He's bold. He walks into places and steals directly from people. He's a highwayman dressed as a gentleman. It's quite effective."

"Have you seen him?"

"No. None of us have. One of us has come close a few times, but we're still waiting."

"Well, he could be anyone," Gareth offered.

"True. But we feel fairly confident that he's a servant who works for a good family."

"Or he could be someone from a good family," he argued.

She opened her mouth to respond, then shut it. Could he be? They had not even considered the possibility. That would certainly be the scandal of all scandals. She shook her head. It couldn't be. No one from a good family would dare. "No. Why would they need to steal?"

"Not all good families have money. You know that, Meg. In the same paper where you read your stories of the Jack of Hearts, there are reports of the Earl of Such-and-Such having to marry an unrefined heiress from America to save his family's name."

Meg simply started at him.

"Why do you look so surprised?" he asked.

"I guess I didn't realize you read those parts of the papers. Keeping up with Society news, are you?" Was that customary for most factory workers? Or only ones who seemed more educated than most, who had alluring hazel eyes, and whose kisses could steal a thought right out of your head?

Gareth shrugged, but did not look at her. "It's comforting to know that even the blessed have their trials." His tone was biting. "I only meant that the Jack of Hearts could be anyone. It could be a servant as you and your friends suggest. It could be the second son of an earl angry at his lousy inheritance. It could be a duke who's lost his fortune and is hell bent on getting it back. Or it could be any of the above, stealing not out of necessity, but out of sport." He shrugged, then leaned back over his box to finish his work. "It could be me," he added.

Her heart nearly stopped. "What do you mean, it could be you?"

"Precisely what it sounded like. I could be the Jack of Hearts."

Her hand flew to her cheek. "Are you?" He couldn't be serious.

He said nothing, did not answer her at all, merely looked up briefly, smiled, then went back to work.

Oh dear. Could he be the Jack of Hearts? Certainly not. How would he get into the social functions? Had he not said that he hadn't been in London that long? The Jack of Hearts had been making his grand appearances for more than six months now.

Meg looked down at the box she was working on. He was teasing her; he had to be. If he were the Jack of

Hearts, surely he wouldn't just come right out with it. Would he? She looked back up at him.

He chuckled. "Get back to work, Meg," he said.

She smiled, but was still uncertain what that comment had meant. It seemed that he was always trying to throw her off kilter in some form or fashion. Be it his words or his kiss.

Despite his refined speech and mysterious previous life in London, Gareth was no more than exactly what he appeared to be, she assured herself. A hardworking, struggling factory worker. Completely unsuitable. Despite his tempting kisses.

Reluctantly she went back to her box. It was coming along nicely. They'd put together several through the course of the evening.

"Have you and your fellow sleuths discovered anything that would lead you to the thief of the original chocolate boxes?" he asked.

So he was interested. "No, we haven't. But we've only just begun. Why? Did you want to join us? Do a bit of sleuthing of your own?" she asked.

"No. As tempting as that might be," he said with a smile, "it is not my responsibility, but rather Munden's. He should have to prove my guilt, but we both know he's not working to do that. Nor do I believe he's intelligent enough to do so."

"I still have a difficult time understanding that you have no desire to prove your innocence."

"There's no reason why you could understand it. In your world wrongs get righted and the innocent are deemed such. But life isn't always like that. People don't always get their happily ever after. I learned a long time ago that trying to force someone to believe one thing about you when they believe another is a futile effort. People will believe what they want of you. Nothing you can do can alter that."

"I don't believe that," she admitted. And she knew firsthand that people didn't always get their happily ever after.

"I've been accused of far worse, Meg. Try not to turn over in your sleep too much on my account."

Accused of what? She wanted to ask, but dared not. Perhaps there was more to him than it appeared. It appeared that the missing boxes weren't the only mystery to solve. She was going to have her hands full.

He could resist the temptation. Gareth sighed heavily as he closed his door. He'd been alone with her all evening and not laid a single hand on her. It didn't mean he hadn't wanted to. She'd brought her maid to protect her reputation, but the woman had slept the entire time. So he had ample opportunity to take as much advantage of Meg's virtue as he would have liked.

He undressed quickly and folded his clothes. The Ladies' Amateur Sleuth Society. The very thought of it brought a smile to his lips. He didn't believe they would be able to uncover the identity of the real thief, but he had to admire her resourcefulness and dedication.

The boarding rooms sat on the Piddington property, right between the factory and Meg's house. The hill blocked the view to Piddington Hall, but he remembered what it had looked like that night he'd walked her home. Stately, large, well manicured, and inviting somehow. There was something about it that reminded him of his own childhood home. But that was a life-time ago.

He'd given her far too much information about his family tonight. It was unlikely that she would discover the truth; even so, there was no reason to divulge that much information. The more he told her, the more he'd trust her, and that was a dangerous game to play.

Women like Meg deserved to be wooed and cherished; he couldn't do either. If he wanted to dally with a woman, he could find someone else. But Meg was the marrying sort, and since he wasn't intending on marrying, he needed to stay away from her. His mind understood that perfectly, blast it; he didn't even want to marry her, regardless of ability to do so. But his body didn't understand. He wanted her despite who she was.

Chapter 6

Gareth had no sooner placed his coat in his locker than Munden appeared behind him.

"What do you have hiding in that locker?" he sneered.

Gareth turned slowly to face him. He leveled his eyes at the portly man, but said nothing.

"I need to search your belongings. Your locker and your rooms," Munden said.

Gareth didn't move, but he felt his hackles rise. "I don't believe I'll allow you to do that."

Munden's eyebrows rose and he fidgeted the cigar with his tongue until it was on the other side of his mouth. "You won't be allowing?" He gave Gareth a nasty grin. "I don't think you have the option. This here is Mr. Piddington's property." He motioned to the lockers behind Gareth.

Gareth stepped to the side. "Be my guest then, but you will not get into my rooms."

"You gonna stop me?"

"This order comes from your filthy head and no one else's. Until I hear an order from an official or Mr. Piddington himself, my rooms are off limits." He took a step forward and reveled in the fact that he stood a good head over Munden. "I'll be at my machine if you need me."

Munden didn't cower, but he also didn't question him further. Gareth made his way out of the storeroom and over to his grinding machine. He knew eyes were watching him, so he kept his own glance straight ahead.

He had nothing to hide. There was nothing in his rooms that would indicate he'd taken those boxes. Regardless of that, Munden for some reason had something against Gareth, and it was unlikely he would let the accusations go.

Gareth was already working on the boxes when Meg arrived. Mr. Munden had caught her as she'd entered the factory, and she was nearly ready to plead with her father to rid the factory of the foul man. There was something about him that unsettled her nerves, but she had no legitimate reasons to want to dismiss him.

She found Gareth sitting at the table positioning beveled mirrors on a velvet-lined box.

"Good evening," she said as she walked into the room.

He did not look up. "Hello," he said.

She removed her cloak and took a seat across from

him. The discussion she'd had with Munden had been about Gareth. She wanted to mention it, but thought better of it. If they discussed something else for a while, he'd be more inclined to confide in her.

"I brought in some chocolates," he said, pointing to the small metal tray at the center of the table. "These didn't mold right, so they won't go to the store."

"Thank you. I actually am rather hungry." She reached forward and picked up one of the misshapen pieces. It was thoughtful of him to think of her in such a manner. "Aren't you going to have some?" She bit into the dark, rich chocolate.

"I prefer drinking chocolate," he said.

"You know, I do as well. With a bit of warm milk, it's absolutely divine." She took another bite. "But I must admit, this is rather tasty."

She gathered her supplies and set about selecting the box she'd work on first. "May I ask you a question?" she said.

He shrugged.

"That night we got locked in the storeroom. What were you doing here? At first I thought it might be customary for employees to work after hours, and that perhaps I was just unaware of that. But as it turns out, it's quite rare and generally only happens under special circumstances."

Earlier today when she'd questioned the workers in the packing block, she'd inquired about just such a scenario. Granted, Gareth worked in a different area of the factory, but most of the same rules applied. "I'm only curious," she added in case he thought she was being accusatory.

"I was helping a friend," he said.

She narrowed her eyes. Until now, she'd assumed he didn't have any friends here. She'd never seen him speaking to anyone other than her and Munden.

"Jamie," he said. "He works at the station next to mine, and that day he'd come in and told me that his wife was birthing their child. I told him to leave, that I would do his lot that day. Doing both took me longer and so I was here after hours," he said. He never looked up while he spoke, just kept his focus on the box in his hands.

She didn't know what to say, but she suspected if she said much it would make them incredibly uncomfortable. It wouldn't matter to him that she was proud and touched by his kindness. And it should matter to her. She went back to her work, and they sat in silence for several minutes.

"I do believe we might finish tonight," she said as she set a completed box to her right.

He looked around the table. "You're probably right. And it won't be soon enough for me. I much prefer the cocoa powder on my hands than the glue," he said.

She grabbed a new box. It was one of the larger boxes that resembled a chest of drawers. "You never told me why you chose to work at a confectionery," she said. She knew she was asking a lot of questions, but she couldn't help it. That was who she was. He had just as much right to decline answering as she did in asking. So she'd continue to toss questions out there and see which ones he'd answer.

He glanced up at her and hesitated, and she wondered if she'd struck a nerve. But then he responded. "I've done many different types of work. Some factory, some not. But when I arrived in London, I heard good things about Piddington's. About the location of the factory and the living quarters and recreational areas." He set his completed box aside and grabbed for another. "I'd never done chocolates, so I thought it might be interesting."

"And is it?"

"I suppose. It smells good. Which is different from most factories. And the living accommodations are nice."

"You still have to pay rent," she added.

"Yes, but I can walk to work and the grounds are lovely. I've never worked anywhere before that had a recreation area for the employees." Then he laughed. "Mrs. Silsby cooks good meals too."

Her father had worked hard and bucked convention to provide a working environment that was safe and healthy for his employees. "It's nice to know that my father provides well for his employees. It is as it should be."

"Well, it is not standard by any means," he said.

"The other places you've worked, they've had poor conditions?"

"Most of them. Every once in a while you'll run into a fair foreman, but they're rare." He looked about the room. "But Piddington's is vastly different. I don't mind this. The work is good and the pay is good. The reading room is my favorite. I've never had access to so many books before."

She smiled. "I love to read as well. The reading room was my mother's idea so many years ago. She was the real book lover in our family. She loved stories and wanted access given to everyone. It was one of those ideas you have when you're dreaming of possibilities.

I don't think she ever imagined it would be a reality, and it's such a shame she didn't live to see it fulfilled. As soon as we moved the factory out here and we had so much room, Papa added the reading room."

She paused long enough to watch him stretch. With his arms over his head, the fabric of his shirt stretched taut, revealing a hint of his sinewy chest. "What did you want to do? I mean, when you were a child?"

Gareth leveled his eyes on hers, and didn't speak for several minutes. "When I was much younger, and my father was still alive, I wanted to box like he did."

"Box? As in a boxing ring? Fighting?"

"Yes. That wasn't really his profession. More of a favorite pastime. But it seemed very exciting to me as a boy. But then we left for Ireland."

"Did you ever box?" she asked.

"No, I've never even tried it."

"So your family moved to Ireland?"

"My mother and us kids," he said.

"But your father did not?" she asked.

"No. We left him here. Shortly after that, he died in a boxing match." He sounded more angry than sad, and she had to wonder if he still carried around the scars of a twelve-year-old boy.

Her stomach lurched. "Oh, how dreadful, Gareth. I'm so very sorry." She wanted to go to him. Pull him close and hold him, but she knew he would not accept the gesture. She could offer no comfort though. She had barely been able to swallow her own loss.

He shook his head. "It was a long time ago. The wounds had long since healed."

But she wasn't so certain she believed that. There was something there between him and his father. Anger or guilt or something she couldn't quite put her finger on. Something unsettled that left Gareth restless and that had ultimately brought him back to London to resolve it. Whether or not he realized that himself.

"So at some point, you must have realized that boxing was not for you. Did you want to do anything else? Even something you felt was out of your reach?"

"No, after that, I knew I only had to find something that paid a decent wage. Something honest," he added. "What about you? You're so full of questions tonight. What were your childhood dreams?"

It was hard to remember who she was before her mother died. She knew she was different. Simpler and full of dreams and big ideas. "I wanted many different things. But I think for most of my childhood, I wanted to grow up and be like my mother. Be a wife and have a little girl whom I doted on."

"And now? Do you still want those things?"

"No," she said quickly. She would be unable to explain to him why she couldn't have those things. Why she'd had to give up those dreams. She wasn't certain anyone would understand her reasons. "Now I want different things."

"Such as?"

"This factory. I want to be a true heir to it. I want my father to leave it in my hands and know it will be well cared for."

"And that is what will happen?"

She closed her eyes a brief moment. How she wished that would happen. "No. As it stands now, when he dies, this will cease being a private business and will become a company. Owned by many, none of whom toil here. None of whom love this place."

"But you love it?"

"In my own way. I love my father. And he loves it. I want to run this factory for him."

"Isn't all of this rather unorthodox for a woman? Especially one of your breeding? I would have suspected a lady such as yourself would have married years ago."

"It is odd, I suppose. Women work in factories, but to have one in charge of the entire outfit? That will be unique. But I'm determined." She ignored his comment about marriage.

"What does your father have to say about this?"

"Every time I've approached him with it in the past, he's switched the subject. I'm not certain if he doesn't believe I'm capable or if he simply doesn't want to burden me with it. Perhaps both. But I'm determined to prove to him that I'll gladly take the burden. That I want to. I don't want him to lose this company. Even in death. Why, do you find it odd?"

He shrugged. "Different. But you're different from any woman I've ever met. If anyone can administer this factory, you can."

The words "thank you" were right in her throat, but she was unable to utter them. He was quite accomplished at pretending he was this uncaring oaf who didn't like people. But she'd seen sparks of a gentle heart on more than one occasion. There was definitely more than met the eye when it came to Gareth Mandeville.

"I spoke with Mr. Munden when I arrived," she said. Perhaps now was the time to broach this subject.

He did not look up.

"Gareth, why would you not allow him to search your rooms if you know it will prove your innocence?"

That pulled his glance up to hers. "Do you honestly think that giving him permission to do so will prove anything to him? No." He didn't give her time to answer. "All it will do is feed his need to have power over me. And when he finds nothing, he'll create some excuse about how I sold them, or I'm storing them elsewhere. I've worked with men like Munden before. He will not give up—this is only the beginning with him."

He was so matter-of-fact. As if it were completely natural to have someone not only assume the worst of you, but, in a sense, pursue you. It wasn't natural and it wasn't right. "Why is he after you?" she asked.

"How the hell should I know?"

The dark stubble on his chin and upper lip gave him a dangerous look, yet Meg felt no fear. He was angry, and rightly so. It was unfair for him to be accused of something while someone else got away with it.

"The Ladies' Amateur Sleuth Society hasn't found anything yet, but we have a plan. I started speaking with the other workers today to see if anyone heard or saw anything about that night."

"I didn't see you come in today," he said.

"Oh, not here. I started with the packaging and molding rooms. Women talk more than men, so any gossip would circulate among them first."

His eyebrows raised slightly. "And?"

She sighed. "Nothing." But many of the women had known who he was. Apparently Meg wasn't the only one to find him handsome. A fact she found rather annoying regardless of how unimportant it should have been to her.

He shrugged. "It's not your responsibility," he said.

"It is my responsibility because the theft occurred

here. I cannot allow a thief to run amok and do nothing about it. Amelia and Willow are going to ask around at some pawnbrokers. We figure if we were to steal something, that's probably where we would try to sell it."

"That's clever," he said.

Her heart seemed to flip in her chest. Perhaps he didn't think her an utter fool. "My friend's husband is an inspector for hire and he has friends at the Scotland Yard, so if we need professional assistance, we can ask them."

"I don't think that's necessary. The authorities haven't even been notified. Besides, I thought you knew how to do this sort of investigating. Being the amateur sleuth that you are."

She thought she detected a light smile play across his mouth, but she wasn't certain. He was goading her. But he was also correct. She did know how to sleuth. She wasn't as clever as Amelia or Willow, but surely she could be of assistance.

He might not feel this investigation was necessary, but she certainly did. Her heart beat a rapid tattoo and she gifted him with a smile. "We will discover the real perpetrator. You can rely on the Ladies' Amateur Sleuth Society."

He smiled, and her stomach jolted. The lines creasing his forehead relaxed, and she was struck again by the perfection in his lips. He was so handsome.

"I appreciate your help, Meg, but you don't owe me anything. So if you and your friends want to ask around or something, I'm not going to attempt to stop you. I doubt very much I'd be able to do so. But don't go to any great deal of trouble."

"You are not the only reason I am engaged in this

investigation, I'll have you know." She took a deep breath and held her chin out. "If this criminal thinks he can run willy-nilly in my father's factory, then he's not prepared to deal with me. That being said, if you're worried about me getting hurt, I can assure you, I can take care of myself."

"No, I wasn't worried about that."

"Oh." That pinched. Why wouldn't he be concerned for her safety? Any decent man would be a tiny bit worried. Or at the very least spend a moment with a furrowed brow.

They worked in silence for several minutes. Each working on one last box. Meg held the last mirror in place, then paused to examine her work.

"It appears we have completed the task. They look nice, don't you agree?" she said.

He looked around the table, but only shrugged in response. He released a great sigh. "I don't work well with others," he finally said. He stood and walked over to her side of the table, close to the door. "I've done enough tonight. Thank you for your help."

"Have you tried it?" she prodded.

He was growing impatient. She could tell by the tight clench of his jaw and the sharp movements of his hand.

"Tried what?"

She stood, but did not dare move closer to him. "Working with others? Don't you have to do that here? What is the difference with me?"

"The difference?" he grumbled. "Let me tell you the difference. The men in this factory dress a little different from you." He came to stand in front of her. He leaned in and put his nose beside her left ear and slowly inhaled. "They smell different from you."

Chills scattered all over Meg's body, and she felt her breasts tighten. *Oh my.* What she'd pegged as annoyance apparently was nothing less than desire. Desire for her, in particular. Her pulse sped up, as did her breathing.

He leaned even closer, and she felt his warm breath on her neck. She closed her eyes just as he took her earlobe in his mouth and suckled it.

"I would imagine they taste much different too, although for that one I have no base of comparison," he said.

Desire coiled so quickly through her body, she feared she would melt into the wood-planked floor. She turned her head ever so slightly, and he grabbed her fiercely and pressed his lips to hers. His body molded against hers, pressing her already sensitive breasts to his chest. He pushed her onto the table and fell over her, all the while trailing hot kisses over her neck, collarbone, and ears.

She wanted him. Wanted whatever pleasure he could give her. It was wrong. Improper. Immoral. And completely irresistible.

His lips met hers and his tongue tantalized her. Teasing, licking, stroking until she thought she would go mad. She reached behind him and pulled him down to her and slanted her mouth, giving him full access. Their tongues stroked and played, and shivers cascaded over her like delicious waterfalls of pleasure.

She felt his arousal push into her belly, and she instinctively pushed against him. Wanting more, wanting release, wanting him.

His hand slid up her abdomen and cupped her right breast. Her back arched instinctively, and she felt her nipples harden. Gracious, she'd never felt such sensations. He kneaded the sensitive flesh, and the tingles between her legs intensified.

With a movement full of impatience, he slipped his hand beneath her bodice and stroked her aching nipple. His mouth left hers and blazed a trail to her ear, then down her throat.

She bucked erratically against him.

"Oh, Gareth," she breathed.

"Blast!" he said, then rolled off her. He stood against the door, with his hands clenched at his sides.

She slowly came to her feet, but had to grab on to the table so she would not fall. "What's the matter?" she asked. "If you're worried about my maid, she's napping. Falls asleep every evening by seven."

He shook his head. "I can't do this," he said. "Not with you." Then he turned and walked out the door.

Not with her? What did that mean? What was the matter with her? She knew she was no great beauty, but neither was she plain or unattractive. So why not her?

More importantly, why did she need him to want her? He was not a suitor, and they were not going to marry, so why did it matter? The easy answer was because it felt good. His kisses and his touches sparked her body.

She'd never before been kissed or embraced in such a fashion, and she loved it. Loved the desire coursing thick through her blood. It wasn't merely the sensations, though; she knew it wouldn't be the same with just anyone.

It terrified her to examine the situation more closely to discover the truth. She was playing a dangerous game, and ultimately she knew she would lose.

* * *

Gareth closed his eyes and let the wind slap at his face. A storm was brewing, and the wind had picked up considerably. He'd gone too far tonight. Why did he find it so difficult to be in the same room with Meg and not touch her? There was nothing that unique about her body. She was a woman. He'd been with women before.

Why were her lips so much more tempting? Her laughter so much more appealing? Her presence so much more inviting? She was an innocent, and he shouldn't toy with her emotions and virtue with such disregard. He could blame her for being a temptress, but he was the true one to blame. He and his selfish nature for taking what he wanted without giving thought to the repercussions. Just as his father had done, and his father before him.

This was not what he needed right now. Yes, he wanted a higher position in the factory, but he certainly didn't want to achieve it by nuzzling the owner's daughter. If anything, that might lose him his current position. This whole fiasco with Munden had really broken his focus on his work. He need only find that focus again and resist the temptations that being near Meg brought.

But she was so different from any other woman he'd ever encountered. The differences seemed more elaborate when he considered her wealth and privilege. Unlike most women of her station who sat around and gossiped and drank tea all day, Meg had plans. Even the silly society she and her friends had formed. It was not something that women of their birth should be doing.

She was unmarried by choice, he assumed. Because

it seemed unlikely that Meg had not had her fair share of eligible suitors. Yet she wanted to forsake the life of a woman and being a wife and mother to take her father's factory. Perhaps he'd been wrong when he'd assumed no one would understand his need to prove himself. It was a noble sacrifice born out of a sense of responsibility, and Gareth couldn't ignore that.

Unfortunately, it was a trait that only made her more appealing to him.

Chapter 7

Meg walked into her family dining room not quite certain what to expect. She had received a summons to dine there for the evening rather than in her father's chambers where she had been eating since his accident. And lo and behold, the answer to her question sat at the far end of the table.

"Papa!" She hurried to his side. "But how did you get down the stairs?"

"Pah," he said gruffly. "The doctor finally listened and brought me some crutches. So I walked. Or rather I hobbled, with some assistance."

"But you could have fallen," she protested.

"Ah, but I didn't. Sit, child, let us dine together as civilized people would."

She gave him a small curtsy, then took her seat at the opposite end of the table. A spot reserved for a wife, but he had never even considered remarrying after her mother died. He'd ached too much. They both had. Which was precisely why it was becoming abundantly clear she had to cease dallying with Gareth.

Every moment without him, she wondered when the next moment with him would arrive. This infatuation was growing stronger by the day, and it should end. But something in her simply didn't want it to.

If she was not careful, her heart would get tangled in something she would have no idea how to undo. She couldn't walk through that pain again. She wouldn't. It was her sunny disposition that had finally eased her father's pain. She'd swallowed her own sorrow in an effort to bring her papa back from the edge. And it had worked. Nothing seemed to make him happier than seeing his Meggie smile. If she got her heart broken again, it might destroy them both.

So it mattered not that Gareth did not want her. Yes, her pride was bruised, but that was for the best. Because she could not want him.

She would help him; she owed him that much. But after that, she would focus all her attention on the factory.

"Tell me, Meggie, how are things down at the factory?" he asked.

"Have you not spoken to Mr. Sanders?" she said. "Has he not apprised you of everything?" She wasn't certain how much information her father had regarding the goings-on at the factory. If he knew of Gareth's predicament, and if so, how much. Would he approve of the way she'd handled things thus far?

He chewed thoughtfully on his bite of pheasant, then wiped his mouth with his napkin. "He has mentioned a few things. Profits are up. We've almost completed negotiations with Wakemore for their condensed milk, so it won't be long before we are in production of the dairy chocolates."

Perhaps he knew nothing.

"Oh, and he has mentioned that there is a thief working there. And that you have become somewhat of a champion to him." His eyebrows rose in clear amusement.

At least he was not angry with her, although when had he ever been truly angry with her? "But Papa, he is not the thief."

"You know this for certain?" he asked.

She did. But she definitely couldn't tell him that. At least not in detail how she knew. "I do."

"How is that?"

"I know. I've asked him, and he says he did not steal the boxes."

"Would not a thief answer that question in the same manner?" he asked.

"I suppose he might. But with Gareth, I know he speaks the truth."

"Gareth, is it?" he asked with an ounce of surprise.

She felt the heat of a blush creep into her cheeks. Never a becoming look for one with hair as flaming as her own. "Mr. Mandeville, Father."

"What has Mr. Mandeville done to land himself in the good graces of my daughter?"

"Mr. Munden has wrongly accused him and refuses to consider any alternatives than the one set to his mind. Mr. Mandeville has no one to champion him but myself. Mr. Munden was going to dismiss him. I couldn't allow that to happen. I know the truth. And if that nasty foreman won't do anything to uncover the truth, then I will do it for him."

Her father looked at her, then he chuckled heartily. His shoulders popped up and down as he shook with deep laughter. "You are so much like your mother, my dear girl. So much like her. Such fire in you." He wiped his mouth with his napkin. "Very well, if you believe him innocent, then you prove it. In the meantime, do take some care with your reputation. I know you're not involved with Society that much, but your mother was, and people still remember her."

She nodded. She knew she ought to be more careful with that. Should at least consider it now and again. But the truth of the matter was, it never entered her mind. Not rarely, not every once in a while. Never. Not once had she ever considered it on her own. Only when Willow mentioned it. She never considered it because it seemed strange to assume that people would talk about her.

Papa was right, though. People did remember her mother. Meg would endeavor to try and think of her reputation and guard it more often. Although since she would never marry, it seemed any great effort would be wasted.

"So you are not angry?" she asked.

"No. I am not angry. But keep in mind that when someone claims innocence it does not mean he is, in fact, innocent. He could very well be the thief in question. If that turns out to be the case, not only will you have been wrong, my dear, but you will be sorely disappointed."

She nodded. "But, dear Papa, I am not wrong." She saluted him with her goblet of wine.

"Very well, Meggie, very well. For your sake, I hope your Mr. Mandeville is as innocent as a priest."

She turned her attention back to her meal, hoping her father did not notice how disconcerted she suddenly felt. Gareth might not be a thief, but he was not innocent. Not when just last night his body had pressed against hers and he'd kissed her and touched her in such carnal ways. Tingles of desire coursed through her. A priest he most certainly was not.

And for the first time, Meg realized that although Gareth was not guilty of stealing the chocolate boxes, there might be far worse sins of which he was guilty.

"The Ladies' Amateur Sleuth Society are a fine lot. We are doomed in love," Charlotte said dramatically.

Charlotte had come to Piddington Hall today to assist Meg with some mending, most notably her petticoat. Meg smiled. "Doomed? How so?"

"Each of us seems to find the perfectly wrong man to fancy."

"Explain," Meg prodded.

Charlotte secured the needle, then set the torn petticoat aside. "Well, there's Amelia, who for the longest time fancied Sherlock Holmes. The man is not even real. You fancy Mr. Mandeville. A man you scarcely know. And myself, well, I'm the most hopeless of all," she said dramatically, then leaned her head back on the settee.

"Jack of Hearts?" Meg asked.

Charlotte winced, then covered her face with her hands. "Isn't that wicked?"

Meg poked her in her side. "No, it's romantic. Nothing wrong with fancying an adventure. That's all it is. But I find serious fault with your logic. First of all, where is poor Willow in this scenario?"

Charlotte turned her body to face Meg. "Willow, for reasons I shall never understand, doesn't seem to be interested in men at all. How is that possible? She's much too involved with her books and the newspapers. I bet she reads every broadsheet in town. That's simply not normal."

"She likes to be involved and know what's going on around her. Nothing wrong with that," Meg said. "Very well, so we shall leave Willow out of this theory of yours. But how do you explain Amelia? She might have fancied Sherlock Holmes, but she is married now. That is hardly doomed in love."

"Yes, she is married. But practically to Sherlock himself!"

"Not true. You know very well that Colin is quite different from the fictional detective." She picked a piece of thread from the cushion and balled it between her fingers. "And he does love Amelia in such a grand fashion."

"You're right about that. So 'tis only you and I that are hopeless, I suppose?"

Meg shifted her position, folding her legs under her to sit. "Ah, but you are wrong about me too. I don't fancy Gareth Mandeville, just so you know. I merely feel guilty that he's being falsely accused and I can't do anything about it."

"Honestly, Meg, there is no reason to pretend. I

know you better than anyone and you are smitten."

Meg tried to laugh it off, but she couldn't. Part of her knew that Charlotte's accusations were true, and that terrified her. "I am not."

"You know as well as I that this fascination is different. You have had fancies in the past as each of us has, but this is different. You actually have a relationship with him. You see him, speak to him on a regular basis. You know things about him."

Meg shrugged. "Not many." At least that wasn't a lie.

"What color are his eyes?"

"Hazel." Meg winced.

Charlotte smiled. "See."

"That doesn't prove anything. I know what color your eyes are too."

"But here's the difference. Most of the time you have to be rather close to someone to determine the exact shade that is hazel, otherwise one might assume the eyes are only green or only brown. The fact that you know there is both mingling together indicates to me you've been close to him. Quite close."

"Well, aren't you the clever detective this morning."

Charlotte laughed. "Do you deny it?"

Meg considered her options. She could lie and then feel guilty for a day or two until she confessed as she always did when she was persuaded to tell an untruth. Or she could be honest. Tell Charlotte everything, how she thought about Gareth more than she ought and how he'd kissed her. More than once.

She knew Charlotte would not judge her. But she also knew that Charlotte would find much excitement in the situation, enough to persuade Meg into feeling equally excited. That was something she couldn't afford. But she needed to talk about it with someone, and Charlotte was her dearest friend.

"You have to promise that you will not say anything until I finish," Meg said.

"All right," Charlotte said with a frown.

Meg watched her friend a moment before beginning. "I have been close to Gareth. Close enough to see the exact shade of his eyes. I can even tell you that the green and brown mix together to form a rich gold that circles his eyes."

Charlotte raised her eyebrows in question, but Meg rushed on. "I can tell you that he has a small scar through his right eyebrow. Or that his lip twitches ever so slightly when he's amused, but doesn't want to be. And I can tell you that his lips are soft and tender." She closed her eyes then to block out Charlotte's face. She needed to say these things, needed to pour them out and set them free else they continue to collect in her brain and drive her mad.

"When he pulls me into his arms, which he has done on more than one occasion, I feel more alive and vibrant than I ever knew possible. And kissing him is as natural as breathing. I know he was born in London and that he has three sisters and a brother, all of whom still live in Ireland. I know he's intelligent and focused and stubborn. And I know that to him, I am nothing more than a sweet diversion." She heard Charlotte intake her breath sharply, but Meg ignored the reaction; there was more she needed to say.

"Ever since that first evening locked in that store-room, I have thought of little else save him, and his presence in my head is crowding everything else. I think of Willow and know how disappointed she'd be in my behavior. And I think of my poor papa who wishes I would settle down and marry. But mostly I think of my heart and how I cannot afford to spend another thought on Gareth Mandeville. I have not yet lost it to him; for that I am thankful. I realized where I was headed the other evening, and I have been successful in tightening the reins on the situation."

Of course, even that was a lie. It was Gareth who had ended their embrace, not she. Which only served to convince her how desperate the situation had become. She could not allow this to continue. She must harden her heart and strengthen her convictions, such as they were.

"The factory and my father are what's important to me. And that's where I will pour all of my energy. So yes, I do know the exact shade of Gareth's eyes as well as many other tiny things I wish I'd never discovered. I will continue trying to solve this crime to catch the true thief and to clear Gareth's name because I feel partially to blame." She opened her eyes then and leveled her gaze with Charlotte.

"Is it all so bad then?" Charlotte asked.

Meg thought on it. "No, it's not bad. I just want to be cautious."

"Would loving a man like Gareth be so bad?" Charlotte said.

"I remember a year after Mama had died, I went down to the kitchen to get something to drink. It was late, I'm not certain what time, but it was dark and everyone was in bed. I passed by my father's chambers and I could hear him weeping. I opened the door to see what was wrong because I thought he might be injured, but it was another type of pain I witnessed. There he was"—Meg smiled ruefully—"great man that he is, on his knees at the edge of his bed. He had the bedsheets fisted in his hands and his eyes squeezed tight and he was wailing, he was crying so much. And then he said her name. Josephine.

"I missed her dreadfully then, but I was but a child without a mother. But my poor papa, a grown man full of strength and wisdom, still so full of anguish from losing her. I decided that evening that as long as I lived I would offer him nothing but smiles. That I would bring him joy the only way I knew." She shook her head. "I am not as strong as he, Charlotte. I know that I could not ever survive such a loss." She swiftly wiped one tear away. "I know that it is not to be my lot in life. I was not designed for love so great because I would not be able to withstand the pain of losing it."

"Meg, I—"

"I know what you're going to say. They don't all end in loss, sometimes people stay happy forever. And that's true, but what if?" She looked at Charlotte. "What if?" She shook her head. "It would destroy me. And that would destroy my papa." Meg patted Charlotte's hand. "Listen to me carry on." She shook her head. "Pay me no mind. I'm feeling awfully sentimental today. It matters not. I will feel quite right tomorrow; I suppose I am tired. Thank you again for agreeing to fix my petticoat. You can take it with you, if you prefer."

She'd never before dismissed her friend. But she'd said far more than she intended and now she needed, very much, to be alone. Bless Charlotte's heart, she understood, because she nodded, gathered her stuff, and left after giving Meg a tight squeeze.

* * *

He watched the tall brunette leave Piddington Hall. Meg and her silly friends. She would not have as much freedom once she belonged to him. He would be her only confidant then. The only one for her to turn to. His hand clenched tightly around a rose blossom.

No need to be frustrated. All was not lost yet. He would figure out a way to work this situation to his benefit. But so far blaming the thefts on that lowly Irishman was not working. Without evidence, nothing could be brought to the authorities' attention. And now Miss Piddington had tangled herself further with the Irish bastard, and that would ruin everything. Months of planning and years of hard work. He couldn't allow that to happen.

He needed more time. More time would produce the perfect plan, and then all would fall into place.

Chapter 8

Meg settled in her seat in Amelia's parlor, waiting anxiously for the meeting to start. She'd received a post that morning for an emergency meeting. She was as grateful as she was curious. It had been a day since she'd dismissed Charlotte, and she wanted to ensure all was right between them. She tried to catch her eye, but Charlotte was not looking in her direction. Perhaps her friend was angry with her.

"Let us recite our oath," Amelia said.

"We solemnly swear to unravel mysteries by ferreting out secrets at all costs," they said together.

"Now, then, let us begin. I called this meeting today because Willow has some information to share that she believes will be most useful to Mr. Mandeville's case. Willow, proceed."

Willow sat at the edge of her seat and pushed her spectacles farther onto her nose. "Now then, I was speaking with Edmond last night about things going on in his life, and he mentioned a particular fellow he ran into recently at a gaming hell."

"Edmond was at a gaming hell?" Charlotte asked, clearly surprised.

Willow frowned. "I was shocked and disappointed in my dear brother as well, but he assured me he had good reason. In any case, he was there playing cards with some fellows, and this one, in particular, was bragging about a recent purchase he made. A rather pricey purchase."

"Willow, where is this going?" Meg sat up straight. She felt excited and slightly annoyed, all at the same time.

"I shall arrive at the point shortly, if you would but give me a moment. As I was saying, this particular gentleman, who is actually not a gentleman at all, recently purchased a racing horse."

Charlotte frowned. "What do racing horses have to do with anything?"

Willow shrugged, then smiled. "Only that this man is none other than Mr. Munden."

"My Mr. Munden?" Meg said. "I mean, the Mr. Munden that is employed by my father?"

"One and the same," Willow confirmed.

Meg shook her head. "But he does not earn enough to make such a purchase."

"Precisely." Willow pointed a finger at Meg. "Where do you suppose he got the funds for such a large purchase?"

Meg felt her eyes grow round. "From stealing and selling those chocolate boxes? Surely they wouldn't earn quite that much."

"They might if you sold them to a competitor who was trying to produce similar products," Amelia offered.

"That's what I was thinking," Willow said.

"Surely he wouldn't dare," Meg said. That would be terrible and grossly unfair to her father.

"Or perhaps this isn't the only thing he's stolen," Charlotte suggested.

"Excellent point," Amelia said.

"So he stole the boxes himself and has been trying to blame Gareth for the crime," Meg said, indignation on Gareth's behalf rising within her. "But why would he do that?"

"His motive is unclear at this point," Willow said.

"This is terrible," Meg said. "What should we do?"

"You need proof that he took those boxes before you can do anything," Charlotte said.

"She's right," Amelia said.

"Well, I believe it's safe to assume that he wouldn't keep any such proof at the factory," Willow suggested.

"Perhaps he has some kind of record at his residence," Amelia said.

"That certainly presents a problem," Willow said.

"Do you know where he lives, Meg?" Charlotte asked.

"No, but my father keeps a file on each of his employees, so the information would not be too difficult to come by."

"Perfect," Charlotte said, a mischievous smile creeping across her face.

"Why do I get the feeling you're about to suggest something that I am not going to approve of?" Willow asked. "You always get that look on your face."

"What look?" Charlotte asked innocently. "I was merely going to suggest that Meg sneak into Mr. Munden's residence and dig around a bit. See what she can find."

Willow put her head in her hands. "I knew it," she said with a muffled voice.

"Then you thought of it too?" Amelia asked.

"Well, of course I did. It's the logical choice to find such evidence. But it's far too dangerous," Willow said.

"Not if you help," Meg said.

"You want me to go with you?" Willow asked.

"Of course not. I need you to help divert Munden's attention. Have Edmond send him an invitation for another hand of cards. Men love those sorts of things. While he's gone, I'll sneak in and poke around and see what I can discover."

"This sounds very dangerous," Amelia said.

"Not any more dangerous than the escapades you went on last year," Charlotte pointed out.

"Yes, but I nearly got killed. And I was going to add that it sounds very dangerous, and exciting," she said with a laugh.

"All Meg needs is a disguise. She's so tiny that with the right clothes, she'll look like a young boy and no one will bother her," Charlotte said.

"Where am I supposed to get the clothes for that?" Meg asked.

"From me," Charlotte said. "Mama has put up trunks of Anthony's clothes; I'm certain we could find something that would work."

Meg's stomach fluttered.

Willow released a great sigh, then leaned forward in her chair. "If you're going to do this, wear dark clothes so you'll blend in more with the dark night," she said. "But I am not approving of this," she added with a point of her finger.

"Do you really think your brother's clothes will fit me?" Meg asked.

"Something of his will. Mama keeps everything, so we have years' worth of clothes. Most of it in browns and blacks, so we can abide with Willow's suggestion."

"You also want to put your hair up," Amelia said. "No young boy I know has flaming curls the likes of yours. You can hide it beneath a hat of some sort."

Meg's hand went to her hair. "Yes, good reminder. Will you help me?" She directed her question to Willow. "Ask Edmond to send an invitation to Mr. Munden? Then you can send me a note to let me know the date he's settled on, and I'll make my plans accordingly." Meg eyed her friend and watched the myriad of emotions cross her face. Helping her do this went against Willow's strict code of propriety and rule following, but she was also a loyal friend, and saying no would be difficult.

Willow's lips went thin, then she gave a brief nod. "I will ask Edmond to send a message to Mr. Munden."

Meg popped out of her seat and raced to embrace Willow.

"If he receives an acknowledgment," Willow continued. "I'll notify you. You will need to go in and out quickly, Meg. And don't speak to anyone. If he catches you, there is no telling what he might do to you. You must take extreme caution."

"Yes, of course." The more Willow talked, the more Meg's nerves raged inside her. But the stakes had risen. Not only was Gareth's innocence at stake, but if Munden was the thief, Meg needed to find out so they could dismiss him from his position.

Her father would never question her ability if she succeeded in this.

"I promise I will take great care. I will stop by later to find some clothes," she said to Charlotte.

Meg looked around at each of her friends and felt nothing but gratitude. People went a lifetime without making one genuine friend, and here she was blessed with four.

She needed to speak with Gareth. Give him this information and see what he suggested they do. She stood. "Thank you, Willow. Thank you to each of you. And Edmond too. I should be going. Mr. Mandeville will find this information all too interesting. See you at the next meeting."

Meg paced her father's office, impatiently waiting until she and Gareth could speak privately. Surely this information about Mr. Munden meant he was the true thief. It all made sense. If he wanted to continue working at and stealing from Piddington's, he had to blame the theft of the boxes on someone else. Gareth was a convenient choice since he was the newest employee and, for the most part, kept to himself.

She stood at the windows overlooking the factory floor and watched the men filter out the front door. She'd been waiting for nearly three hours to speak with Gareth, and the moment would be here quickly now. On her way into the factory, she's stopped by his machine to tell him she needed to see him at the close of the day. He'd looked rather irritated by the whole scene.

Meg stepped back to the desk, then walked over to

the bookshelf. She ran her hand across one shelf of books. Some of her mother's favorite volumes, worn-out, well-loved leather-bound books. Kept here in her father's office because ordinarily he spent so much time here. And he always needed a piece of her nearby. At home in his bedchamber, he had a handful of other editions.

She picked up the framed photograph that sat on the shelf next to the books. The image in her palm did not do her mother justice. Without color in the picture, the vibrancy of her rich auburn hair wasn't accurately portrayed, nor was the softness of her skin. But if Meg closed her eyes, she could almost remember the sound of her voice, almost recollect the joy in her laugh. A wave of longing washed over her.

"Oh, Mama," she said softly.

A knock at the door startled her.

Meg jerked her hand away from the photograph as if caught doing mischief, then she chided herself. No, sentimentality was not mischievous. Nor was it the proper business countenance she wished to convey.

She allowed her hand to drop to her side, straightened her shoulders, and turned her back on the photograph.

"Come in," she said.

A few seconds later Mr. Munden stepped into the office. Her stomach flipped over. "Mr. Munden, I wasn't expecting you," she said.

"I saw you up here and wanted to come ask about your father. How's he doing?"

What did he care how her father was doing? He was stealing from the man. She set her chin and met his eyes. If he was going to be dishonest, then she'd force him to do it to her face. "He's well, recovering quite rightly, I do believe," she said.

He nodded. "That's good." He glanced over to the windows, then slid his hands into his pockets. "When are you expecting he'll return to work?"

"Shouldn't be too much longer." She actually didn't know that for certain, but perhaps his pending return would spur Munden to confess.

"That was a nasty fall he took," Munden said. She thought she detected a slight glimmer in his eyes.

Meg frowned. Nasty fall, indeed. Oh, gracious, was it possible that Munden had caused her father's accident to get him out of the way at the factory? Without her father's watchful eye and daily management, Munden's duties had increased, as had his freedom. "Yes, it was a nasty fall."

Munden nodded. "Give him my best. I'll be off now," he said, then turned and left the office.

Meg watched him leave and clenched her fists at her side, then caught herself. She was not a violent person, and even if she were, what could she do to him? He was more than twice her size. She ordinarily didn't mind the fact that she was so small, but only a moment before it had seemed a serious hindrance.

Granted, even if she were as tall as Charlotte, she probably could not do much to defend herself against the bulky Mr. Munden.

"What the hell did he want?" Gareth said from the door.

She hadn't even heard him open it.

Gareth must have read the momentary confusion on

her face because he continued without giving her a chance to respond. "Munden?" he repeated. "What did he want?"

She shook her head. "He was asking about my father. He wanted to know when he was coming back to work."

Gareth nodded. "What was it you wanted to discuss with me?"

Seeing Munden had rattled her, and she'd nearly forgotten what she needed to tell Gareth. Nearly forgotten that they had the first clue in the case.

"I've discovered a bit of information. Helpful information," she added, then sat behind the desk.

He followed suit and sat across from her. "And?" he asked.

"It appears that our Mr. Munden made a hefty purchase recently. One he could not afford with his salary."

"What sort of purchase?"

"A racing horse."

Gareth released a low whistle. "I've never been in the position to investigate the price on such a creature, but I suspect you're right and they're not cheap. How did you find this out?"

"Willow's brother. Apparently he saw Munden at a gaming hell and the man was bragging about it."

"So you have no other proof than the man's own boasts?" Gareth asked.

Meg frowned. "No, I suppose not. Edmond, he's Willow's brother, is a fine fellow, very honest, you see, and he would never make up something of this sort."

"I didn't mean him. I meant Munden. He seems precisely the sort to invent such things to make himself appear more important than he actually is." Gareth rubbed his one forearm and then the other. No doubt working those machines all day made his arms ache.

She didn't miss that his sleeves were rolled to his elbows, revealing well-formed arms smattered with dark hair. "You certainly have a point there. But it seems to make sense. He steals the boxes, sells them and pockets the cash for a later purchase, then blames you for his crime to deflect suspicion from himself."

His eyebrows raised. "You've certainly figured all of this out, haven't you?"

She shrugged. "With the help of the society."

Gareth leaned back in the chair, arms rested behind his head. "Do you believe those boxes are worth that much?"

"I asked the same question." She relayed the potential plan of selling the concept to another factory.

"That would make him a thief and a traitor," Gareth said. "Weighty accusations, Miss Piddington, with no actual proof."

She pursed her lips. "Did I mention, I also suspect him of causing my poor father's accident? Removing my father from this office for a few months would certainly give him the freedom to do his debauchery."

"Debauchery?" He smiled, and she caught herself staring at his mouth. "You do have quite the imagination. I hate to present the obvious, but you've criticized Munden for making accusations about me without proof. Now you're doing the same with him. You need evidence for your suspicions," he said.

He was right, but it was different somehow. Different because she liked Gareth. More than she had any right to. But despite that, she knew they needed proof about Munden regardless of how she already knew and believed him to be guilty.

"We've already thought of that too and have the perfect plan," she said.

He steepled his fingers under his chin. "I'm intrigued."

"I will sneak into Munden's residence and look around. Find paperwork or something from the purchase of the racing horse or perhaps confirmation of him stealing those boxes. Once we have that verification, we can confront him and your name will be cleared."

"You can't be serious," he said. When she didn't deny it, he came to his feet. "No, it's too risky, not to mention illegal." He shook his head. "It's too dangerous, Meg."

"But if it will clear your name, isn't it worth it?"

A deep frown creased his brow. "Not if you get caught or hurt in the process," he said. "I can't allow that."

Oh, so he was concerned with her safety, and that meant he cared for her. Her insides warmed. At least a fraction.

"I will wear a disguise to protect myself."

He stood and walked the short length of the carpet. "You don't know how to break and enter," he argued, then he hesitated, his expression changed as if he was almost afraid to say more. "Do you?"

"No, I don't know how, but how difficult could it possibly be?"

He stopped pacing and looked at her. "You really are serious about this," he said. He rubbed his forehead.

"Indeed."

"I'm going with you," he said firmly.

Her heart—not to mention her pulse—leaped at his words. To hide her sudden anticipation, she insisted, "I will be safe. I don't need you coming along to act as a nursemaid." Although she was secretly hoping he would come with her.

"You can't argue with me about this. If you're insistent on this, I'm going with you. You're not getting yourself killed on my account. I don't have time to feel guilty about that."

She felt her excitement wane a little. Here she had just accepted that he was concerned for her well-being. Began to believe he actually cared about her, if only a tiny bit. But his concern wasn't built on warm feelings toward her, but rather a desire to not feel guilty. He didn't want to feel responsible should anything happen to her while she flitted around the city on his behalf.

He released a puff of air. "What about Munden?"

"Already taken care of." She gave him a sweet smile.

"Proud of yourself?" he asked.

"Quite."

"Very well, explain how you will get him out of the house."

"Edmond will send an invitation for another game. Munden apparently enjoys a good game and shouldn't be able to resist a personal invitation. Especially from the son of a viscount."

She thought she detected a slight flinch, but it was gone before she could be certain.

"It is settled then," he said.

"Yes," she said. Her stomach was rolling with excitement. This must be how Amelia felt as she and Colin chased after the man who had stolen her father's prized antiquity. Nervous and scared, but exhilarated all at the same time.

She didn't want to consider how her excitement had increased now that Gareth was going to accompany her.

"Do you know where he lives?" he asked.

She picked up the file from the top of her father's desk. "I looked it up. He's not too far from here, but we'll have to go into the city. I'll send you a message when I have everything set," she added.

"No, it might be intercepted, and that's too risky. Come and retrieve me," he said. "You have better access to carriages, and then we'll ride into London and get this over with."

A tremor of excitement shot down her spine. This was going to be a real adventure. But she couldn't help noticing that Gareth seemed to have an uncanny insight into how to proceed with their plan.

"Have you done this sort of thing before?" she asked.

He met her gaze and nodded. "Once before."

She felt her eyes widen. "To steal something?"

"Yes."

"Did it work?"

He chuckled. "No, I got caught."

Brilliant.

Meg eyed Charlotte as she dug in the trunk. "Sorry, I do believe everything will be dreadfully wrinkled. Dear Anthony is growing so quickly that his clothes are often tossed in trunks and stored. Stored for what? I haven't any idea. It is not as if my parents will have any additional children." She stood abruptly and turned to face Meg. "How very odd that would be. Considering I am old enough to have my own children now." She went back to digging. "I've found a shirt. I'm looking for some trousers now," she said. Her voice echoed a bit from being so close to the inside of the large trunk.

Meg smiled. "I appreciate this."

"Well, this whole scheme was my idea. I must say, I'm thrilled that Mr. Mandeville is going with you. I feel much safer knowing he will be at your side. Here we are," she said, then stood and turned, clothes in hand. "I believe these should fit nicely." She shook them out before handing them over.

"Should I try them on, to make certain, in case we need to look for alternatives?" Meg asked.

"Good idea." Charlotte watched her a moment, then added. "Go on then. Try them on."

"In here?"

Charlotte looked around. "No one is in here. And Mama and Frannie are off this afternoon having tea with one of Frannie's friends."

"Give me a hand, then." She presented her back to Charlotte so that her friend might assist her with the buttons on her dress. Quite a different situation from the night that Gareth unbuttoned her. An occasion she'd replayed in her mind several times since that night. She could close her eyes now and remember the thrill of excitement that had trailed through her body as he'd unbuttoned her dress. Good heavens, if she wasn't careful with her thoughts, Charlotte would wonder where all the blushing came from.

"How is Mr. Mandeville?" Charlotte asked as if she could hear Meg's thoughts.

"Doing well, I suppose. We finished the boxes. I think they came out rather nice. Considering neither of us had ever done that sort of work before."

"There we go." Charlotte helped Meg pull the dress over her head. "Now then, I do believe you'll have to take your shift off, as that won't work with the trousers. Oh, and your petticoat, obviously."

Meg removed the petticoat and then slipped out of her drawers. Now she stood there in nothing more than her shift. There wasn't a good way she could bunch this up beneath the trousers, so she tossed it on the floor as well. Quickly she pulled the trousers on, then the shirt. After fastening everything, she faced Charlotte.

"Well? How do I look?" she asked.

"That will never work. You can see your breasts through the shirt. We should bind them." Charlotte went back over to the trunk and pulled out an old nightshirt and ripped a piece of fabric from the bottom hem. "This should do it. Wrap this around you."

"Are you quite serious?" Meg asked.

"Of course I am. You don't want anyone walking about to notice that you have breasts while you're wearing that getup, do you?"

"My breasts are not large enough to notice."

"Trust me, I can see them clearly. It will be worse that night because of the chilly night air."

Meg felt herself blush. "Honestly, Charlotte." Meg snatched the fabric from her friend and wrapped it around her chest, then tucked the end under her arm.

"What? It happens to all women, I imagine," she said with a smile.

"You're terrible. Completely incorrigible." She held her arms open. "Better?"

Charlotte tried to hide a smile, but ended up roaring with laughter.

"What? Is it that bad?" Meg looked down to see as much of herself as she could manage without a mirror.

"It's not the clothes. It's the hair. You need to put your hair somewhere."

"Amelia suggested a hat," Meg said.

Charlotte poked around a bit in the room and came up with a tweed cap. "Try this."

Meg wound her hair up and held it to the top of her head while she maneuvered the cap with the other hand. Eventually she was able to get it secured on her head and then went about poking stray hairs into the sides. "How's this? It's not perfect, but I'll secure it with pins when we go that night. But for now?"

"For now it creates a clear picture."

"Do I look like a boy?"

Charlotte tilted her head a few times. "If it were dark and I didn't know any better, I probably would assume you were a boy. Oh, we forgot one thing."

"What?"

"Shoes."

"That would have been interesting. I can see it now. Me hiding in the London's dark alleyways with my trousers, hat, and pink satin slippers." She giggled.

Charlotte held up a pair of shoes. "These will probably be too big, but you can always stuff them with some paper or something."

Meg took them. "I guess I'm all set then."

"Are you nervous?"

"A little. But I'm more excited than anything. I thought Amelia would be the only one of us that would ever do some authentic investigation. I wish you could go with me," Meg said.

"I don't believe I would ever pass for a boy. I am far too tall."

"Yes, you would be quite the strapping lad," Meg said in a falsely deep voice.

"Good luck and be safe."

"I shall. Gareth will make sure we're safe. I'll report everything at the next meeting." Meg quickly removed the masculine clothing and slipped back into her dress. She backed up to Charlotte to give her access to her buttons. "Thank you for the clothes." She turned to go, then stopped. "Charlotte, about the other day at my house, I—"

Charlotte held up a hand to stop her. "Don't say another word. There is nothing to concern yourself with."

Meg squeezed her friend, then went on her way. She needed to take care she didn't relive Gareth undressing her while she was with him. Charlotte might ignore any blush she'd seen, but Gareth would inquire as to her thoughts. He'd want to know what daring thought entered her mind to create such a stain. In the future, she would endeavor to not remember what it was like to have the dashing man see her practically naked.

Chapter 9

⌒⌒

I t hadn't taken them long to set things in motion with Mr. Munden, and the night they would break into his living quarters finally arrived. All was arranged; her disguise, the hackney, and Gareth would be waiting for her.

Meg stood in front of the mirror eyeing herself. She'd never before seen herself in a pair of breeches, and while they were strange, they were somewhat comfortable as well. She'd certainly be able to do more in them than she ever could within the confines of a skirt.

Perhaps after tonight she'd have several pairs made and wear them around the house, or even at the factory. They might come in handy were she to help with certain aspects of the factory work. Or riding a bicycle, for that matter. No wonder men were so fond of them.

She wound her hair up and secured it with several pins, and then stuffed it inside the tweed cap to hide it.

It was time. Time to go and retrieve Gareth. And join the ranks of the other thieves in this town. She should probably feel guilty about this evening's activities, but she didn't. Excited and nervous, but not an ounce of guilt. They were doing this for a good purpose, and that mattered above all else.

She peered into the hall, and all was dark. She hoped everyone slept and no one would notice her sneaking out of the house dressed as a boy. As it was, she'd already had to hire a hackney so that she didn't have to explain anything to their own drivers. She crept out of the house and down the hill where she met the carriage. She couldn't very well have them drive up to the front steps—that would have alerted everyone.

She instructed the driver to stop at the boarding rooms as she climbed in. Tonight they would not only clear Gareth's name, but she was doing a service for the factory and her father. What better way to prove to her father she was ready for more responsibility at the factory than to catch a thief?

It didn't take the brougham long to pull up to the boardinghouse where Gareth rented his rooms. He was waiting outside, and when she opened the door, he slid in across from her.

Even in the dark carriage, she could see Gareth eyeing her from head to toe. "So this is your disguise?" he asked as the carriage lurched forward.

"Perfect, don't you agree?"

"You still look like a woman to me."

"Yes, but you know that I'm a woman." More than anyone, he knew. He'd touched her body and held her against his own. Something she was even more aware of than usual in the quiet intimacy of the carriage. "But a stranger will not notice."

"You can put on a boy's clothes, but it doesn't erase your curves or the delicate features of your face. You're too soft to be a man."

She watched him form every word. Slowly, as if each was specifically chosen. What else had he noticed about her? She had to clear her throat before speaking. "I'm supposed to pass for a boy, not a man."

"Where did you find the clothes?"

"From Charlotte's younger brother." She had to remind herself to breathe. Hoping to distract herself from temptation, she wiggled around the seat. "I find them rather comfortable. I could certainly wear these on a regular basis."

He raised his eyebrows.

"I doubt many would even notice."

"Trust me, they'd notice," he said.

She let her eyes settle on him and viewed his yet again stubbled chin and cheeks. What was so unbecoming on other men made him look positively dashing. But it was not his unshaven face that made him appear dangerous. No, that honor went to his eyes. Eyes that dared her to look. Dared her to touch. Dared her to want things she knew she had no right even thinking about.

"How did you get out of the house dressed that way?" he asked.

She shrugged sheepishly. "I snuck out."

"So your father doesn't allow you complete freedom?"

"Of course not. He's indulgent, I'll admit that, but he is certainly not flippant about my welfare." Unlike some men who probably didn't care at all. "He would be sorely disappointed in my behavior tonight," she admitted.

"Well, that stands to reason."

"But I'm doing this for him as much as for you. I want to prove to him that I'm responsible."

"By breaking the law?" It was a statement more than a question.

She did have to wonder if the end justified the means. Only time would tell, and she hoped that if her father ever learned of this outing, he would not be too disappointed by her lack of judgment. "Of course not," she said. "By catching a thief."

He gave her a wry smile, but dropped the subject. "Where are we headed?" he asked.

His husky voice slid across her skin like a caress. She cleared her throat. "Mr. Munden lives not too far into London."

"I take it from the expression on your face that it is not the most savory part of town."

"Indeed," she said.

"Are you frightened?"

She frowned. "Of what?"

"Meg, do you not know what happens to ladies in those unsavory parts of town?"

"You'll protect me. I'm not concerned." That wasn't entirely accurate. Her hands were shaking fiercely, but no need for him to believe her to be a ninny. Since this escapade was, after all, her idea.

"I see."

"You would prevent anyone from hurting me. Would you not?"

He looked away from her. "I'm not the gentleman you believe me to be," he said, his jaw clenching.

"I never accused you of being a gentleman. I simply don't believe you're a beast." Still amazed to have each leg encased in tight fabric, she wiped her hands across her pants leg. "Are you going to try to convince me that you're a rotten man and that I should be afraid of you?"

"No. I know you'd never be afraid of me. I've seen the way you look at me."

Her heart felt as if it had fallen into her shoes. He'd seen the way she looked at him. That meant he'd seen her fascination, her attraction, her longing. She fought the urge to bury her face in her hands.

"Precisely how do I look at you?" she asked, unable to resist knowing how he would describe it.

"With no fear or repugnance. You look me in the eyes."

How could she not look in his eyes? It was improper for her to be so bold, but she could not resist them. Could not resist staring into their brown and green depths and almost forgetting her own name. "Why would I look at you any other way?"

"I am an employee, Meg. Surely that has not escaped your attention."

"Our station difference?" She waved a hand in front of her. "Simply because I was born into a wealthy family and you were not. That matters not. My father always taught me that people are the same no matter where they sleep. You and I—we are no different."

She met his gaze, and it became all too clear how untrue that statement was. They were very different. He'd be hard and sinewy where she was soft and round.

Dark where she was light. She took a deep breath. Perhaps tonight had been a bad idea.

"We are plenty different," he said. But something told her his reasons would be far from the ones she thought of.

The carriage rolled to a stop.

"We must be here," he said. They both leaned forward to climb out of the carriage, but he stopped. "I want you to listen carefully to everything I say and keep next to me."

She was so close now, she could feel his breath on her cheek. Gracious, how was she going to make it through this night with her virtue intact? Were it up to her, she'd give it to him right now, right here in this very carriage. His reputation and her heart be damned.

She put her hand over her mouth. What was the matter with her? Perhaps she wasn't as concerned with her reputation as Willow was, but there was no reason to be completely flagrant with herself. Staying close did not mean anything more than staying near him while they were doing this specific task so that she might remain unharmed.

It was protection, not desire. Protection, not desire. She repeated that three more times in her head. The inky night closed in around her as they stepped down from the carriage. There was no lighting in the alleyway. A shiver ran up her spine.

"It should be this one, right over there." She pointed straight ahead of them.

"Let's walk around the back of it and see if there is a back door," he suggested.

She nodded and followed him forward, treading on his heels in the process.

Gareth stopped, looked down at her feet, and then back up at her. "Those ridiculous shoes," he muttered. "When I said stay close, I did not mean walk on top of me. You can step back some. I only meant, don't go anywhere without me. I want to keep an eye on you."

She gave him a weak smile. "Sorry."

He turned and started walking again.

She touched his shoulder. "Gareth?"

"Yes?"

"I am a bit nervous now."

His features softened, then he nodded. She felt his fingers touch hers as he reached down and grabbed her hand. "You're safe."

So there they were walking, fingers entwined, around the back of a dimly lit building. In any other situation, this might have felt as a courtship would, but the rat scurrying past her right foot ruined the romantic image. Shallow water splashed as they stepped through a puddle. Thank goodness she had on these thick-soled shoes rather than her delicate slippers.

He stopped abruptly and pulled her against the brick wall. Meg could feel the cold mortar through her shirt. Two men walked by, talking loudly and laughing. They disappeared down another alleyway, and Meg released the breath she'd been holding.

"Goodness, I thought for certain they'd seen us," Meg said.

Gareth eyed her, then stepped away from her to put a small amount of distance between their bodies. "They were too deep into their cups and would not have noticed that you were a woman."

The rhythmic thump of her heart still pounded in her ears. It was going to be a long night. They needed to get in there quickly and out just the same.

They stepped around the corner into the alley with the back doors leading into the flats. It took no more than a gentle shove on Gareth's part to open the correct door. And then they stood in a dark hallway. They walked forward, shuffling quietly through the darkness. Thankfully some light from the moon filtered into the front of the room, making it bright enough for them to maneuver without having to light their candle. There were two rooms off to their right.

Moving along the shadows, they made their way to a room that housed a desk and one tattered chair.

"This is a good place to start," Meg said into Gareth's ear.

"Do you have the candle?" Gareth whispered.

"Yes." Meg fiddled in her bag and retrieved some matches and lit the candle. It presented enough light for them to see as long as they stayed close by each other, but not so bright that too much light would shine through the window and give suspicion.

"What do we do now?" she asked.

Gareth nodded to the beat-up desk against the wall. "We'll start there. Look through the drawers; I'll sort through the papers on the top."

They moved over to the desk, and Meg set the candle on the desktop. She opened the first drawer and rifled through the contents. It was mostly odds and ends: a pencil, ink container, papers, and a few coins.

"What precisely are we looking for?" she asked as she opened another drawer. It seemed her nerves had robbed her of the agenda for the night.

"Any sort of paperwork that would prove he stole the chocolate boxes," Gareth said.

"Of course." She nodded, then went back to the current drawer.

"Meg?" he whispered.

His whisper of her name caressed her as if it had been his hand.

"Hmm?"

He held her stare for a moment. "We're going to be all right."

She nodded. And in that moment, she knew they would be. He'd made a promise to her. Not in so many words, but she knew he would not allow any harm to come to her. He would protect her. In most situations, she would not enjoy needing support or protection, but it was evident in this scenario she would be a fool if she said she could manage it on her own. He'd been so wise to come with her tonight. Although part of her didn't think she would have even gotten out of the carriage had she come here alone. Some sleuth she was.

Gareth must think her an utter fool. This was her brilliant scheme, and she'd done such a poor job holding her nerves together. She wasn't even certain what she was so afraid of.

She read paper after paper, searching for a receipt or anything that would connect Munden to the theft. Toward the back of one drawer, something caught, preventing her from opening it all the way. She reached in and maneuvered it out. A stack of folded parchment. She unfolded it and scanned the first sheet and then the second. Her heart slammed against her chest.

"Gareth?"

"Yes."

"What do you make of these?" she asked as she handed him the stack.

Gareth examined the sheets a moment before he looked up and met her gaze. "It looks like some sort of accounting. Sheets from a ledger."

"My father's accounting. That's a sheet from my father's ledger," she said. "Seven sheets in total. They must have been cut from my father's ledger book. Why would Munden take these pages?"

Gareth inspected the parchment's edges. "It's as if he slid a knife right into the book and sliced the pages out." He looked up at her. "He's taking the money that goes with them. That has to be the only reason why he would take them," Gareth said. "Munden is pilfering funds and hiding his tracks by removing the ledger sheets. Who records in this book?"

"My father and his director are the only people I know that have that sort of access to the book." She wracked her head trying to think if she'd ever heard her father mention Munden or anyone else doing any of the accounting.

"Does Munden have access to it?"

"I'm not certain. Until my father's accident, I only visited the factory on occasion. Not enough to know Munden's regular routine. But that night we were locked in the factory together, I had come there to retrieve one of the ledger books for my father. If Mr. Munden took those boxes, then he would have had access to the ledger book as well."

"Without these pages, there is no record of these funds. We can assume these are the only pages that are missing, so he hasn't been doing this for too long." Gareth said.

"This certainly explains how he was able to purchase that racing horse. That animal belongs to my father," she said defiantly.

"The horse or Munden?" Gareth asked.

Meg gave him a deliciously wicked smile, and Gareth resisted the urge to pull her to him. "I'd prefer only the horse. Although it might cause great amusement to watch Mr. Munden graze on the lawn of our country estate."

Blast it, she was attractive. That red hair drew him in until he wanted nothing more than to bury himself in it. It was mostly hidden at the moment, bundled up beneath that silly cap, but tiny curls around the nape of her neck had escaped. He wanted her. With an urgency he'd never experienced with any other woman.

"What shall we do with these sheets?" she asked, holding up the bunch.

"We should take them with us. We'll put everything back where it goes so it might take him a while to notice they're missing. But when he does, it will drive him mad. He'll know someone is on to him."

She smiled. "This could be fun."

"Yes, it could. We have a few more minutes to look around before we need to leave."

Gareth continued digging through the rest of the items littering the top of Munden's desk, but found nothing relating to the sale of the chocolate boxes.

He did find something that resembled a receipt for the purchase of the racing horse. He pocketed the scrap of paper, then picked up an envelope.

"That son of a bitch!" Gareth said, as he read the contents.

"What? What is it?"

"This." He handed her the letter.

"A gift for you," she read aloud.

> *The Irishman must take blame.*
> *Or else it will be a shame.*
> *For when it is through.*
> *More money's your due.*

She looked up at Gareth. "A riddle?" she asked.

"Or a bad poem."

"Someone paid Munden to accuse you? Now it makes sense why he won't let the accusations go. He wants the rest of the payment," she said.

Gareth nodded. "Can't even make a decision himself. He was probably grateful to point the finger at me for something like this while he's stealing money. No doubt if he were ever accused of taking this money, he'd blame that on me as well."

"Who do you think it is?" she asked.

"I have no idea. I don't know anyone in this town. I can't imagine why they would have selected me out of the rest of the workers at the factory."

"Perhaps because you're the newest and no one knows much about you."

"We should leave," Gareth said. "We've found enough information."

Meg tucked the ledger sheets into her bag.

"Snuff out that candle."

She did as he said. Gareth stood for a moment, allowing the darkness to settle in around him before he attempted to move. He could see Meg's outline in front of him, but little else.

"It's quite dark," she said, her voice shaking with nerves.

"Indeed. We'll be in the carriage before you know it." He stepped beside her and grabbed her hand. He'd held it as they'd entered the building, and that seemed to have eased her fears.

They stepped into the hallway, and Gareth heard the back door open. Instinctively he grabbed Meg and pushed her against the wall, then covered her with his own body.

"Shhh," he whispered into her ear.

Gareth's heartbeat seemed to mimic Munden's footsteps as the man moved closer toward them. They were enough in the shadows that if the man wasn't paying too close attention, he just might miss them.

They had proof of his theft, but they had no weapon to protect themselves, and while Gareth was in choice shape, Munden was an imposing man.

Munden entered the house, singing loudly.

Six times did his iron, by vigorous heating.
Grow soft in the forge in a minute or so.
And often was hardened, still beating and beating.
But each time it softened it hardened more slow.

Gareth winced. He was certain Meg would miss the bawdy tune's meaning, but he needed to get her out of here now.

Gareth could feel Meg's breaths, short and tight, against him. She was terrified. He, on the other hand, felt something entirely different. The familiar heaviness as his erection swelled. He hoped she could not feel him pressed up against her, or that she was too frightened to notice his hardness. He tried not to move, tried not to move against her. Tried to keep still so as not to alert her to his arousal and not to add to the stimulation. But it was a battle of will because all he wanted to do was bury his face in her glorious red hair and lose himself in her dampness.

Munden stepped into another room still singing, and Gareth took the opportunity to pull Meg down the hall and out the back door. He closed the latch silently, then turned to face her. Her eyes were wide, but she was smiling.

"*That* was close," she said.

She didn't know how true those words were.

Chapter 10

He led her to the carriage and closed the door behind them. At least in the safety of the carriage, he wouldn't have to press his body against hers.

"I thought for certain he would see us there. My heart was beating so fast." She grabbed his hand and put it against her chest. "Still is," she said breathlessly, her eyes lit with excitement.

His eyes moved to her chest as if somehow he expected to see his hand pulse with the beat of her heart. Instead he felt only the hint of her breast moving up and down. He tried not to notice how it felt rising against his hand. Tried not to remember how it had felt the last time he'd held it in his hands.

He snatched his hand away. He needed to get away from her before he did something they both regretted.

"Can I have the ledger sheets?" he asked, in hopes that discussing Munden's crimes would divert his thoughts from laying her back on that seat cushion, slowly peeling off her breeches, and entering her quick and hard.

Her smile melted away. "Why?"

He shifted in his seat. "I thought to keep them safe."

"I want to show them to my father." She frowned, clearly confused. "How else can we prove that Munden is guilty of stealing money from the factory?"

The diversion was not working; he still wanted her. "I thought you would want to do that, but I feel as if we should wait before you discuss this with your father."

"But he's stealing, Gareth. I can't knowingly allow him to continue working there knowing he takes money from my father. Why would you even suggest such a thing?"

"Because he's the one the real culprit has been in contact with. We'll likely never discover the criminal's true identity if Munden is gone. I need to know who's trying to frame me."

She was silent for a moment before responding. "I still don't like it, but I suppose you're right. We'll simply have to make certain Munden isn't given any private time with the money or the ledger book. I can see to that most of the time, but when I can't be at the factory, you'll have to keep an eye on him," she said. "And we mustn't allow this to continue for very long. He doesn't deserve his wages."

"I can watch him, but I can't do much more than that. If I confront him, he'll suspect something," he said. She was so intense, so loyal, so passionate. No matter how unconventional and dangerous her schemes were, she had one motive. To help others. At the moment, that meant him and her father. He'd never before had anyone go to such lengths for his benefit. He wanted to be grateful, show his appreciation, but he simply couldn't bring himself to do it.

"Maybe he knows who sent him that note." She dug around in her bag. "Oh no, I thought I put the note in here. I must have dropped it."

"We don't need it. It didn't make all that much sense in the first place."

"Perhaps we can think of a way to pry some information from Munden," she suggested.

"Let's wait until we see if the information we have can be more useful," Gareth suggested.

She nodded. They sat in silence for a while as the carriage rattled through the streets. Gareth couldn't see her full features since the curtains were pulled, but everything about her tonight was burned into his memory.

The way her breeches molded against every curve; he would have had to be blind not to notice that. He'd known she had a rounded bottom, but seeing it outlined was almost more than he could bear. But even more than that, he tried to ignore the reminder that her delicious little bottom had been in his hands. Briefly, yes, but he had touched her that night in the factory. He hardened with the thought.

Slinking around in the dark with her had done nothing to aid his good intentions of keeping his hands to himself.

The way she'd smiled up at him, her glorious hair tucked beneath that hat. The way she'd felt pressed against him. Her warm breath on his skin. Then she'd put his hand on her breast. Blast it, how was a man supposed to act the gentleman in that sort of situation?

Then it occurred to him. He might have been born a gentleman, but he'd never behaved as such. He needed to touch her. If only for this one night. He knew he had no right, but he would not take more than she was willing to give. His abdomen tightened with the thought, and with an undeniable impulse, he reached across and pulled her to him. He situated her until she straddled his legs.

"What are you doing?" she asked. It wasn't an accusation; there was no fear in her voice, merely a question as if she'd simply asked him about the weather.

"I'm tired of this," he said as he reached up and pulled the cap from her hair. He dug through the mass and removed each pin. A waterfall of red curls fell down her back. "I'd prefer you not ever wear a head covering of any sort or pull your hair up. It's so beautiful." He ran his hands through the silky mass and wondered how it was that she managed to get her hair that soft.

A bump in the road slid her farther onto his lap and he groaned in response. He reached up and pulled her face down to his and kissed her. He was so hungry for her, he hoped he had enough restraint to at least keep her virtue intact.

Her lips were pliant and soft, and he wanted so badly to be controlled and patient, but found he could not. Instead he took her with a ferocity that shocked even him. His tongue slid inside her mouth and caressed hers until he thought he would spill beneath his own trousers. A mere kiss had never aroused him to such a degree.

She didn't seemed bothered or frightened by his forcefulness; she met him with every moment, every kiss. Her hands snaked their way around his neck and now clung to his back. She bucked a few times and made contact with the hardness in his trousers. She moaned and rubbed herself against him.

All the while kissing, she moved against him and he fought with every bit of his control to keep from losing himself completely. She could find her release and leave this carriage with her virtue intact. He would simply enjoy seeing her writhe with pleasure.

He grabbed her buttocks and pulled her even tighter against him, and she released a throaty growl. Moving his mouth from hers, he traced his tongue against her jaw, then down her neck to her collarbone.

Unbuttoning her shirt, her found her breasts bound with a strip of fabric. It explained why he hadn't felt their entire fullness earlier. It didn't take long for him to tear it out of the way and cover one aching tip with his mouth.

Her breasts were perfect—enough to put a little weight in his hand. It was the rich color of their centers, though, that nearly rocked him over the edge. Dusky pink. He stopped himself before he growled. Never before had he seen such luscious nipples. He suckled hard and she cried out. Her fingers dug into his back.

Her bucking against him became erratic as her control slipped further away. He held her hips and rocked her in a steady rhythm until her release hit her. She shook in his arms, then fell against his chest. An innocent with her first release.

God, he wanted her. Wanted to be inside her. But no

matter how thick his desire, he would not ask her for that. He would not become a complete cad. He'd already taken more from her than he had any right to.

She lay against him while her breathing slowed, then she cautiously leaned back. He smoothed a curl away from her face. Her eyes were heavy lidded and she gave him a satisfied smile, not unlike a cat who'd just had its cream.

She licked her lips before she spoke. "I'm not quite certain," she said. "But I feel as if I must thank you."

He chuckled in spite of himself. "So you enjoyed it?" he asked.

"Very much."

"You have perfect breasts," he said.

She looked down at them, then back at him. "Indeed? I always figured them to be too small."

"No." He weighed both of them in his hands, tormenting his arousal. "Perfect."

"There is more to all of this, yes?" she asked.

"Much more."

Her eyes widened. "Are we going to do more?"

He swallowed hard. God, he wished. "No. Not tonight." He pulled her shirt closed to remove the tempting morsels from sight. Not ever. He shouldn't ever have laid a hand on her, but damn, she was a temptation. More tempting than anyone he'd ever encountered. He would do well to stay away from her. But he knew he wouldn't be able to do that until they solved the mystery surrounding those chocolate boxes.

"Gareth?"

"Yes."

"Are you playing the gentleman?"

If only she knew the truth. A gentleman playing a

peasant playing a gentleman. It was enough to confuse even him. "Something like that," he said.

She scooted off his lap and sat next to him. His arousal had not diminished, so he leaned forward to hide it from her view.

It wasn't much longer before the carriage pulled up in front of his residence. He turned to her.

"Stay away from Munden at the factory. I don't trust him. And now you know too much. That could be dangerous."

She grabbed his arm before he could step down from the carriage. "Thank you for helping me tonight. I would not have been able to do this on my own."

He nodded, then turned to leave. He knew she would question everything now. It was in her nature to do so. Why he touched her. Why he hadn't completed what he'd started. Damn, if he hadn't made one hell of a mess.

She had expected him to protect her. And he had. He'd protected her from the men on the street and from the drunken Munden. But with himself, he seemed unable to do the same. Her confidence in him never wavered. She expected the best of him, but he knew that eventually she'd see the truth, see the selfish bastard that he was, and then where would that leave him?

Meg raised her hand and recited the oath. She was still tired from not getting enough sleep the night before. But how could she? She'd become a criminal, discovered a thief, uncovered a clue that led to an even bigger thief, and then Gareth had done sinful, amazing things to her body. She still tingled. She hoped the girls would interpret her silly grin as excitement about the case. Perhaps they would even have insight into how to put the rest of the pieces together, to solve this mystery once and for all.

Because the memories of last night were still so vivid, she needed some distraction before she discussed it. She didn't want to slip, share more than she intended. So they could discuss the Jack of Hearts first. That would give her enough distance to calm her nerves, plan her words better. It was a perfect excuse as well since the Jack of Hearts had actually made the front page of the *Times*, and there was much to discuss with that mystery first. It was a nice reminder that she had existed before she'd met Gareth. Regardless of how he filled her mind now, she still remembered how to think of other things. All was well; she, like the other ladies, was intrigued by the masked thief.

"Meg, we are all quite eager for you to fill us in on the details of your excursion last night," Amelia said.

All eyes turned on Meg. She swallowed, then took a deep breath and smiled. "We will get to that." She hoped she successfully hid her nerves. "But first, shouldn't we discuss the Jack of Hearts?" She passed a pleading look to Charlotte.

"I know we've all seen it," Charlotte said. Thank goodness for her dear friend.

"The front page," Willow said.

Charlotte smiled. "People are beginning to take notice."

"What do you expect when he robbed a duchess? He's disgraceful," Willow said.

Jack was a perfect diversion for her friends, so enthralled were they with him. And she would join the conversation and it would slow her pulse and alleviate Gareth's plague on her mind.

"He never harms anyone. I'm not even certain he carries a weapon," Charlotte said.

"That doesn't make any sense," Meg said, attempting to add to the discussion. "Why would you relinquish your jewels to someone who doesn't threaten you with a weapon?"

"He does use a weapon," Willow said. "Remember, from the second article we found? When he stole Lady Babcock's diamond and ruby earrings. She distinctly said he carried a pistol. She said he aimed it right at her."

"Willow's right," Amelia said. "If I remember correctly, he aimed the pistol right at her heart." Amelia shuddered.

"Wretch," Willow muttered.

"Well, he's never used that pistol," Charlotte protested.

"We don't know that," Willow said. "We only know that no one has been injured thus far, or if they have it has not been publicized." She sat straighter. "He's nothing more than a well-dressed highwayman."

Meg smiled. It was somewhat comforting to know that despite the upheaval in her own life, the rest of the world was as it should be. Willow and Charlotte constantly disagreeing—their new favorite subject about which to do so, the Jack of Hearts.

"Have we been collecting the information we've learned of him in some common list?" Meg asked. She certainly hadn't been taking notes, but she wasn't the sort to do that type of thing.

Willow reached in her bag just as Amelia unfolded a sheet of parchment. Alike in so many ways, those two.

"We know that our baiting him doesn't work," Meg said.

"Not completely. We know that he hasn't taken Charlotte's bait," Willow said.

Charlotte frowned. "What is that supposed to mean?"

"Nothing to reflect poorly on you, my dear, I can assure you," Willow said. "What I've noticed is that you're the one we've sent out to bait him, believing that with your beauty and some well-placed jewels, you might prove a temptation."

"But you don't believe she's a temptation?" Amelia asked.

"No, I do think she is." Willow leaned forward. "But what else do we know about Charlotte when she goes out in public? What happens?"

"She's surrounded by other men," Meg said.

"Precisely!" Willow said.

"You think that because I have suitors all about, it is scaring him off?" Charlotte asked.

Willow nodded.

"Perhaps it's mere coincidence, but on four separate occasions, he has waited until you're in a different room, or have left for the evening before sweeping in to take his bounty. It makes perfect sense to me," Meg said. "Excellent observation, Willow."

"I agree," Amelia said.

"Do you suppose that means he knows me? The Jack of Hearts?" Charlotte could not hide her excitement.

"Could be," Willow said. "Or it could be mere coincidence."

Charlotte rolled her eyes. "Pesky men. Perhaps I can try to rid myself of them the next time I attend a function. Put myself in a position that might be slightly more tempting for the rogue."

"Honestly, Charlotte, it's really not in your best interest to continue to put yourself in harm's way," Amelia said. "We can discover his identity other ways."

"Perhaps we should give it a go again," Charlotte suggested. "We only once attempted to lure him together. I simply don't feel we gave that plan a real chance."

Every eye turned to Willow since it had been her original idea to try such a tactic. They had attended the theater and worn their best jewels in an effort to entice the thief, but Jack had not shown up.

Willow nodded. "Perhaps it is time again. But I do think we should all go. Wherever we decide." She looked around the room.

They each nodded. They might even be able to discover more about the stolen boxes, see if anyone had heard anything. And catch a glimpse of the Jack of Hearts. Meg's pulse beat rapidly. Adventures at every turn.

"Let us be on the lookout, then, for the perfect social engagement to attend," Amelia suggested.

Meg smiled. "It is time this gentleman thief met some ladies to contend with."

They all laughed.

"Aside from Charlotte's suitors distracting him, what else do we know of him?" Meg asked.

"He dresses well," Amelia said. "As a dandy would."

"He's young, at least that's what Lady Danbridge told me," Charlotte said. Both Willow and Amelia quickly wrote the information down. "She said he smelled of elegant tobacco and hair cream and that despite the mask covering the majority of his face, his lips were uncovered and he had the most sinful mouth she'd ever seen."

"Charlotte!" Willow said.

She opened her eyes dreamily and smiled. "What? I'm only repeating a story from one of the wealthiest members of Society." She shrugged her innocence.

Meg knew, all too well, who owned the most sinful mouth, so she could certainly argue with Lady Danbridge.

"Tobacco. Every man in London smells of tobacco," Willow said.

Gareth didn't, although Meg would certainly not tell them that. He smelled of fresh cocoa with a hint of musky soap. Rich, clean, and fragrant. Meg stopped herself right before she sighed. She really needed to get a hold on herself before she took this too far. It was one thing to enjoy pleasures of the flesh with Gareth, but in doing so he'd robbed her of her peace of mind and he'd taken over her senses. She knew she was treading on dangerous ground, and if she wasn't careful she'd soon find herself as heartbroken as her poor papa.

And then she'd be lost.

"But hair cream is not used by every man," Amelia noted. She smiled wistfully. "This would be a brilliant case for Sherlock, don't you agree?"

"Have you read the latest?" Meg asked. She had received her copy of *The Strand* yesterday, but had been too busy to even open to the first page.

"Not yet. I'm far too busy with my own detective

story. Lady Shadows is in thick trouble right as we speak," Amelia said. "Now if I could only complete this volume, it will be ready to go in the post."

"You're going to be a glittering success," Charlotte said.

"Absolutely. I cannot wait to read it myself," Meg agreed. Her dear friend had finally gained enough courage to begin her own detective stories after being so enraptured with Mr. Conan Doyle's for so long. It would be such a joy when her detective would be printed alongside the famous Sherlock Holmes.

Amelia smiled. "Such wonderful friends you all are. But this is not about me. We are making good progress with the Jack of Hearts this morning."

Indeed they were making good progress. More than they had in months. This new article was very helpful, and while Charlotte had not yet seen the masked robber, the more she spoke of her evenings out, the more she remembered others' comments of him. Before long they had twice as many notes about him and a new plan.

"Now then, we have that settled for the moment," Amelia said. "Let us discuss the more pressing case. Willow and I went and spoke with three separate pawnbrokers, and while all agreed they would be interested in such an item, none had seen them or heard of their sale. Sorry we couldn't find some information you could use," Amelia said.

Meg sat up in her seat. She'd stalled long enough, it was time she shared with them the events from last night. With the exception of some very specific, very passionate details. "We, that is, Mr. Mandeville and I discovered some rather helpful and intriguing information last night when we snuck into Mr. Munden's residence."

"What did you find?" Charlotte asked.

"Unfortunately, nothing about the stolen boxes. But we did find an anonymous letter instructing Munden to accuse Gareth of the theft. Well, it was more like a riddle and we assume it originally came with money."

"So someone else is trying to pin the crime on Gareth," Amelia said.

"Paying Munden to do it," Meg clarified.

"Interesting development. So the money that came in the note, do you think it would have been enough to purchase the horse?" Willow asked.

"I doubt it, as it mentioned giving him an additional payment if he succeeded in blaming Gareth. But we also discovered several sheets cut from my father's ledger book. Apparently Munden has been taking some funds for himself, and he steals the pages from the book so no one is the wiser."

"That's terrible," Amelia said.

Charlotte shook her head in disgust. "That would certainly afford a racing horse."

"I haven't added up the entire amount, but I would imagine you're right. Gareth didn't want me to have Munden removed from his position at work until we discover the identity of the person who sent the anonymous note. He said since Munden is the only known contact, we should keep him close by." She still didn't like that. She wanted to have the despicable man dismissed immediately. But no doubt Gareth knew what he was talking about in this situation. And he had a right to know who was trying to frame him.

"So what next?" Amelia asked.

"I'm not certain," Meg said. "We took the ledger sheets to use as proof for later. Not knowing who sent him the note might stall our current investigation though."

"That's a really good idea," Amelia said. "Your poor father though. To not only be injured, but to have a man like Munden working for him. He will be very proud of you, Meg, when this is all finished and you've rid his factory of this ne'er-do-well."

Warmth spread through Meg. "Thank you." She certainly hoped Amelia was right.

"Somehow you need to coerce Munden into telling you what he knows. He must know or have an idea of who sent the note," Willow said.

"Yes, but how to persuade him to share the information?" Amelia asked.

"Seduce him," Charlotte said softly, as if she were speaking to herself.

"What?" the other three said in unison.

Charlotte eyed them a moment, then she nodded. "Yes, it could work. It's simple; you need only seduce him." Charlotte waved her hand casually. "Men like Munden are the easiest ones of all. More than likely all you'll need to do is flutter your eyes at him a few times and he'll tell you everything you want to know."

"That's too risky," Willow said.

"She's right. It could be very dangerous," Amelia said. "We don't know what this man is capable of. Trust me, you do not want to dally with men akin to Munden. Even if you are only pretending to dally."

"It wouldn't have to be risky. Mr. Mandeville could protect her," Charlotte said.

"Munden will not talk to me if Gareth is anywhere near me," Meg said.

"He doesn't have to know Gareth is near. Isn't there somewhere you can speak with Munden that would allow Gareth to hide himself?" Charlotte asked.

Meg thought for a moment, then nodded. "There is an armoire in my father's office. It would be large enough for Gareth to hide in. I don't think Gareth will agree, though. And I most definitely do not know how to seduce a man." They might not believe that if they had seen her and Gareth the night before in the carriage.

"You don't actually have to seduce him." Charlotte came to sit next to her. "But you know how to flirt. Make him comfortable. Make him want to divulge information to you. You can do that. You've always been at ease around men."

"It still sounds risky to me," Willow said.

"Yes, but don't you agree that with Gareth there, she will be well protected?" Charlotte asked.

Willow pursed her lips. "How are we to know that this Gareth fellow can be trusted to protect Meg? Perhaps he will want to take advantage of her himself."

Meg felt the blush creep up into her cheeks, so she grabbed her teacup and held it close to her lips.

"He has had ample opportunity to do so, were he going to," Charlotte said. "Isn't that right, Meg?" Charlotte crossed her right leg over her left, and in doing so kicked the back of Meg's leg.

Meg jolted. "Certainly. He would never harm me," she said.

"It's settled then. Now, on to the next problem. The seduction. It is simple, I assure you," Charlotte said.

"It is nothing more than a game. Men enjoy being toyed with—you pull the right strings and they'll do anything you ask of them, just as a marionette would."

"Honestly, Charlotte, you make them sound completely without thought," Willow said.

"They are not without thought, but she's right," Amelia said.

Willow fidgeted with her spectacles. "That may be, but you shouldn't toy with your virtue in such a flagrant fashion."

"Willow, this can work," Charlotte said. "Do not fret. No one will know about this. It will be a secret between Meg and Mr. Munden. If Munden tells, no one will take his word over Meg's; besides, she has the excuse of working in her father's stead. And Gareth, of course. But he won't tell anyone."

"He's quite good with secrets," Meg said.

"You'll want to make eye contact," Charlotte continued. "But look away as well. Smile at him, but not a full smile, just a hint of a grin." Charlotte mimicked her own instructions and Meg realized she'd seen her friend smile in such a fashion on hundreds of occasions. It always worked perfectly. But what worked for the exquisite beauty might not work for all women. "It will make him want more and keep him focused on your mouth," Charlotte said.

"I can't believe I'm hearing this," Willow said.

"You should take notes." Charlotte pointed playfully at Willow. "You never know when skills such as these will come in handy. There is a reason the Lord gave women wiles in the manner in which He did."

"Certainly not for this," Willow argued.

"Yes, precisely for this," Charlotte said. "Now then,

let us continue. If you are sitting near him, you could touch him on the sleeve. Nowhere else, you don't want to be too forward. Drop your voice a little lower, almost a whisper. Oh, and you can lick your lips if you see him watching them."

Meg tried to mentally record every suggestion.

"Charlotte, how do you know all of this?" Amelia asked.

She shrugged. "Tips I gathered from here and there. When you don't have money, it's important that you have other ways to lure men in to secure a good husband." She rolled her eyes, then laughed. "My mother."

That explained plenty.

Chapter 11

Gareth stood and threw his arms up. "Absolutely not. It's out of the question."

Meg acknowledged that this might do it. Might convince him she was totally mad, which, of course, she wasn't. She was doing all this for him. But it would definitely take some convincing to persuade him to go along with her plan. "You haven't given me an opportunity to explain," Meg said.

"First the breaking and entering into Munden's house and now this?" He pinched the bridge of his nose. "If I didn't know any better, Meg, I'd think you were training to be a spy." He exhaled loudly. "Where do you come up with these ideas?"

She wasn't certain if it was a legitimate question or not, but she decided not to answer. "There is no risk involved; I will be completely safe," Meg said.

"How can you be certain? We don't know what Munden is capable of."

"You'll protect me," she said. She believed that too. Regardless of whether his motive was keeping her safe or proving his own innocence, she knew he wouldn't allow any harm to come to her.

His jaw clenched. "I appreciate your faith in me, but precisely how am I going to do that when you're in this office alone with him?"

"You'll be in here with me."

"He won't reveal anything if I'm in the room with you, you know that."

"Yes, and if you'd keep your mouth shut for ten seconds, I could finish explaining the plan," she said, more loudly than she'd intended.

His eyebrows rose, and a slight smile settled on his lips. He sat back in the red chair and crossed his feet at the ankles. "By all means." He swept his arms open. "Miss Piddington, enlighten me."

His arrogance was surely justification enough for her to throttle him, but she needed him to go along with this plan, else it wouldn't work. "Thank you," she said, unable to resist giving him a smirk. "Now then, I'll invite Munden up here for a chat and try to sweet-talk some information out of him. All the while you'll be hiding there." She pointed to the large mahogany armoire behind her. "That way you can hear him. If he attacks me or something and I must call for help, you need only pop through the doors and be the hero."

"I am not qualified to be a hero," he said dryly.

She nearly argued with him, but she restrained herself. It was bad enough that she thought more of him than she ought, she didn't need to alert him to the matter. "More than likely, there will be no need for you to be. Munden might be a thief, but he's never been inappropriate with me," Meg said.

"But you intend to play the coquette with him?"

"Yes. To get information from him."

"And you don't think that flirting with that sort of man might cause you trouble? Meg, he's used to getting what he wants."

"Well he certainly will not get anything from me."

"I wasn't implying that he would. But don't be surprised if he tries to take something you're not willing to give. Regardless of whether you're offering. Men sometimes mistake flirtation for an invitation to sin."

She leveled her gaze on him. Had he done that with her? Was that why he'd taken certain liberties with her? Because he thought she'd offered them? She hadn't done that, but neither had she warded off his advances.

"I see," she said.

"I didn't mean all men." He rubbed his temples. "I only want you to be careful. You are too green for your own good."

"I'll be careful," she promised.

"Have you considered how I can get in here without him seeing me climb the stairs? Those windows"—he pointed to his right—"don't hide much, unless you wish me to crawl in."

She had not considered that. The windows only showed the upper half of the room, but still, Munden would see Gareth come into the office and not leave. "We'll have to distract him. What about your friend?"

"Jamie?"

"Yes."

Gareth shrugged. "I suppose that might work."

"Will you do this with me?"

He thought for a moment before he spoke. "I still don't think it's a good idea. It feels too risky. And I'm not certain it will make a difference. Why do you think Munden will tell you anything?"

"You might think otherwise, but other men find me engaging. I can generally persuade them to speak with me with little difficulty." There was no reason to tell him that Charlotte had given her seduction tips.

He shrugged in resignation, but his expression was tight as he spoke and his words terse. "We can try it, but I don't want you doing anything foolish. Stay behind that desk and he can sit over here as I'm doing." His jaw clenched as he took a deep breath. "There is no reason why you would need to touch him."

Why did it matter one way or another if she touched him? She wasn't foolish; she wasn't going to allow things to progress further than an innocent pat on the arm. Mr. Munden was a hulking man she had no desire to speak with, let alone touch. But her investigation mandated she do this. So there was no reason—and then it hit her. Gareth was jealous. Meg felt the thrill of the situation course through her. He didn't want her to touch Munden because he was jealous. Jealous. On her behalf. She smiled.

"I'll be careful. And you can rescue me should the need arise."

"I can hardly wait," he said wryly. "When are we doing this?"

"At the end of closing tomorrow. I believe I'll wear something special."

He rolled his eyes. "It's a wonder your father is not

in Bedlam from having to care for you with all your antics for so long. How you have managed to keep yourself out of serious trouble is remarkable."

"You find me entertaining," she said, hoping he would confirm it to be true.

"I find you something. Not quite certain I would classify it as entertaining."

"You are no fun at all," she said.

"I disagree. You think I'm quite fun." For the first time in the conversation, heat edged the exasperation out of his expression. "I believe I've proved that on more than one occasion."

He had her there. And she had the blush to prove it. A large part of her wished he'd come across the desk and prove it again.

It felt as if a battle were raging inside Meg's chest, her heart was beating so rapidly. Gracious, she couldn't remember the last time she was this nervous. Far more so than the night they'd sneaked into Munden's house. Of course, she'd insisted that her nerves were inconsequential when Gareth had asked. She refused to allow a jumbled stomach to prevent her from completing this task. She was a sleuth; she would persevere, even in dangerous situations.

Charlotte had given her plenty of tips on how to interest a man. Meg had even worn a party dress under the pretense that she was leaving here to attend a function that required such attire. The pretty lavender dress complemented her complexion perfectly, and it didn't hurt that the cut accented her female features. No doubt the gown would have the desired effect. Gareth had already commented on it. And his eyes had said more than his words. He'd looked ready to devour her when she'd removed her cloak and he'd caught sight of her cleavage.

She turned to look at the armoire doors, and wondered if Gareth could see her. She gave him a flashy smile. A knock sounded on the office door, and she started.

She moved to stand behind her father's desk. "Please enter," she said.

Munden opened the door and stepped inside the office.

"Close the door," she said, trying to make her voice sound husky.

She eyed the foreman from head to toe, and words caught in her throat. He was portly and grimy and not attractive by any stretch of her imagination. Instead he reminded her of a great sweating bull.

She offered him a smile in spite of her disgust.

"What did you want to see me about?" he asked.

"I have a favorite hobby, a secret hobby, and it seems as though we might share it." She lowered her eyes, then slowly let them slide up to his face. "I heard recently that you have purchased a racing horse." She said the last two words in a whisper.

His eyes widened ever so slightly. He shifted his stance and poked his hands in his pockets. "Where did you hear that?"

"A friend." She waved a hand in front of her. "It matters not. The point is, I love racing horses." She walked around to the desk and propped one hip against it. "I find racing exhilarating to watch. And I've always wondered what it must feel like to ride atop such a beast, with my hair blowing in the wind and . . ." She released a dramatic breath. "Now see, I've gone on and on. Do forgive me."

He eyed her warily, but she didn't allow her smile to waver. Eventually his shoulders sagged a little and he leaned forward. "I didn't realize, Miss Piddington, that you felt so strongly about this."

She leaned forward and lightly touched his arm. "Oh, but I do." She leaned back. "I realize it's not all that ladylike of me to want to ride such a fast horse. But I can't help myself. Will you keep my secret?" She released a low giggle. This was easier than she thought it would be. No wonder Charlotte had her pick of suitors.

He smiled, which looked more like a leer, and it sent shivers up her arms. And not the welcome sort of shivers.

"Of course I can," he said. "I'm good with secrets."

She knew that was true. "Might I ask you a question, Mr. Munden?" she asked sweetly.

"Of course."

"I certainly don't mean this in a nasty sort of way, but I was wondering how you were able to afford such a beast? I realize my father pays you quite well for your position, but perhaps not as much as would be required for such a purchase. Did you, by chance, find a seller who gives bargain prices? Because I would love to make a similar purchase, but with my allowance it would be difficult."

He seemed taken aback at first, but she kept her smile firmly in place. He cleared his throat. "I made some investments that turned out well for me," he said.

Investments! Stealing money was not an investment.

"Oh." She tried to look disappointed. "Were I to discover I could afford such a creature, could you put me in contact with your seller?"

He looked down at his feet. "I don't remember his name," he said.

Meg reached to touch his arm. "Are you quite certain of that?"

"Yes." He stood and moved away from the chair. "I should be going."

"Oh, Mr. Munden." She reached out and touched his arm. "Don't go. Not yet."

He looked at her bare hand resting on his coat sleeve and nodded.

"I hear that Lady Glenworthy was pleased with her chocolate boxes," she said. If she could trick him into talking about Gareth, he might give her the information she sought. "Perhaps Mr. Mandeville is good at something."

He snorted. "Bloody Irishman."

"You do understand," she cooed, "that the only reason I forced you to retain his position was because my father wanted to keep him on in case he would lead us to what he did with the boxes." She looked around and leaned in. "My father believes that he sold them to a competitor." She let her eyes go wide. "Can you believe that?"

Munden took a cigar out of his pocket and stuck it in his mouth. "Course I understand, Miss Piddington. Your father is smart. He knows what he's doing."

"He wouldn't have allowed Mr. Mandeville to continue to work here had we found any real evidence. Tell me, what clued you in on him as the thief?" she asked.

He shifted on his feet.

"It's quite all right if you tell me, Mr. Munden. I won't tell. I promise." She crossed her heart with her right hand.

He leaned closer to her. The smell of tobacco and rotting teeth sprang tears to her eyes and she fought to stay put and hide her revulsion.

"Someone sent me an anonymous note letting me know he was the one that took the boxes," he said.

"Anonymous? Are you certain you don't know who it was from?"

"No. Maybe it's from the blokes he sold it to. You know the ones from the competitors," he said.

"Perhaps you're right. Very clever you are. I'll make certain to put in a good word with my father about you."

He smiled and turned to go.

"Oh, and Mr. Munden, I'd very much like to see your horse someday. Perhaps you would notify me when you will be racing him," she said.

"I will." He nodded, then left the room.

Gareth waited until the office door closed before he stepped out of the armoire and shut the double doors behind him.

"Well, that wasn't very helpful." He walked over near her and leaned against the desk.

"No, it wasn't." She glanced at the window. "Will he be able to see you?"

"No, you can't see this far into the office from downstairs."

She nodded in relief. "I was certain he would give me a little more. Sorry, I—"

Then a knock at the door sounded. Meg felt her eyes grow wide. "You have to hide," she whispered.

He knelt right where he was and scooted under the desk a bit. "Stand in front of me and he'll never know."

She nodded. "Yes?" she said.

"I'm sorry to bother you, Miss Piddington, but I did remember one thing," Munden said.

"Yes?" She felt a hand clasp her ankle. *Oh my.*

"I remembered that it was a gent out in Yorkshire. Bunkle or something such name," he said. "The one who sold me the horse."

The hand slid up the back of her stocking-clad calf to the back of her knee. She clutched the desk to keep from falling into the seat behind her. "Oh, of course. Very good," she said, her voice breathy. "Thank you, Mr. Munden."

Tiny circles Gareth made with his fingertips sent shivers spiraling through her body.

"Are you all right, miss?" Munden asked. "You seem a little agitated and out of breath."

"No, all is fine." More than fine if she was honest. Gareth's hand slid up the back of her drawers and now sat behind her knee. Munden nodded. "I found that fellow from Yorkshire one day when I was in a pub. He was at the next table talking about his horses. About how they came from good stock and their sire had won several races." Munden rubbed his hand against his beefy neck.

She could feel the warmth of Gareth's touch through her stockings. She wanted Munden to leave, but she certainly couldn't ask him to do so. It was her idea to start this conversation.

Munden gave her a wide grin. "We'll see how mine does in his first race."

The desire was flowing rapidly through her blood

and she had to fight the urge to clench the desk and cry out. Gareth's hands had moved so far up now, his hands were wrapped around the insides of her thighs.

"I suppose I should be going," Munden said.

Thank goodness.

"Have a good evening, miss."

"You as well, Mr. Munden," she said, her voice sounding far too shaky.

He turned and left the office.

She knew she should step away from Gareth, but she was afraid to move. Afraid she'd fall. Afraid he'd stop. Afraid he wouldn't.

He said nothing, so she remained quiet as well. And soon she felt his other hand slide up the back of her other leg, until his hands rested beneath her bottom. He kneaded her flesh a bit before curving his hands around her hips until they touched the front of her legs. Very near the center of her being.

He smoothed his right hand across the juncture of her thigh and hip, and cupped her gently.

"Sit down, Meg," he said, his voice rich and deep.

She opened her eyes, not quite recognizing that she'd even shut them, and felt for the chair behind her. She complied and sat, and in doing so, she could finally see his face. His glorious hazel eyes had darkened to a sultry brown and the shadow of a beard darkened his cheeks. In that moment, she knew she would do anything he asked of her. She might not be strong enough to survive this, but she also wasn't strong enough to walk away.

He knelt before her, hands still up her dress.

"Should we lock the door?" she asked.

"No, I think he's gone."

She nodded.

He moved his finger to the slit in her drawers, all the while never taking his eyes off hers. He barely touched her flesh, and she jumped. His hands were warm and delivered such delicious sensations that she wasn't quite certain what she should do. He'd brought her to release once before. In the carriage, where he'd held her against his hardness and stroked her with almost agonizing pleasure.

Tonight would he take his own pleasure? They were completely alone in the factory. All the workers had long since left, and she'd heard the front door close as Munden took his leave. Unlike the evenings she'd worked here on the boxes, she had not brought Ellen with her.

His finger found the outer edge of her opening and gently teased the area.

"Already wet for me," he groaned. "You are the most tempting woman I've ever encountered."

"Honestly?"

"Oh yes. Such naughty things I want to do to you," he said.

Her heart raced in her chest, pounding an uneven rhythm. "Such as," she breathed.

"This," he said, as he slid his finger into her.

She clutched his shoulders and cried out.

He moved his finger in and out until she was rocking against him in the chair. *Oh my.*

"I see," she managed to say.

"And this." He removed his finger and slid it to the nub hidden beneath her folds. He made a slow circle with it and she cried out.

"But most of all, right now, I want to do this." He

picked her up and scooted her to the edge of the chair. With one swift movement, he hiked her skirt up and found her center with his mouth.

Oh sweet heaven, she never knew there were such things. Sensations sparked through her body like gunfire as his tongue made its great exploration.

It was hard to determine precisely where his tongue was, the pleasure was too intense and spreading through her so quickly. She bucked against him, and even went so far as to raise one of her legs to brace on his shoulder.

The pleasure grew and grew until she was unable to contain her moans, and soon the office echoed with her pants and cries. As his tongue laved across that little nub, his finger slid back inside her and she felt a jolt shiver through her abdomen.

The feelings were intensifying, and she knew her release was coming. Could feel it rising and building until she was certain she would explode into tiny pieces at any moment.

It crashed over her quickly. Waves and waves of pleasure rocketed through her and she clutched his hair. He kissed her tenderly on the thigh, then lowered her skirts.

She was unsure how to look at him then. What she should say, how she should proceed.

"You are so beautiful," he said, his voice quiet and intense. Almost as if he blamed her for such a thing.

"Gareth, I—"

"Don't say anything. I will probably regret this later, but I couldn't resist you. I find that to be true much of the time." His eyes narrowed. "What sort of spell have you woven around me, witch?"

It wasn't a legitimate question, and she had no answer to bestow on him. She had certainly not tried to bewitch him. She did not know how to do such a thing. Although she had certainly wondered the same about her reaction to him. At times it seemed as if it was he who had created the spell. That seemed unlikely, though.

One thing she knew for certain, no matter how she feared the repercussions, she would never regret this. Never regret allowing him to touch her. To love her body.

Chapter 12

$\sim\!\!\infty\!\!\sim$

Meg sat at her dressing table while Charlotte put a jeweled clip in her hair. The four of them had met at Meg's house to ready for the concert. Although with the exception of the jewels she was loaning Charlotte, the other three girls were ready when they arrived.

Meg wore a rich purple dress with a plunging neckline and black lace trim.

"This matches your dress perfectly. You look lovely," Charlotte said.

"As do you," Meg agreed.

"We all look lovely," Amelia said cheerfully.

"Willow, do take your spectacles off," Charlotte said. "You look so much prettier without them, and you only need them for reading."

Willow bristled. "I feel quite fine with these on. Thank you." She straightened them on her nose.

"I was only trying to help," Charlotte said. "There is no need to get short with me."

Willow nodded in acknowledgment.

They all had on their finest gowns, and Meg and Amelia had supplied jewels for each of them to wear. Tonight they were attending a vocal concert in an attempt to lure the Jack of Hearts. It took a half-hour carriage ride to arrive at Charing Cross Road, and they chatted the entire trip.

It had been several months since the four of them had attended something together. Poor Charlotte had taken it upon herself to do all the work on the case, as far as attempting to catch the Jack of Hearts in the act, while the rest of them tended to their own business. They all knew she'd done so not out of a great sense of bravery, but rather because of a heightened fascination with their nemesis.

While not nearly as excited or nervous as she had been the night she'd ventured into Mr. Munden's residence, Meg could feel the hum of adventure in the air. They made their way to their seats, and soon the lights dimmed.

Meg could hear the music and could see the soloist, but her mind was drawn away. Neither the excellence of the performance nor the purpose of tonight's outing could keep her mind from wandering to Gareth. Tall, seductive Gareth with his sensual eyes and sinful mouth. Keeping her mind off him was an exercise in futility.

The first part of the concert had concluded and they stood in the lobby for the intermission. The music hall was abuzz with activity and Meg took in her surroundings. Charlotte hailed a footman who brought over a tray of champagne.

"To us," she said, holding up her glass, "the Ladies' Amateur Sleuth Society. May we always find adventure and friendship wherever we go."

They toasted, and Meg took a sip of the refreshing liquid. The bubbles tickled her lips as she held the glass to her mouth. Had Gareth ever been to such a performance? So many things about him remained a mystery. And the closer she came to solving this case, the more she realized that eventually she would complete the task and she would no longer have reason to call upon him. All those little things she wanted to know, those curious little facts, would remain unknown.

"Any sight of him?" Amelia inquired, breaking into her thoughts.

"None," Willow said. "But the night is not over. We mustn't forget that the times he's come into theaters, he's always robbed those in their box seats, not in the lobby. Perhaps he's waiting until the intermission is over."

"How's the chocolate business?" an unfamiliar voice asked. Meg was about to answer when another voice did it for her.

"As it turns out, an excellent investment," the second voice said.

They were both women and the conversation had caught the attention of the rest of sleuths as well.

The two women having the discussion were behind Meg, and she wanted to turn and see their identity, but she couldn't do so without being too obvious. Not only that, but most people knew who she was, and she didn't want the fact that she was standing right there ruin her opportunity to listen in on this private chat.

"The two gentlemen I'm funding," the second voice

said, "have developed a new and rather exciting idea for packaging." The voice was not familiar at all, no matter how Meg struggled to place it. "Keepsake boxes," the lady whispered.

Meg felt her eyes go round and Amelia actually released a loud "Oh," but no one seemed to notice.

"I only just saw them this afternoon, and they're divine. The development of these could put the Leighton Brothers in serious competition with the rest of the confectioneries," she said.

"I'm certainly glad to see this investment turned out better than your last three, Mildred."

"As am I."

The lights flickered, indicating it was time for them to return to their seats, but Meg and the other girls remained where they were while the rest entered the auditorium.

"Who was that?" Meg finally asked. "I couldn't place either voice and I so desperately wanted to turn around and look at them."

"Mildred Sommerset," Charlotte said. "I don't recall anything in particular about her, but I know I've met her once or twice. She's wealthy, but I'm not certain why. I believe she's a widow. I didn't recognize the other woman."

"I didn't know either of them," Willow said.

"Nor I," Amelia said. "But they certainly had some interesting information to share. Do you know anything about the Leighton Brothers?"

"I've heard the name, but not in a while. They're a smaller confectionery and rather new, only starting up in the last year or so," Meg said. "I'd have to ask my father for more information."

"Sounds as if the thief might have sold those boxes to the Leightons," Willow said.

"Indeed," Meg said. She would have to go and see Gareth tonight, tell him of this information. They needed a plan of how they could visit the Leightons and prove the boxes had been sold to them. She would not allow someone to steal her father's ideas and profit from them.

"We should get back in there; the music is starting," Amelia said.

Meg had no mind for the music after that. She barely heard one note and was eager for the evening to end.

"We had no luck again," Willow said as they waited for their cloaks.

"Don't fret," Amelia said. "The Jack of Hearts is a clever one. It's simply impossible to predict when he'll strike."

"She's right. But it was certainly fun to be out with all of you." Meg smiled. "The information we overheard sounded promising. I am most eager to share it with Gareth and see how he thinks we should proceed."

"Indeed," Charlotte agreed. "This could be the missing element needed to solve this case."

"I suppose for that reason, the evening was not a complete loss," Willow said.

"We mustn't forget, it was also vastly entertaining to watch dear Charlotte swat all those men away like pesky dock flies," Amelia said with a giggle.

"Yes, yes, entertaining," Charlotte said drolly. "Might I point out that you three are not any more tempting to dear Jack than I." She crossed her arms over her chest, clearly pleased with herself.

"He is proving to be quite elusive," Meg said.

"Perhaps I'll invite Detective Sterling over for dinner and see what the Yard thinks about him," Amelia said. "Care to join us, Willow?"

Willow shuddered. "I don't believe I will. But I do appreciate your hospitality."

Their cloaks arrived, and they stepped out into the cool night air.

"The three of us can share a hackney. Meg, there's no reason for you to ride all over London dropping us off. It's late and you have a longer ride to get home," Charlotte said.

"Are you certain? Because it's no trouble at all," Meg said.

"No, you go ahead," Willow said.

"Very well." She kissed them each on the cheek and then climbed into her carriage. "Good night."

She must find Gareth and tell him all that she'd learned tonight. She couldn't ignore the bit of thrill coursing through her at the thought of his seeing her in such a dress.

Gareth was sitting on his bed, leaning against the wall when he heard the knock. He glanced at the clock; quarter after midnight. Who else was up at this hour? He was only awake because a certain siren with flaming hair wouldn't give his mind a single moment's rest.

He stood and walked to the door, not even bothering to don a shirt. Whoever it was that dared to rouse him at this time of night could very well take his state of undress.

He cracked the door, then opened it all the way when he saw that it was the siren herself. "What the devil are you doing here? At such an hour?"

"I had to see you," she said.

"How did you even get in here?"

"I told Mrs. Silsby that I had an urgent message for you from my father," she said.

"And she believed you?"

"Are you going to invite me in, or do I have to stand out here whispering in the hall?" she urged.

He stepped out of the way to give her entrance to his rooms.

"Mrs. Silsby trusts me implicitly. She was our house-keeper for years."

"This is not the way to keep your reputation intact, Meg. Are you trying to start a scandal?" he asked.

"You're the one who's undressed," she said.

"I was going to bed."

"Why are you still whispering?"

He cleared his throat.

She removed her cloak to reveal a deep purple dress with a plunging neckline that molded to every luscious line of her body. His mouth went dry, and he became very aware of the fact that he was not fully dressed.

"You're not fully clothed yourself," he said, then added, "it's a nice gown."

She smiled prettily. "Thank you. We went out to-night to lure the Jack of Hearts, but were unsuccessful."

"The four of you went out in your fancy gowns to try to tempt a thief?" He chuckled in spite of himself. "Quite risky, don't you think?" He paused briefly, then said, "that's a foolish question when it comes to you. It is as if you thrive on the daring and perilous."

"He never came, so it mattered not. But I did discover another bit of information that might help us with our investigation."

He knew he should feel grateful. She'd been willing to help him when she scarcely knew him. She'd always believed his innocence. He owed her so much, but instead of feeling gratitude, he felt only annoyance. Irritated that she was in a position to discover such information.

And irritated with himself because if he'd only tell everyone the truth about himself, he too would have such opportunities. But he would never use that name, because to do so, he'd have to take all the responsibility that came with it. That was something he wasn't prepared to do.

He leveled his eyes on her. "What did you discover?"

"While we were at the concert, we overheard a conversation between two women." She filled him in on the details of all she heard.

Gareth found himself smiling. She was a clever sleuth. A vaguely familiar feeling constricted his heart. He could have sworn it was pride.

"What do you know of the Leighton Brothers?" he asked.

"Very little."

"I haven't heard anyone speak of them here. That doesn't mean someone doesn't know something about them," he said.

"I plan to ask Papa about them tomorrow. See if he knows anything specific. After that, we can formulate our next move," she said.

Red, springy curls fell seductively around her shoulders, while the rest of her hair was pulled up in an elaborate coiffure. She looked so beautiful, it was almost painful to look at her. It was beginning to get a little uncomfortable in his breeches as his arousal was straining against the fabric.

Draped across her neck was a stunning amethyst; the gem made an arrow to her tempting cleavage. Although he would have found it without the directions. Her breasts rose and fell with her breath and he found he was nearly entranced by their rhythm.

Without giving much thought to the consequences, he grabbed her by the wrist and pulled her against him. "Did you not think this dress would tempt me, minx?"

He did not give her opportunity to answer before he lowered his lips onto hers. The feel of her body tightly encased in that velvet dress pressed against his naked chest was intoxicating, and he groaned into her mouth.

Her kisses were exhilarating. Soft, plush lips melted with his own and the fire of her tongue shot blood pouring into his groin. God, he wanted her. But to have her, he'd have to continue taking what was not his to take. Gamble with her feelings as if she were nothing more than a game of chance.

He was more like his father than he wanted to admit.

He ended the kiss, but did not step away from her. He held her close to him, breathing in the scent of her

hair, his eyes still closed. How quickly she had be-
witched him.

"You should go," he whispered. She must be so confused. Pushed and pulled at his whim. He should apologize, but found no words for it. He wouldn't touch her
again, no matter how tempting. He wouldn't play with
her emotions in such a reckless manner. She meant too
much to him now, and he wouldn't hurt her that way.

She nodded against him.

He grabbed her cloak and helped her back into it.
"Is the carriage still here, or would you like me to
walk you home?"

"No, he's waiting for me."

"Very good. I hear your father is coming back to the
factory soon. He must be recovering well."

She nodded. "Quite well. It won't be too much longer now."

She stood there a moment longer. Perhaps waiting
for him to say something else, but he was at a loss. And
he certainly didn't want to say something he'd regret.
Something he could never take back.

"Good night, then," she said, then slipped out of the
door.

"Good night," he answered, but the door closed before she could hear.

He'd blamed her dress and he'd once before accused
her of bewitching him. But the truth was, none of this
was her fault. He had a hard time resisting her, but that
was his own damn weakness. A sliver of moonlight
spilled onto the floor.

He paced the short length of his room, the wood floor
feeling cold to his bare feet. He wanted to tell her the

truth about himself. Wanted her to know about his title and his father and how he'd ruined everything. Wanted her to know that taking the title would destroy him. But telling her would serve no purpose.

There was a truth he could deny no longer. It had started as desire, just his flesh needing to touch her flesh. Then she had awakened a protective instinct within him. But it was more than that now. He didn't want to put a name to it, but he'd be a liar if he said he wasn't beginning to care about Meg Piddington.

Yet another reason that he needed to stop giving in to temptation. Stop being weak and allowing the desire to pull him over the edge and pull her into his arms.

Meg leaned against the closed door, her eyes squeezed shut. They were playing a dangerous game, both of them. He for reasons he had yet to disclose, and she for her own. She risked so much every time she allowed him to kiss her or touch her. Risked her carefully decided plans for the future.

For every time they kissed, she wanted one more. Every touch he gave, she wanted him to touch her elsewhere on her body. Never was she left satisfied when it came to Gareth. More. She always wanted more. This was the most dangerous of all because she knew if she ever lost her heart to him, she'd never be happy. He could never, would never love her, and knowing that would eventually break down her spirit.

She'd guarded her heart for years against trifling things, thinking that she'd done a good job protecting herself, when in reality, she'd never once been tempted.

Not really. Not with the one man who could make her risk it all and who, in the end, would take everything she gave without having anything to give in return.

If she wasn't more careful, this relationship was going to end in her greatest fear.

Chapter 13

Gareth walked in silence next to Meg as they made their way around the factory grounds. He kept his hands in his pockets and his eyes forward. He'd said nothing when she asked him to take this walk; he'd merely nodded and followed her out the door.

"I asked you to walk with me because I thought you might enjoy some open air. That factory can get dark with the limited windows," she said.

"Thank you," he said.

There were so many things he wanted to say to her. So many apologies and explanations, but the truth was, he wasn't certain he could come up with a good explanation. He'd lain awake for hours last night thinking of their passionate kiss. About the many times he'd pulled her into his arms only to push her away moments later.

He could only hope she knew that he was not a callous man and that he meant her no harm. Their attraction, the pull between them confused the hell out of him. He'd never before met a woman he couldn't resist. In the past, he'd always been the one to say when and where, always been the one in control.

And while so far with Meg, he'd managed to control when he touched her and when he let her go, he seemingly had no control over the intense desire for her. The lustful need to put his hands on her body and his mouth on hers. So far he'd been able to resist the intense longing to plunge himself deep inside her, but he wasn't so certain he could resist it much longer. Which was why he couldn't allow himself even the slightest taste of her lips. Why right now, he stood with his hands stuffed in his pockets.

He knew she felt it too. What he didn't know was whether it was unique to him. Would she react as strongly with any man who made such advances on her? Was her flesh ready for any man's touch, or was it his touch and his alone that left gooseflesh in its wake?

They ended up at a bench at the edge of a pond. It was a ways from the factory, so they were alone, secluded from everyone. It was the perfect spot for a seductive rendezvous, he couldn't help but notice, but today he would not touch her. Better to end it now before it grew out of control. He'd rather walk away knowing, or at least believing, that she desired him. Walk away before that desire waned and she no longer looked at him with hungering eyes.

It would happen eventually.

"I spoke with my father," she began. "About the Leighton Brothers. He didn't know many specifics either. Only that they're a fairly new confectionery and have been trying several new recipes looking for something that would separate them from all the rest. I didn't mention the conversation I heard in detail. There is no reason to alarm him of a possible traitor if we discover this has no merit," she said.

"The Leighton Brothers seem to be quite secretive," he commented. "What shall we do now? I want to investigate this matter further to discover if the chocolate boxes came from here."

"I agree, we must do something," she said. "I've thought on this awhile, and I've come up with a plan. But you will need to be the one to see it through as I can't risk being recognized."

He picked up a fallen twig and began plucking the leaves off it. "What would you have me do?"

"Meet with the Leighton Brothers. Charade as an investor and persuade them to show you the boxes. You'll be able to determine, on sight, if the boxes are Piddington's."

Once all the leaves were removed, he flung the twig into the pond. "Charade as an investor? Do you think they'll believe me?"

"I'm certain of it. All we need to do is put you in some fancier clothes and you'll pass for a wealthy investor in no time." She gave him a shy smile. "You have the arrogance for it."

He smirked and elbowed her in the side. "Why will they agree to see me if they already have an investor? What did you say her name was?"

"Mildred Sommerset. Even if they have an investor, they certainly won't turn away another one. I think if you try to schedule an appointment ahead of time, they'll have too much time to research you. It seems it will be better if you simply drop by because you were in the neighborhood, so to speak." She stood and walked to the edge of the pond, then turned back to face him.

"Associate yourself with Mrs. Sommerset. Tell them that she was bragging about her investment and how lovely the Leightons were to work with and that you would like to make a similar investment. If they're as hungry for funding as they appear to be, then they should jump at the chance." She walked back toward the bench.

"You certainly have all of this figured out," he said.

She chewed at her lip. "I didn't sleep much last night." She met his glance and didn't look away or say anything else for a moment.

He hadn't slept last night either. And instead of feeling guilty for causing her such withdrawal, he instead thought of all the sinful things they could have done to each other while awake in the darkest of night.

"It was easy to formulate this plan. I've given it a lot of thought and it is my belief that we should follow through with this," she said.

He considered her for a moment in silence as he fought his urge to immediately agree. He couldn't help but wonder: did he want to help her because it was the right thing to do or because he merely wanted to spend more time with her?

He suspected it was the latter. But did it matter either way? He wouldn't—no, couldn't—refuse to help her. Not when he knew if he refused her plan, she'd develop some other scheme to investigate on her own.

"What do we do first?" he asked.

"We need to go shopping." She started up the hill as if she was ready to leave.

"Now?" he asked.

"Yes, I believe so. The sooner we can purchase something for you to wear, the sooner you can visit them. Aren't you ready to move past this?" she asked.

Clearly she was ready. Ready to be rid of him. Ready to be finished with this task she'd taken on. It had been exciting in the beginning, but now it was another burdensome duty for her. She would not say it, she would never walk away until she'd exhausted all methods of proving his innocence, but she was tired of this. He could see it in her weary eyes. Eyes that had once been bright and cheerful and full of challenge, now would scarcely look at him.

He stood and followed her up the hill. "We need to stop by my room so I can gather some funds," he said.

"That won't be necessary. I have plenty of money."

"I realize that. But it is your money. I will use my money to purchase my own clothes." He would not argue with her about this. He would not take her money. He'd taken enough from her as it was.

The newly purchased pants, boots, and jacket were so black, Gareth looked like midnight itself. Unless you glanced up to see the shock of white at his neck, tied perfectly.

"You look . . . wealthy," she told him. And sinful. And so desirable, she wanted nothing more than to run her fingertips all over him. She felt the heat of her blush creep up her breasts and into her neck.

He stepped out of his room. "Are you ready?"

Her mouth had gone dry, but she managed to nod. As he helped her into the brougham, she focused on keeping her eyes averted.

She watched the Piddington Confectionery disappear out the window of the brougham, trying to avoid glancing at Gareth's long legs encased in the tight black fabric. Good heavens. A movement from him caught her attention and brought her eyes to his face.

He fidgeted with his collar.

"Are you uncomfortable?" she asked.

"No. Do you think they'll believe I'm an investor?" he asked.

It was on her tongue to tell him that they'd believe anything that he told them, but she decided not to. "You certainly look the part."

He smiled at her.

She sucked in her breath.

"You like this look," he said. He was quite pleased with himself.

She tugged on her skirt. "You look very handsome," she said tightly.

"Handsome? Is that all? Because I could swear from your expression that there was another word floating in your mind. Dashing, perhaps?"

"Sinful," she said in a huff.

He arched one eyebrow. "Sinful?"

"Are you teasing me? Because you are not a teaser. In fact, you have rarely shown signs of even having a sense of humor, let alone that you know how to tease a person. Yes, you look so handsome in that, I'm finding it incredibly difficult to concentrate on anything else. But there is no reason why you must torment me further."

As soon as the words left her mouth she wanted to snatch them back.

Oh no. What had she done? She'd said way too much. It was not entirely news to him that she might find him attractive since she'd allowed him such liberties in the past, but she'd never come right out and said anything about that.

She was nearly afraid to look him in the eye.

But instead of apologizing and ending the conversation right then, he looked at her and laughed. Heartily.

"I'm sorry," he said. "You should have seen your face."

"There is no reason to laugh at me."

"But you are so upset with your reaction. It's amusing."

She looked away.

"Meg, it's only a pair of black pants and a jacket. There's nothing that different about me."

He was wrong. It was different. The differences were slight, almost too small to even notice, but she'd seen them. The slight angle he held his chin. The small rise of his shoulders. The clothes made him feel different about himself. And either he hadn't noticed or he didn't want to admit it.

The carriage pulled to a stop outside a brick building that ran the length of one block. There was a small, hand-painted sign out front that read, "Leighton Brothers. Chocolates and Other Delights."

Gareth ran his hands down his thighs. "This is it," he said.

"Are you nervous?"

"No. I'm not convinced they'll believe me, but I'm not nervous."

"I'll wait in here," she said. She wanted to go in with him. Play a role as well, but what if they knew who she was? She couldn't risk it. "Make certain they show you the boxes."

"I will." He opened the carriage door. "I will be back in a short while."

She watched him walk into the building and disappear behind the doors. The area was not the nicest in London, but it was better than many spots. The building must have been for another factory of sorts and the Leightons had purchased it. It didn't look as if they'd finished remodeling the entire factory. Perhaps they were working as they could afford.

The streets were fairly quiet, not offering too much for her to watch while she waited for his return. Two little boys, scruffy and dirty, ran by her window and then across the street. She could hear the horse's hooves clicking on the street. It was getting restless, as was she.

She had no timepiece with her, so she wasn't certain how long it took, but eventually Gareth stepped out of the factory and back into the carriage.

He shook his head. "Not our boxes," he said.

Meg felt as defeated as he looked. His face had lost the light from before, and now his brow furrowed and his lips set in a line.

"What happened?"

He shrugged. "You were right, they were eager for another investor. I mentioned Mildred's name and both men jumped to their feet. At that point, they would have shown me anything." He reached up and loosened his tie. "After I saw the boxes, I told them I'd be in touch. But they weren't our boxes. Not even the same quality. So if they start selling them, Piddington has nothing to be concerned about."

Meg nodded. She had been so certain that this was the break they'd been looking for. The final piece to the puzzle. But it was not to be. So they were still left wondering who took the boxes and why they were going to such lengths to pin their crime on Gareth.

If she was completely honest, she wasn't totally disappointed with the outcome of this jaunt. Once they solved this case, they would no longer need to work with each other.

"I'd wager you did a brilliant job in there," she offered.

His beautiful hazel eyes met hers. Such longing in them. Longing for too many things for her to name. But she was not one of those things. Whatever had spurred his initial desire for her had waned. He was civil to her, even kind. But he had not touched her in days. Even earlier when he'd teased her, it had been harmless, as if she were a girl he'd just met.

It was for the best, she knew that. But she missed his touch. Missed his kisses. Missed being the object of desire.

Chapter 14

G areth had no sooner stepped up to his machine than he was summoned to Mr. Piddington's office. There was no mention of Meg, but no one else had ever used her father's office. Then again, she'd never sent another worker for him, had always stopped by his machine herself and requested his presence. He climbed the stairs, all too aware of the eyes that followed him.

He knocked once before an unfamiliar voice replied, "You may enter."

Meg had said her father was healing quickly, but this seemed a little fast. Gareth opened the door and stepped into the office. He spotted Munden first, grinning widely. Behind the desk stood another man. A man far too young to be Mr. Piddington.

Gareth frowned. "What is this about?"

"Mr. Mandeville, I am Henry Sanders. Mr. Piddington's factory director. Mr. Munden here called me in this morning to attend to some unfortunate business."

Henry Sanders was not a tall man, but he was slim as a rail and his light brown hair was thinning on top, although he did his best with the comb to disguise that fact. Gareth suspected the director was close to his own age, perhaps a few years older.

"Unfortunate business?" Gareth asked.

"It appears that you are in a bit of trouble," Sanders said.

Gareth released a great breath. "If Mr. Munden has called you out here because he believes I took those chocolate boxes, I could have saved you a trip. He has no proof and I maintain my innocence."

"Do you have an alibi, sir?" Henry asked.

"No," Gareth said tightly. At least not one he could use.

Sanders nodded. "That is a pity, Mr. Mandeville, as there does seem to be some incriminating proof that was discovered recently."

"What proof?"

He held up a box that had been on the chair behind him. One of the missing boxes.

"Where did you find that?" Gareth asked.

"In your locker," Munden said, then hid a laugh behind a wheezing cough.

"That is enough, Mr. Munden," the director chided.

Gareth felt rage coiling through his stomach. "You son of a bitch," he said. He took a few steps toward Munden.

"I wouldn't do something you might regret," Sanders said. "Nothing will be done today, as far as your position here, Mr. Mandeville, but I'm afraid I must bring this to the attention of Mr. Piddington. I will be leaving for a meeting with him at the conclusion of this one. Is there anything that you would like me to tell him on your behalf?"

"Yes. You can tell him that this sniveling bastard has toyed with the wrong man, and I will see this righted."

Sanders nodded, but his expression never changed. "Will that be all?"

"That will be all," he mimicked. "Now if you don't mind, gentlemen, I'm going to work."

"Very good. I will report back with you tomorrow and let you know how Mr. Piddington wishes to proceed."

Gareth said nothing, simply turned his back and slammed the door behind him. The bastard had planted that box and then called in Piddington's workhorse to do the dirty work. Had the anonymous benefactor provided Munden with the missing box?

Munden was the thief in this factory. The secret lay in discovering the identity of the author of that anonymous note. Why had he stood by and done nothing while Meg and her friends did all the work? It was his own damn fault he was in this predicament.

It might not be the same situation his father had been in, but like his father he'd taken the lazy route, and look where it had landed him. Thank goodness Gareth didn't have a wife and children who could be affected by his lack of action. He'd been a fool to sit idly by while someone worked very hard to frame him, and if he didn't work quickly, they were going to succeed.

"What did you wish to speak with me about, Papa?" Meg asked as he entered her father's study. His leg had healed enough that he was now able to maneuver the stairs without the assistance of servants.

He waited until she'd taken a seat in the leather chair. He wasn't smiling, and that concerned her. He'd had a similar somber look the day he'd told her that her mother was not coming home.

Today would bring bad news; she could smell it in the air.

"What is it?" she asked.

"Sit down and then we'll visit. Meggie, you are not going to be pleased, but it seems your Mr. Mandeville is, in fact, guilty."

Her heart dropped into her stomach. "But how could that be?" What could possibly have happened since the last time she'd seen Gareth? It made no sense. He'd been with her and there was no way he'd gotten back into the factory later that night. He was innocent. She was certain of that.

"Munden called Henry to the factory this morning to handle the situation. Apparently the foreman discovered one of the missing boxes in Mr. Mandeville's locker at work."

Munden was still working to frame Gareth. Had he received another note? She frowned. "But Papa, why would Gareth keep something he'd stolen in a place where people could find it? Not only that, but I believe Mr. Munden had searched Gareth's locker on a previous occasion and found nothing."

Her father nodded. "I agree it doesn't make sense, but people that steal rarely do," her father said. "I'm sorry, Meggie, I know you wanted him to be innocent."

"What are you going to do?" she asked.

"He will lose his position." Her father took a deep breath. "I can't overlook this."

"Has anyone spoken to Gareth yet?" she asked.

"Henry spoke with him this morning. Apparently Gareth was none too pleased."

"Well, obviously not. You wouldn't be too pleased either if someone was manipulating evidence to blame you for a crime." She did nothing to hide the sarcasm from her voice.

His eyebrows raised. "So you are still maintaining his innocence?" her father asked.

"I most certainly am." She folded her arms across her chest. "This isn't about me being right. It's not an issue of my pride. It's an issue of truth."

"I do believe this will end in disappointment for you, Meggie," he said.

"Perhaps." Her father had never spoken words of greater truth. Although disappointment was an understatement. This had started, more than anything, as a quest to snare a thief and prove to her father that she was responsible enough to manage the factory. Along the way, though, it had become much more. A man's future was at stake. A man she cared for.

She would prove Gareth's innocence, and then he'd be out of her life and she'd have to recall all those reasons she'd sworn off marriage. She wasn't about to stand by and allow Gareth to be wronged this way. But she needed more time.

She went to her father and knelt beside his chair. "Do something for me, Papa."

"Ah, my girl, when you look at me that way, I have no choice. But within reason, please," he said.

He was always so good with her. "Allow me one

day. One day to set this right. Before you dismiss him. If I cannot do so, then you may continue with your plans."

"Very well. One day, Margaret, that is all you get. Do you understand?"

He only ever called her by her given name when he was trying to be firm. She smiled and kissed him on the cheek. "Yes. Thank you, Papa. Oh, how I love you." And with that, she came to her feet and ran out of the room. There was much to be done and very little time to do it. What she needed now was some counsel. She summoned a carriage, then raced to her room to gather her cloak and reticule. Perhaps Charlotte would know what to do.

Meg spent the entire drive trying to come up with something to save Gareth's future. She could easily go to her father and tell her all they'd discovered about Munden, although she'd have to convince Gareth to give her the ledger sheets. But—without the note they'd found—that only proved Munden was stealing money; it did nothing for the accusations of Gareth's theft.

Now, somehow, they had one of the boxes as proof. Despite Munden's guilt, she still needed to prove Gareth's innocence. She knocked on the drawing room door at the Reed town home, and immediately it opened.

"Meg!" Frannie, Charlotte's younger sister, embraced Meg enthusiastically.

"Frannie, let her go before you knock her over," Charlotte said from across the room.

Frannie did as she was instructed, then glared at her sister. "Stop calling me that!" she said, then smiled at Meg. "I apologize. It's been so long since you've stopped by."

"Yes, it has. I think you've grown even taller," Meg said. It was remarkable how the two sisters favored each other in stature, but the resemblance ended there. Charlotte had glossy-straight hair the color of a raven's wing, with contrasting bright blue eyes, whereas Frannie had blond wavy hair with exotic brown eyes. Different, but both strikingly beautiful.

"You must be almost to Charlotte's height by now," Meg said.

"Nearly," Frannie agreed.

"I'm assuming this isn't precisely a social call," Charlotte said, looking up from her mending.

"I need advice," Meg said.

Her friend set her mending aside. "Frannie, go play with your dolls," Charlotte said.

"I do not find you humorous." Frannie glared at her sister.

Charlotte took a deep breath. "I apologize, dear sister. Frances, would you please allow myself and my friend some privacy to discuss something?"

Despite their seemingly hostile relationship, Meg knew that both sisters would do anything for each other. Meg felt a pinch of jealousy to have never known what it would be like to have siblings.

Frannie gave her a forced smile. "Certainly, dear sister."

After the tall blond had left the room, Meg turned to Charlotte. "You shouldn't goad her so."

"I know it. I simply can't help myself."

"She certainly has grown. I don't suppose I've seen her for a while," Meg said.

"I think she's grown nearly a head taller in the last year. But I don't think you came to discuss my pesky younger sister."

"No, I didn't." Meg paced the length of the faded Persian rug. "I'm at a loss for what to do."

"I can't help you if you don't tell me what it is," Charlotte pointed out.

Meg stopped, then gave her a quick smile. "You're right. I'm so nervous though." She recounted the discussion she'd had only an hour before with her father. "So you see, I'm the only alibi he has, but to do this would ruin me."

"Are you that concerned with that?" Charlotte asked.

"To be honest, I don't know."

"Some time ago, you decided you would never marry. Do you still feel the same?" Charlotte asked.

She still felt the same. Still had the same desire for her own family. And still believed that was not to be. Unfortunately Gareth had made those desires hard to ignore these past few weeks. More than ever she wanted to allow herself the joys of being a wife and mother. But the joys would not last and the pain that would follow could possibly destroy her. She couldn't afford the risk. "Yes, I still feel the same. I have no desire to marry," she lied.

Charlotte nodded, but there was no agreement on her face. "Being a ruined woman would certainly give you some freedom. Allow you to work at the factory without anyone thinking twice about it."

"I suppose you're right. So you think I should give him the alibi, then?"

"That's not what I said. I was merely pointing out something you might not have considered." Charlotte set her gaze on Meg. "There is also the possibility that Gareth will do the honorable thing and marry you."

Meg's heart gave a small catch. She hadn't even considered that. "No, that will never happen."

"How can you be so certain?"

"He was adamant about this point the first time I tried to give him this alibi. He made it quite clear that marrying me was the last thing he wanted to do," Meg said.

"But that was before you knew him, correct? He might have changed his mind since then."

So much had changed since then, but Meg knew none of that would mean anything. "But I don't believe it would matter to him."

"Is he so heartless to leave you deserted and ruined?"

Gareth wasn't heartless, but he had warned her that he had no desire to marry her. Making this decision without him would seal her fate, and she wouldn't blame him for turning away from her.

"I don't think you should be quite so insistent on that. You never can tell what a man will do. What of all the embraces you've shared? They must mean something to him." Charlotte frowned in concern. "*You* must mean something to him."

Meg wouldn't even allow herself to hope for such a thing. Her friend meant well, but Meg knew that Gareth did not love her and never would. He'd told her before. "He finds me desirable," she admitted. Had even gone so far as to accuse her of bewitching him. "But it is desire, nothing more."

"You obviously know him better than I do," Charlotte agreed.

Meg fell back into a yellow armchair. "Oh, Charlotte, what do I do? I can't allow him to lose his job. And if it were only Munden we could expose his theft and be done. But they involved my father. Supposedly they found evidence in Gareth's belongings." She rolled her head to face Charlotte, who sat in a matching yellow chair. "What would you do?"

"I'm not certain. I suppose it would depend on how important this man was to me. And whether or not sacrificing my own future would right this wrong."

Meg winced. She wasn't certain she knew the answer to either of those questions. "That's not helpful."

"I'm sorry."

"What would Willow say? Willow would know the right thing to do," Meg said.

"Indeed. She would probably first chastise you for putting yourself in a position to be a man's alibi."

Meg smiled. Willow had indeed chastised her for such a thing already. But little did any of them know precisely how ruined she actually was.

"Then she would probably tell you that telling your father the truth was the only solution."

"Do you really believe that?"

"I think so. You could always pay her a visit and ask," Charlotte said. "To make certain."

"No. As much as I dearly love her and could use her counsel, I'm not certain I'm prepared for one of her lectures at the moment." No doubt Willow would know the perfect decision for her to make, but Meg couldn't bring herself to ask.

"I understand. I'm sorry I couldn't be more helpful. I'm afraid this is a decision only you can make."

Meg realized she was right. She was asking someone to make this decision for her because she was terrified she would make the wrong one. "You're right. I know you are. Perhaps I should go. Evidently I have some serious thinking to do. Tomorrow morning, I must tell my father whatever my decision is." Meg had expected Charlotte to have a definite opinion, the perfect advice on what to do in this scenario. Her friend still had the capability of surprising her. Perhaps she was wise beyond her years.

"Best of luck. No matter what you decide, it will be the right choice."

"Well, isn't that convenient." She gave Charlotte a smile. She appreciated her friend's attempt at lightening her load. "One more question," Meg said.

"Of course."

"Should I tell Gareth?"

"Will he try to stop you?" Charlotte asked.

"Yes. Of that I am certain."

He would definitely try to stop her. She acknowledged that his decision had the potential to change his life, but the odds of that happening were slim. It might change, but not to the degree hers would. His reputation wasn't in danger the way hers was. No one would give a second thought to him if he ruined her and then refused to marry her. At least no one who knew him.

"If you are, in fact, going to present this alibi to your father, then no, I wouldn't tell him."

She nodded, then quickly hugged her friend. "Thank you."

"Let me know what you decide."

"I shall." Meg stepped out onto the front steps of her

friend's house. She had much to decide and not much time to do it in. Charlotte was right not to offer too much advice. This was her decision and hers alone. And that was precisely how she'd make it.

Chapter 15

Meg stared at the mirror. She'd spent the better part of the morning arguing with her reflection, and that was after a relatively sleepless night tossing over the same decision. She knew now what she was going to do. It was the only decision to make, and she felt certain it was the right one. What she didn't know was the outcome of such action.

She would know soon. Telling her father across the breakfast table might not be the smartest plan, but perhaps some warm jam would brighten his mood. Granted, her father had always been rather indulgent with her, but she didn't suspect he would be in this situation. Instead, she expected he would be nothing less than severely disappointed.

As much as she loved her father, his disappointment did not matter nearly as much as the freedom of another man. And she was the only thing that stood between

Gareth and his position with Piddington Confectionery.

She took a deep breath, then stood. It was time.

He walked around the empty factory floor, surveying what would soon be his. Miss Piddington had gotten herself compromised with the wrong man, and now they weren't even planning on telling anyone. If things had gone as planned, she would have been compromised with him and they'd be planning their wedding now. But the blasted carriage wheel had made him too late for that. And that fool he'd hired to lock the door hadn't even looked to see who was inside. Bloody fool is what he was.

The original plan had failed, and he needed another way to get his hands on the factory in a more permanent sense. Day-to-day operations simply wasn't enough. He wanted more. Had earned more. Deserved more. He would come up with an alternate plan, and then Meg Piddington and the factory would be his.

It was more than past time. He'd worked so hard. Slaved, and for what? Well, no longer would he be anyone's slave. Soon he would have it all.

He chuckled to himself, then wiped a line of residual cocoa powder from the edge of a grinding machine. After so much careful planning, things were, at last, going to work to his favor. It wouldn't be long now. His plan was falling perfectly into place.

Meg watched her father carefully and waited until his mouth was full before she spoke.

"I've labored long and hard over this, Papa, but have decided it is well past time that I be honest with you.

Gareth could not possibly have stolen those boxes that night because he was with me." She said the words so quickly, they ran together. Uncertain if her father had understood her, she waited.

Lines of confusion wrinkled his forehead. He reached for his glass, so she spoke again.

"Alone, Papa. We were together alone."

"Meg, what the devil are you talking about?" he finally sputtered.

"The night the chocolate boxes were stolen."

"Yes, yes." He waved his hand. "I gathered that much. But what is this nonsense about the two of you being alone together? You scarcely know the man." And then as if he'd thought the worst, he came to his feet and threw the napkin on top of the table with such force that, had it been made of glass, it would have shattered. "Are you telling me that he took advantage of you?"

"No, nothing such as that. Do sit down. All will be well."

He eyed her a moment more before falling back into his seat. "Continue," he prodded.

"Yes, well, it was the night that you sent me to retrieve your ledger book. I heard a noise in the downstairs storeroom—the one the workers are using for their dressing room. I followed the noise, and when I went in the room to investigate, the door shut behind me and locked."

Her father eyed her and then nodded. "And Mr. Mandeville was already in the room?"

"Yes."

"Why was he in there so late, did he say?"

Her father didn't look pleased with the situation, but she could certainly imagine that things could be worse.

"He said he was working late that evening and had finished shortly before I arrived and was gathering his belongings to go back to his rooms."

"Did you see if he had anything unusual with him?"

"No. Only a coat, I believe," she said. "Apparently he was working late to cover the hours for one of the other men. This other man, Jamie I believe is his name. Yes, well, Jamie's wife was giving birth and Gareth agreed to do all of Jamie's grinding for the day so he could leave and be with her."

"I see. That seems honorable enough. What happened after you were locked in the storeroom?"

"I don't know how long we were in there, but after some digging and moving things about, we discovered a small window. So he assisted me to the window and I crawled out, then came around to the door and let him out. He walked me home and then he left for the boarding rooms."

Her father waited awhile before speaking again. As if he were balancing all the facts she'd given him. "How can you be certain that he did not go back to the factory after he walked you home and steal them? Or perhaps he had already taken them," he said.

"No, the boxes were there in the storeroom, ready to be delivered. I saw them myself. As for him going back, that's impossible. I locked the factory door when we left, and Gareth doesn't have a key. I think whoever took the boxes was still in the factory when we left that night. I think they were waiting for us to leave.

"There is something else you should know," she added. "We know that Mr. Munden has received funds for him to pursue Gareth as the thief of these boxes.

We're not certain why or who has paid him, though."

"How is it that you know that?" he asked.

She certainly couldn't admit to him that she'd broken into Munden's residence, so she'd leave that part out. "We came upon an anonymous note that instructed Munden to do so. It must have included money as it indicated more was to come. Unfortunately we don't have the note in our possession."

"Interesting development. It does appear that you have an alibi that clears Mr. Mandeville of stealing the boxes." He sighed, a sound heavy with resignation and, she feared, disappointment. "And it seems equally evident that someone was trying to frame this theft on him. I find this troubling that there would be such deception among my employees." He rubbed his hand down his face. "I'd love more than anything to just make this disappear for you. To walk over to the Confectionery and tell Sanders and Munden that Mr. Mandeville is to retain his position, no questions asked. But you know I do not work that way. Sanders is practically my partner, I most certainly could not make a decision without giving just reasons for it. Especially when they have proof that points to Mr. Mandeville's guilt. If I allow you to present Mr. Mandeville with this alibi, your reputation will be shreds. It will be difficult, if not impossible, for you to make a good match. Do you understand that, Meg?"

Of course she understood it. She'd been sorting through the details over and over again. No marriage meant no children. She knew it was unlikely that she would marry, but being faced with the certainty of the situation was harder than she'd anticipated. It was for the best. For she feared that marriage would only end in devastating pain, and she knew she wasn't strong enough to endure such a thing.

"Yes, Papa. I've given this quite a bit of consideration. And it's important to me that I do the right thing by coming forward with this."

He sighed and nodded. "Then I will not forbid you to do so. Make certain you know what this decision could do, Meggie. This could hurt you more than you're anticipating."

At least she did not love Gareth; that would save her some heartache. "I know." She stood quickly, then walked to his side. Leaning down, she gave him a soft kiss on the cheek. "I do love you, Papa. And I hope I am not so much of a disappointment to you."

He cradled her face in his hands. "Nothing you could do would make you a disappointment." He rose and steadied himself on his cane. "Let us be off, then. I will not allow you to do this alone."

"But your leg," she protested.

"Is almost healed, and I'm tired of being stuck in his house. You can assist me."

She nodded and watched him walk next to her out of the house. He was slower, but seemed to be maneuvering without pain or problem. They took the carriage down the hill, so he wouldn't have to try to manage the cane on the grass.

Her stomach was rattling with nerves so much, she was nearly nauseated. She hadn't wanted to do this with Gareth. He would try to stop her as he'd done before. She knew not what sort of response to expect from any of the men. But she suspected Gareth's reaction would be the worst.

* * *

Why hadn't he just left when he could have? Found a new job and been done with this predicament? Not only would it have saved him from Munden's accusations, but it would have kept him away from Meg. Granted, Piddington was a nice factory, paid better than most, but at what cost? And he never would have gotten one of those staff positions.

Gareth stepped into the factory fearing it might be the last time he did so. Mr. Sanders had no doubt met with Mr. Piddington by now, and Gareth's fate had been sealed. He knew he could fight it, but frankly, he was too tired to do so.

He didn't bother making his way to his station, nor did he go to his locker and remove his coat; instead he immediately climbed the stairs to Piddington's office. He'd rather have done with this now. Besides, this way he could at least choose the time of his dismissal. He took a modicum of pleasure from depriving Munden of that.

He knocked on the door, but it wasn't closed all the way, so that it slowly swung open under the weight of his fist. Munden and the director were inside having a heated discussion. A heated discussion with Meg. What the devil was going on?

"Mr. Mandeville," Sanders said with an even tone. It was evidently not so much a greeting as it was more of an alert to the other parties in the room. That's when Gareth noticed a third man, sitting in one of the chairs in front of the desk. Mr. Piddington, he assumed.

Gareth nodded, then met Meg's gaze. She looked more serious than he'd ever seen her. A mixture of concern and resignation flickered across her face, leaving her brow furrowed and her mouth puckered. She'd come here for one last plea, no doubt, and she'd lost. His heart thumped against his chest, and he wanted to walk to her and assure her all would be well.

But that was not his place. After today, it would no longer matter to her how his life played out. She wouldn't owe him anything; he'd ensure she understood that before he walked out of her life for good.

"So is it true, then?" Munden asked, glaring at Gareth.

"I don't follow," Gareth said. "Is what true?"

"What Miss Piddington has told us?" Munden asked.

Gareth took a few steps inside the room, then closed the door behind him. Something was wrong.

Meg wouldn't look at him; instead she was closely examining her fingernails. Sanders eyed him suspiciously. And Munden looked angry enough to strangle him. Her father was not looking at him; the older man kept his eyes on Meg.

Gareth leveled his gaze on Meg. "What have you done?" he asked her quietly. But he already knew the answer. Already knew that she had just changed his life forever.

She lifted her eyes to his, they glistened with tears. "I told the truth," she said.

It felt as if she'd kicked him right in the stomach, hard enough to rip the wind from his lungs.

"Is this true, Mr. Mandeville?" Sanders asked. The thin man's lips were pursed in disgust.

"What exactly did she tell you?" Gareth asked.

Sanders cleared his throat. "She said that on the night of the theft, the two of you were locked in the lower storeroom alone. And that after some time you were able to find a way out. She also said that the chocolate boxes were in the room when you left. Since she locked the main door on her way out, there would have been no way for you to get back inside to steal the boxes. Did I capture the gist of the story, Miss Piddington?" He directed his question to Meg, but never took his eyes off Gareth.

Still her father said nothing. He would have expected the man to throttle him. Unless he was waiting. Waiting for Gareth's reaction, waiting to see if Gareth would do what was necessary.

"Yes," she said.

He would give this to her, she wasn't backing down. She'd been given the perfect opportunity to walk away from this. Apparently Meg wasn't in the habit of walking away. And she hadn't fallen into a weeping pile on the floor as many women would have. Instead she was strong, and in different circumstances he would admire her for that. But she'd just ruined his life. With one swift decision, she'd stripped everything from him.

She knew what this meant; he'd warned her about it before. But she hadn't cared, she'd done it regardless.

"What do you have to say for yourself, Mr. Mandeville?" Sanders asked.

He released a slow breath. He couldn't lie. It wouldn't repair the damage she'd done. She'd maneuvered him into a corner, like a well-placed chesspiece, and he was out of plays.

"What the lady says is true. We were locked in the storeroom together," he said. Meg still stood there, not looking at him. But he watched her, watched her closely as he'd have to do from now on.

She was to be his wife.

But he couldn't ask her here. He needed to speak with her father first. Alone. There were things he needed to know, things Gareth wasn't yet ready to tell Meg. And he needed to look different. If he was to become Viscount Mandeville, then he would need to look the part.

There was much to be done before he could take Meg as his bride. He took one last look at Meg, then turned and left the office.

Chapter 16

M eg had dawdled before making her way home, choosing to walk along the property for a while and clear her mind, rather than return in the carriage with her father. She wasn't too keen on seeing anyone at the moment. She had deliberately chosen to be a ruined woman. No father would wish that for his daughter.

It was not as if she expected Gareth to save her, to declare his love and beg for marriage. But for him to just turn and walk away. Facing that alone would have been hurtful, but to face it with three other people in the room, including her father, had been humiliating.

This was her decision, though, and she had to live with it. She stepped onto the front stoop of her house and opened the door. What of other people's reactions? She couldn't help but wonder what the girls would say. She knew Willow would be supremely upset, but how would Amelia feel? Charlotte had been rather evasive as well. Unlike her, as she was ordinarily so frank. Meg hoped that in the end, they would support her decision and her new status as a ruined woman, and that it wouldn't, in turn, cause them any undue embarrassment.

She entered the house to find the housekeeper pacing at the door. She started when Meg entered. "Oh, there you are. Your father wants to see you right away, in his study, Miss Piddington."

"Thank you." She knocked on the door and her father immediately beckoned her entrance.

He was not alone. Henry Sanders stood next to her father's desk, ever the dutiful servant. Her father sat behind the large desk; he looked tired and perhaps a little sad. He nodded and gave her a smile.

"Papa," she said. "Mr. Sanders."

"Meggie, because of your heroic presentation earlier, it appears that Mr. Mandeville has taken the route of a coward and disappeared."

It pinched to hear her father put into words Gareth's actions. Part of her hoped that his anger would cool and he'd come back. She knew he wouldn't return to marry her, but it would be nice to know that he wouldn't hate her forever.

"Henry, on the other hand, is quite concerned with the effect of this alibi on your reputation."

"That is very kind of him." She looked at Henry. "Of you. But I assure you, I shall be fine, so you need not fret over me." She pasted on a smile. "I have thoroughly enjoyed my time working at the factory and now I shall be free to do so. By your side, Papa. I want to learn everything there is to know." In time that would be enough. She'd learn to accept it as enough.

"But what of your future, Miss Piddington? What about a family?" Mr. Sanders asked.

Gracious, it appeared that poor Henry Sanders was still harboring feelings for her. He'd approached her two years before expressing an interest in a courtship, but she had sweetly declined. Ever since then he'd been nothing but professional with her, so she assumed he had found other interests, perhaps another woman. Henry Sanders was a lovely gentleman, the most loyal of employees, but he was not the sort of man Meg wanted to marry, even if she were to change her mind about marriage.

There was nothing in this man that would make her blood race as Gareth had. Nothing about him that called out to her, daring her to care. If Meg were honest, she knew there wasn't a man in all of England who would make her feel as Gareth had.

"Oh, Mr. Sanders," she said with a smile. "I hardly have enough of a reputation as it is for this to tarnish it all that much. In a few months, it is likely no one will remember such a thing." She wasn't completely positive that was true, but there was no reason to encourage his attentions.

"That would be nice, but we know that the gossips in this town are not quick to forget such things," her father warned. "With the expansion of the factory, our name will be noticed more often. I have no doubt if you were more active in Society, you would have your selection of men. Not only with your charm and beauty, but we do have a fortune."

She knew he'd wanted her to find a good match. He'd wanted all the things for her that any decent father would want for his daughter. But she'd chosen a different route, and she could only hope that in the end, it proved to be the right decision. "I'm not overly concerned," Meg said.

Henry took a step toward her. "I would like to offer you the protection of my name," he blurted out. He held both hands out to her a moment, then pulled them back to his body.

Was that meant to be a proposal? If so it was the most unromantic proposal ever uttered. She could save herself now. Protect her reputation and be a married woman. To someone who no doubt would be a gentle husband, but nonetheless would forbid her to work at the factory. Perhaps it was the responsible thing to do, but she couldn't bring herself to do it. Even though it would be the safest marriage, a marriage guaranteed not to bring pain. It would also bring no happiness. There would be no point. She couldn't do it.

"Dear Mr. Sanders, you are too kind and flatter me. But I cannot accept such generosity." She did not look at her father for fear of seeing pain in his eyes. No doubt he would approve of the match. "I am grateful you would make that sacrifice for me, but I can't allow you to do so. I shall endeavor and make a nice, quiet life for myself."

Henry's lips tightened. "Is there anything I can say or do to persuade you?" he asked. He looked to her father as if expecting the man to urge her to change her decision. But her father said nothing.

"I don't believe so." She walked to him and stood on her toes to kiss his cheek. "I feel nothing but gratitude for such an offer. I won't forget it."

With that she turned on her heels and quickly left the room before her father said anything. Most fathers would have insisted that their daughter take such an offer, take any offer, regardless of the sort of match it would make. Any match would save her reputation now. She had to admit it wasn't the worst offer she could receive. He had a well-paying position and was a kind man who had nice eyes. But in the end, she couldn't justify marrying him.

She wasn't likely to forget it, as it had been her first proposal and would probably be her last. As far as proposals went, it wasn't at all how she'd expected one would go. She'd actually witnessed a few in times past. All to Charlotte. Meg had stood by her friend's side while two viscounts and a baron had asked for Charlotte's hand. Not all in one evening, but Meg was nearly certain it had been in the same week.

Gareth paced the parlor while waiting for an audience with Mr. Piddington. He'd worked for the man for nearly four months and he had yet to actually meet him, as Piddington had been injured the very week Gareth had started his position. He'd said nothing in the office when Meg had compromised them. But it wasn't too difficult to imagine how he would react. Wealthy, entitled, arrogant—they were all the same.

Gareth realized after he'd left the factory office how it must have appeared to everyone. That he was deserting her, running away from his responsibility. He should have reacted better, but there was naught he could do about that now except hope that Piddington took him at his word today. Gareth had even secured them a special license to marry by the end of the week.

He didn't belong in this house; he could tell that simply by looking around the room. Being dressed in his expensive suit should have helped make him feel as if he belonged more, but it didn't. He tugged on the jacket. Money clung to everything in sight. The room was tasteful, it was quality, even to his untrained eye. This was the life he could have had. The life of a wealthy viscount.

Had his own father not been a selfish bastard.

Gareth hadn't ever planned to use his title. Hadn't wanted to become that person, take up the reins, become his father's legacy. He'd wanted to forget. Be his own man. Prove he could be in this town and not succumb to temptations. But marrying his greatest temptation would be like walking on fire—he'd never know when it would completely consume him.

He'd never been much for trying to prove to people he was worthy. He rarely gave a damn. As it stood, no one knew of his title. No one knew who he really was, and since he had no fortune, the title meant nothing. But now everyone would know. There was no way to hide from it any longer.

But Meg had sealed his fate, and now he had no choice. He'd use the bloody title and then he'd be saddled with it for the rest of his life. It didn't matter that he didn't want it, that he knew there was nothing but destruction when it came to a titled life of leisure. He'd seen it firsthand with his father; living the life of entitlement came with devastating consequences. Before he told Meg, he needed to ensure that all would be well. He wanted to see a solicitor, take the small amount of money he'd saved and establish the family estate. She would inherit money from her father, he knew that, but she would be his responsibility now, and he wouldn't leave her with nothing. He needed to ensure that he knew how to handle things and that he wouldn't become his father. He couldn't do that to her.

Despite taking on his title, he had no plans of entering Society. Knowing Meg as he did, it wouldn't be much of a sacrifice for her either. Her and her friends' silly investigation of the masked jewel thief seemed to be the only reason she ventured into Society as it was.

A few more moments later Mr. Piddington entered the room with the assistance of a cane. "I used to be quite spry," he said as he made his way to the chair. "But as you can tell, I'm still hobbling around. Would you like something to drink?"

"No, thank you," Gareth said.

Piddington nodded at the butler, and he bowed out of the room, closing the door behind him.

The man wasn't at all what Gareth expected. He'd worked at enough factories in his life to know that most owners were fat men who screamed at their servants and wasted money on food and liquor and ladies. But Mr. Piddington was tall and trim and while clearly a man of advanced age, looked to be in the best of health—with the obvious exception of the injured leg.

"Mr. Mandeville, I don't believe we've been formally introduced." He nodded, then situated his wrapped leg in a more comfortable position. "I have heard much about you though."

Despite the circumstances, Gareth chuckled at what must surely be a gross understatement. Or maybe it was nerves. He'd never asked for a man's daughter before. "Of that I have no doubt, sir. Mr. Munden is not my greatest fan."

"Not from Munden." There was a quiet but steely strength in the man's voice. "I actually haven't spoken to Munden since I've been away from the factory. It appears you have quite the champion in my daughter, Mr. Mandeville."

No doubt if the man wasn't injured, he would have challenged him to a duel. "Your daughter is why I made this visit, sir," Gareth said.

"Indeed?" Mr. Piddington absently rubbed his right knee above his cast. "Bloody thing has been itching for a week. It's driving me mad." He gave it a good scratch, then moved his hand away. "Mandeville, do sit. With you standing way over there, I feel as if we are not even in the same room."

Gareth liked the man, despite the current situation. He only hoped that the man liked him when the day was done. He did as he was told and sat.

Piddington crossed his arms over his chest. "Now then, what was it you wanted to discuss about my daughter?"

"I see no reason for us to pretend you don't know what has happened between Meg and myself," Gareth said.

"Very well," he said with a chuckle. "You left awfully quickly earlier."

"I realize how that must have looked, but suffice it to say, I had my reasons for leaving."

"Why don't you tell me yourself what happened the night in question."

Gareth slowly inhaled. "We were locked in a storeroom together. Nothing occurred. Her virtue is intact, sir, if that is your concern." It wasn't completely intact, Gareth acknowledged, but nothing save that first kiss had happened that first night.

"She said the same. Unfortunately the people in this

town can be quite nasty and won't care if her virtue is literally intact or not. The circumstances will ruin her reputation as soon as the word is out, and I won't be surprised if it's spread in the broadsheets tomorrow." He took a moment to scratch at his leg again.

"We're not very active in the social scene," he continued, "but my late wife was and the biddies will have a day with my poor Meggie." He released an ironic laugh. "Oh, they all buy my chocolates, but they won't think twice about gristing my daughter in the rumor mill."

Gareth knew all too well the sting of the gossip's tongue. He hadn't been too young to miss all the nasty things people had said about his father. And then consequently about his mother when she'd taken her children out of town. He couldn't allow that to happen to Meg. She might be infuriating at times, but she didn't deserve that.

He cleared his throat. "It is not my intention to allow your daughter to be ruined."

"What are you suggesting?" Piddington asked.

The man was certainly not making this any easier on him. Surely he had guessed why Gareth was here. "I seek your permission to wed her."

Piddington released a low whistle. "That's the second proposal today."

"The other being from whom?" Gareth asked.

He frowned. "My factory director, Mr. Sanders. I always knew that Henry had a fondness for Meg, but I never imagined he'd make his intentions known."

Gareth eyed Piddington, unsure of what to feel or say. "He asked Meg to marry him?"

"Yes."

"Then I am too late," he said. Dejection inched into his chest.

"Quite the contrary," Piddington said. "She declined."

"Why would she do a crazy thing like that?"

Piddington laughed. "That's Meggie. She's headstrong and reckless. Very much like her mother in that way." Piddington narrowed his gaze. "Tell me, were you relieved, Mr. Mandeville, when you thought someone else was handling your responsibility?"

It wasn't an accusation, but rather an honest question, and not one full of judgment or strife. It deserved an honest answer. "No, sir, I wasn't."

"Tell me, then, why you believe you deserve my daughter?"

"I never said I deserved her. But I played a part in ruining her reputation. She put that reputation on the line to salvage mine and I owe her this courtesy."

"Women do not want to marry out of courtesy."

"Duly noted." But it was all he could offer her.

"I do not mean this to sound crude, but your station in life is considerably lower than my daughter's. Why would a father allow such a match?"

"I work in a factory, Mr. Piddington, because it is honest, hard work. I work at your factory because your wages are the best and because the extra allows me to send some funds to my family. But do not be so hasty to assume anything about my station in life based on my position with your factory."

Piddington's eyebrows raised. "Explain."

"As greatly reluctant as I am to use this, as it will only result in unwanted effects on my life, I must be honest with you about my family lineage. While I have no funds, nor estate to offer, I have a name and a title that should afford enough protection of Meg."

Mr. Piddington's eyebrows raised in surprise. "You have a title?"

Gareth drew in a great breath. The gossips had spent considerable time discussing the viscount's wicked ways and how his debauchery and gambling had destroyed his young wife and five children. Once Piddington knew he was that Mandeville, he might not agree to the marriage. Gareth reached into his pocket and retrieved the special license and held it out to her father.

"My father was a viscount," he began. "I inherited the title when he died. I was twelve."

Her father glanced at the license, nodded, then handed it back.

"I mostly grew up in Ireland with my mother's family," Gareth continued. "We had lost the estate and all the money and there was no way to pay for my schooling, so I have no formal education, but I can assure you that I'm not ignorant."

"I don't think anyone would accuse you of being ignorant." Perhaps Piddington did not recognize the name and did not remember all the harsh things said about his family.

Piddington thought a moment before speaking again. "I can see that you were quite reluctant to share all of that. I respect your honesty and your honor. You may marry my daughter. If she will have you."

"Thank you, sir. I have one other request."

"Which is?"

"That Meg not know about my title. Not yet. I need time to decide how best to tell her. I'd prefer to have everything decided before I discuss it with her."

"I can assure you that Meg can handle this information. But I will respect your wishes," Piddington said. "A question for you, Viscount Mandeville?"

Gareth cringed at the name, but nodded.

"Do you care for my daughter?"

Now that Gareth hadn't expected. Who would have pegged Piddington for a sentimentalist? But then Meg had said that her parents had a great love. How did he answer such a question? He desired her, but her father wouldn't want to hear that any more than Gareth wanted to share it. He did not love her, nor could he ever, but he found her company enjoyable and he didn't want her to come to any harm. He cared about her, he couldn't deny that.

"Yes, I do."

"Very well. If you can persuade her to say yes to your proposal, you may certainly wed her."

"She'll say yes," was all he said.

Chapter 17

$\sim\!\infty\!\sim$

Her father had said Meg had gone to her friend Charlotte's for the afternoon. So Gareth currently sat in a carriage on his way to London. Now was as good a time as any to secure his bride.

Piddington had loaned him the carriage and instructed the driver on where to take him. When it rolled to a stop in front of a brick town home with a black door, Gareth chastised himself for not rehearsing the right words to say. Admittedly this was not to be a proposal with promises of love and sweet whispers, but it would have been nice to have something prepared. This was about honor and responsibility. That was the difference between Gareth and his father. Gareth knew he had responsibilities, and he would never walk away from one.

Gareth knocked on the door and was greeted by a young girl. He hadn't lived in Society since he was very young, but he knew enough to know that this family was financially limited, despite their good name, to be unable to hire a butler. He and his family had never had any servants either. Disgraceful behavior in the eyes of many of London's elite.

The young girl's eyes widened. "May I help you?"

"Is this the Reed residence?"

The girl sneered. "Are you here for Charlotte?"

"No, I'm actually looking for Meg Piddington. Is she here?"

"She is, indeed." The girl gave him a big smile and allowed him entrance. "They're in the parlor. Follow me. My name is Frances."

"Well, Frances, thank you for your assistance," Gareth said, then introduced himself.

Frances opened the parlor doors with great drama, then introduced him with all the enthusiasm of a royal footman.

Meg and Charlotte both popped to their feet.

"Gareth?" Meg said. "What are you doing here?"

"I need to speak with you and it couldn't wait." He leveled his gaze on Charlotte. "I beg your pardon, Miss Reed, I do realize this is your home, but would you allow me a few minutes of Meg's time? Alone?" No one could ever accuse him of not having manners when he needed them.

The tall beauty smiled. "Of course." Then, with great reluctance, she shuffled her sister out the door and closed it behind them.

Meg still stood. Her features pleaded with him to explain his presence. She waited a few moments more before speaking.

"Have you come to chastise me? Because I've

honestly had enough of that today." She began to pace. "I do realize that you, above all others, have the right to chastise me, but could you consider me well punished?" She stopped and looked at him.

He started to speak, but before he could say anything, she continued. "Oh, go ahead, I know you're furious with me. But you should take a moment to see things from my perspective. I honestly was doing this for your own benefit. I know you won't stand up for yourself to anyone, and I find that incredibly frustrating. You didn't steal those boxes, and there is no legitimate reason why you should lose your job because of some anonymous person's feelings against you. So you may be angry with me if you must, but I felt it was the right thing to do."

He listened to her carry on for what must have been three full minutes. She was so energetic and expressive and he could feel himself being pulled into her presence. The very aspects of her that he'd expected to drive him mad on that first night were now the things about her that just made her Meg. Unique from any other woman he'd ever encountered. She was mesmerizing, and the attraction he felt to her was undeniable. One thing could be said about marrying Meg; they would light up the nights with their passion.

She stopped walking and turned to face him. He nearly expected her to stamp her foot.

"Are you finished now?" he asked.

She swallowed. "Yes," she said quietly.

"I did not seek you out to chastise you. I do have better things to do with my time than that."

"Oh," she said.

"But I did come to discuss something with you. Your

admission has put us in a damn precarious position. It's not the decision I would have made, nor choose for you to make. There is no good reason to sacrifice oneself for another. Most people don't deserve gestures of such kindness. But it is done and now we must live with the repercussions."

Her features were etched in confusion.

Ah hell, he'd never proposed before and he was already bumbling it up. Another reason that he should have at least thought about what to say before he got there. Honor, responsibility, and passion. There were worse attributes to find in a bridegroom. The list had grown since this morning. Surely those elements were good seconds to promises of eternal love.

"I've come here to ask for your hand," he said quickly.

"My hand in what?" she asked.

"Don't be coy, Meg. Marriage. Your hand in marriage."

"Are you quite serious?" she asked. Then she frowned. "I thought you despised me."

"I won't lie to you, Meg. I'm angry about this." He rubbed his hand down his face. "I also know why you did it. Now it is my time to do the honorable thing."

"Honor," she repeated.

"Yes. Women do not dream of wedding for honor. They want love and other promises, but I cannot make those promises. You are as level-headed as any female I've ever encountered, so certainly you were not lounging about imagining marriage proposals in the form of soliloquies of love."

She bristled. "Of course not."

"So you agree?" he asked.

She shrugged and walked to the window. "I don't see the point. I appreciate your effort in trying to salvage my reputation, but there is no need. I'm quite content to stay in my father's home and continue working at the factory. It's what I wanted."

"I don't believe that for a second. You told me there had been a time when you wanted a family. Wanted children. I don't think you've given that up, at least the desire for it. I may not be able to give you everything, but I can give you that." It was the truth. He could go days and not speak to anyone and scarcely notice. But Meg began to fidget if the world around her had been quiet for very long.

Meg said nothing for a long while, simply stared at him.

He stepped over to her. "I'm not going to beg you, Meg. But I won't allow you to ruin your reputation on my behalf." He put his hand on her back. "I can't. I've already spoken with your father—"

She stiffened. "When did you see my father?"

"This morning. He's already agreed to the match."

She blanched, as if he'd struck her. Pulling back the curtain, she looked out the window. "I see."

"It is settled then," he said.

She nodded.

Gareth had never seen her so defeated. As if she'd lost every friend she had. Was the prospect of marriage to him that horrifying?

Two proposals, and neither was the material of dreams. She'd gone to Charlotte's this morning because she couldn't bear to see her father at the moment. Not only had she intentionally ruined herself, but she foolishly rejected a proposal meant to save her. She'd been going over her decision again and again in her mind, and while Charlotte had convinced her that she'd been right to decline Henry's offer, Meg was uncertain. She hadn't wanted to say yes, but she had done a poor job being responsible thus far. Had she thought more of her responsibilities from the start, she would not have been in this situation and would have received neither proposal.

And so when Gareth had arrived with the same question for her and approval from her father, she couldn't deny him. She couldn't say no to a second attempt to save her name.

Two proposals in one day, and in the end, she had accepted one of them, and while he made no promises of love, Meg knew she'd made the only decision she could under the circumstances. She was trying to pinpoint the specific emotion coursing through her body when Charlotte burst through the door.

"Well, what did he want?" she asked.

"Did you even wait until he had stepped outside?" Meg asked.

"Oh, honestly, Meg, does it really matter? Come on, I'm dying here, please put me out of my misery and tell me what it was that he wanted."

Meg thought on it a moment. How did you tell your best friend that you'd accepted a marriage proposal? Especially under such conditions. Charlotte had received more proposals than any other girl Meg knew, yet she had declined each of them, waiting for the one man who would light her on fire. Meg had accepted the second proposal she'd ever received, and it was nothing more than a duty of honor.

Granted, many marriages were built on such agreements, and they endured and even blossomed. At least she and Gareth had a friendship of sorts; that was more than some women achieved. She'd done the right and responsible thing, yet she felt unsettled.

"I must say," Charlotte said, "he is a most handsome man. I can certainly understand why you fancy him so much. What was so important that he traveled all the way to my home to see you?"

"He came here to ask me to be his wife and I accepted," she said and looked away so she would miss the disappointment in her friend's eyes.

"Are you happy about that decision?" Charlotte asked guardedly.

"I thought after declining Henry's proposal, another would be pushing my poor father's patience. He won't admit it, but I know he was heartbroken about the compromise. I think he believes me that my virtue is still intact, but to think that my reputation could be ruined—it was a lot for him to absorb. In the end, I could have made a worse match."

Saying yes to Gareth's proposal had been the easier choice. She recognized that. It was no great sacrifice to marry a man with whom she had shared passionate embraces. But it was also a more frightening choice. Henry would have been respectable and . . . safe—she would never have worried about pain or loss. He was a kind soul, but Meg knew she never would have loved him. With Gareth she wasn't so certain.

She'd already been treading on dangerous territory by giving in to the passion between them. She'd be a fool not to recognize that her heart was in serious trouble. Now she wasn't so certain she knew how to protect herself.

"That's absolutely true. I only want to make certain you'll be happy."

Meg smiled. "You know me, I'm always happy. I can make do with any situation. That's who I am." That had always been true about her. Even when she'd mourned as a child, she wouldn't allow herself to be too sad for too long. She was always afraid of those darker feelings, always afraid they would pull her under and she wouldn't be able to survive.

"Gareth better endeavor to make you happy, else he'll have me to answer to," Charlotte said.

"I thought you'd be disappointed in me."

"For what?" Charlotte actually looked shocked. "For doing the responsible thing? Meg, the fact that I remain unmarried might seem courageous to some, but so often it feels like such a folly. I believe, in my heart of hearts, that he's out there waiting for me, but what if I'm wrong?" She shook her head. "No, you had the courage to recognize a decent man when you found one and you did the right thing for yourself and for your family. I respect that."

"Thank you. I certainly hope you're right and that this was the right decision, because at the moment, I'm not that positive."

Chapter 18

It had been three days since he'd seen Meg and since she'd agreed to be his wife. Two more days and they'd be husband and wife. She'd been surprisingly absent from the factory. Planning for a wedding took a lot of time, he supposed.

But the time had come. He could wait no longer. He had to tell her today. Gareth pinched the bridge of his nose. Once the announcement hit the papers, the whole of London would know. It was only fair that Meg hear it from him rather than from reading it, or hearing it from a friend.

She was going to be angry, and he couldn't say that he blamed her. She would see this as a lie, a truth he'd withheld from her. But for him, it was part of the fabric of his being. He'd never intended to take that title, never intended anyone would know his true identity.

He'd been in this parlor once before, a few days ago

when he'd spoken to her father. He'd never seen anything beyond this room. It didn't take long for the butler to retrieve her, and she entered the room in a flurry. She wasn't dressed as he'd normally seen her, in her well-tailored dresses. Today she wore a simple gown of soft yellow and her glorious hair hung down around her shoulders. He thought he detected bare toes peeking out from beneath her hem.

"Gareth?" she asked breathlessly. "I wasn't told it was you, only that I had an urgent visitor."

He took in the sight of her. She was refreshing, a breath of air, and despite his reluctance to admit it, being near her seemed to lift the heavy weight from his shoulders. She always had a smile for him. He'd never known anyone like that before. That would all end as soon as she heard his news.

"You look lovely," he said.

Her hand moved to her hair. "Oh, I must look a fright. I've been helping to clean out the north wing."

"No, I meant it. You look lovely." She looked simple and carefree, ironic considering that their situation was anything but.

"Oh, thank you." She reached behind her and twirled two locks from the side of her head and secured them away from her face.

He rubbed his palms on his pants. Did she have to look so damn pretty today? Because all he wanted to do was pull her to him and lose himself in her kisses. He wouldn't have to deny himself of her temptations for much longer. Soon they would be married and he would have her anytime he wanted. Assuming she didn't do something drastic after his confession, like kill him.

"There is something I need to tell you," he said.

"All right." She crossed the room and sat down in one of the wing-back chairs. Somehow she'd folded her legs up underneath her.

"The announcement of our pending nuptials will hit the paper today." He glanced around the room. "You will discover when you read it that I'm not who you think I am."

She frowned. "What is that supposed to mean?"

"Precisely what I said."

"I think you're Gareth Mandeville and you work at my father's factory." She held fabric from her dress in her hands and fidgeted with it. "Is that not correct?"

"No, it is. I am those things. That is my name. But there is more. More I haven't told you. Haven't told anyone. Well, one person knows." He turned from her and walked over to a table. "May I?" he asked, pointing at the decanter of brandy.

"Please."

"Do you want one?" he asked, after he swallowed a glass, and then poured himself another.

"I'll wait. Gareth, you're making me nervous."

"I'm a viscount," he blurted out.

She came to her feet. "You're a what?"

He nodded, then took another sip. "You heard me correctly. I am a viscount."

Her eyes narrowed. "Is this some kind of a jest?"

"No."

"I don't understand." She fell back into the chair. "How can you be a viscount?"

He should probably go to her and comfort her, but that was something he couldn't make himself do. He wasn't the comforting type. It was best she learned that now before she started to expect certain behaviors.

"I don't understand. Why would you lie about this? Why would you lie to me?" she asked.

"I didn't lie, Meg."

"You didn't lie? What would you call this, then?"

"I simply didn't tell you everything about myself. No doubt there are things about yourself that you have not told me." She had every right to be angry with him. He knew that. But it was his secret to keep, and he would not make excuses for his decision.

"Oh yes, let's see. I bite my fingernails, on occasion I don't brush my hair, and . . ." She paused and held her dress up to her ankles. "You caught me; I have a fondness for walking around without shoes. Yes, that's all the same."

"I understand your anger."

"You don't understand anything," she said bitingly.

He didn't. She was right about that. She had compromised them to save his reputation and now she'd have to marry a man she didn't want. A man who had lied to her. A man who would probably lie to her again if it served his purpose. Would she forgive him if he told her he couldn't help it? That he was doomed to be a selfish bastard who only looked out for himself and ways to serve his needs?

"How is it possible that you have a title?"

"My father was a viscount; when he died, I became a viscount."

She rolled her eyes. "I don't need a lesson in birthright, Gareth. I meant, what are you doing working at a factory?" She put her hand to her chest, suspicion flickering across her face. "Are you spying on us?"

"No." It was on his tongue to ask her if she really believed him capable of that—she should know him better. But that would be a slap in the face. She knew him, probably better than a lot of people, because she'd actually taken the time and effort to learn things about him. And they'd spent so much time together. But he'd still kept this from her, and one secret would erase all the other things he'd shared. "Nothing like that. I work because I have to. Because without a paying position, I wouldn't have any funds."

"But aren't gentlemen supposed to invest their funds, not toil and labor themselves?"

He stiffened. "I am not above working with my hands. And you have to actually have funds to invest, or that plan doesn't work." He walked over to her, but didn't reach out to touch her. "I didn't do this to trick you. It wasn't meant to hurt you or anything like that. I kept this a secret for my own reasons, that did not and will not have anything to do with you or this marriage. No one knows about this. I never intended to take this title. It has brought nothing but misery, and I didn't want it to have that sort of power over me. I'm sorry you feel as if I've betrayed you, but this isn't about you. I only wanted you to know the truth before you become my wife."

She said nothing for a moment; she only watched him guardedly. "I have one question."

"Anything."

"Did you set all this up so you could marry me for my money?"

He knew how this looked. He'd be a fool not to. The penniless viscount who happened to land himself a wealthy heiress. He went to her then, unable to ignore her need to be comforted. And his desire to comfort her. He knelt beside her chair and took her hands in his.

"No. I did not. I never even knew that your father had a daughter when I took the position at Piddington's. And the missing boxes, and getting locked in with you, not planned. I am not marrying you for your money, nor do I want your money. I will continue earning my own. Once we are married you'll be a viscountess. The title means little to me, but a great deal to the rest of Society. I wanted to be honest with you before we were married."

She nodded but did not respond further. His comfort was not enough. He was not enough.

He stood. "I'll leave you to your thoughts about this. And I will see you in two days at the church. I do hope that you won't be angry with me forever," he said, then he turned and left.

She wouldn't be angry forever. He knew that. Meg was a naturally happy person. She wasn't a fraud, she simply had a naturally cheerful disposition. Even so, she deserved to be angry right now. Once she digested everything, the anger would clear. It had to. Because he couldn't live with himself if he was the reason Meg Piddington stopped smiling.

Meg was angry, shocked, and confused. A viscount? She wouldn't have been any less surprised had he told her that he was the crown prince.

And her, a viscountess. Her Ladyship.

That was almost laughable. On the surface, this was exactly the kind of match the pushy mothers of heiresses all over England dreamed of making for their daughters. She had been raised in a good home with plenty of privileges, but once her mother had passed on, all her education about catching a husband had ended. She knew nothing about being a wife. And even less about being a viscountess.

Ah, Mama, now would have been a nice time to have a talk. She very much needed some guidance. What did you do with a marriage based on a man's sense of responsibility? And how could she protect herself when she knew that losing her heart to him was only a kiss away? Was the heartbreak of loving someone without his returning that love as great as losing the love of your life?

It wasn't merely his lie that had her upset. He didn't want to marry her, and that hurt. It was clear that she would never be more to him than an obligation.

Evidently all those moments when she thought he trusted her, the moments he shared with her meant nothing to him. She closed her eyes and took a deep breath. Now a part of her would always wonder if he was telling her everything. Or if he was keeping some things to himself. Keeping her out of the corners of his life, only allowing her to touch the places he designated.

Could she live within his boundaries? She'd never been very good at following rules. So if Gareth wanted a true viscountess for a wife, he would be sorely disappointed. And at the moment, Meg didn't care. Let him be disappointed for a change.

Two days later she was married. The evening of the wedding, Meg wandered aimlessly up to the north wing, feeling lost and adrift. Alone.

Ellen came in and assisted her with her gown. She said nothing to the maid as the woman busily hung up the dress and put away her stockings and petticoat.

"That will be all, Ellen, thank you." Meg didn't look at her. She couldn't bear to see the pity that no doubt lined her maid's features. Everyone in the house knew he wasn't here, that he couldn't face his bride on their wedding night.

Meg heard the door close as Ellen left.

Her father had given them the entire north wing of the estate, insisting that the boarding rooms were not fit for a married couple. He was most accommodating to the viscount. Meg knew in her heart that the civility had little to do with Gareth's newly disclosed title and everything to do with the fact that he was now her husband. Her father had never been pretentious, and while he enjoyed his money, he certainly didn't believe it made him any worthier than the men working in his factory. Similarly he didn't feel that a family name or title made a man any grander than anyone else. But it was all the buzz with the household staff that she had married a real gentleman.

So she still lived in the same house, only it didn't quite feel much like the same house since she was in a different room, on a different floor, in a very different role. Her father claimed it was no different than how things would be handled if he were to leave his estate to a son.

But here it was going on midnight and she had not seen her new husband since they'd exchanged vows. Supposedly Gareth was at his boarding room retrieving his belongings, but Meg had been in that room and there was no conceivable way it would take this long to gather everything. Her father had offered for him to move in immediately upon announcement of their engagement, but Gareth had declined, and had remained in his rooms until today. He didn't seem interested in claiming special treatment now that he was related to the factory owner.

So here Meg sat, a wife, and her husband was not even home. On her wedding night. Not precisely how she'd imagined things would be. Thoughts of desertion flitted through her mind. He would have protected her with his name, but would he still maintain his freedom? She tried to believe that was a possibility because she didn't know him the way she thought she had. But she knew, deep in her bones, that he would never do such a thing.

He would never love her, but she knew he would never leave her.

But that didn't explain where he was. And the longer he was absent, the steadier her anger became. Perhaps he didn't want to be married—well, this wasn't a perfect situation for either of them. But he owed her the common courtesy of being here on their wedding night. At least so that things would appear as though it was a legitimate union.

He was, no doubt, walking around trying to reconcile the reality today brought. They were married. Man and wife. Forever.

Despite her own reluctance to marry and her firm belief that she never would, she had, as any other young girl, allowed herself the freedom to dream of this day. She and Charlotte had spent entire evenings spinning wildly romantic tales of the proposal and the wedding and the wedding night. But none of her wild imaginings ever included an absent husband.

Would he consummate their marriage? Or was this to be nothing more than a business agreement? Meg looked over to the bed at the filmy piece of clothing lying atop it. She and Charlotte had gone shopping as soon as the wedding plans were in place and she'd purchased a few necessities. Namely prettier undergarments. Their thinking was that there was no sense in having a husband to undress you if he could not appreciate the entire experience. Now she thought better of it, and it seemed of more importance that she herself be able to indulge in the silkier bits of material.

There was no reason she should not enjoy her purchases simply because her husband had fled. She removed her plain chemise. Standing at the foot of the bed in nothing but her skin, she reached over and fingered the beautiful silk fabric. It felt as smooth and slippery as water in her hands. She closed her eyes and pulled the shift over her head and shivered as it slid down her flesh.

The silk felt unlike anything she'd ever felt, softer than any silk stockings she'd ever owned. She was no novice when it came to fine materials and fabrics. Her father had always seen to her comfort, but this—she ran her hand across her abdomen—was pure pleasure. A glance in the mirror confirmed her initial thought that it would be as good as being unclothed. It was completely transparent, shading her body no more than if she stood naked in the rain.

She deserved to wear it. With or without her husband and a silly fantasy wedding night. If Gareth ever did return, he would go to his own room. There would be no passionate kisses, no long embraces or words of love. With all her good intentions, she'd landed herself in a charade of a marriage with a charade of a husband.

Meg sat at the dressing table and began undoing her

hair. It took her several minutes, but she managed to finish taking the pins out, then let the mass fall over her shoulders. The release sent tingles across her scalp and brought some relief to the nagging headache she'd had since that morning. She combed her fingers through her hair to untangle the stubborn curls. Then she walked over to the bed. Perhaps a good night's sleep would make her feel better.

There was part of her that felt as if she should be sad. Sad at the turn her life had taken, but no tears came. Instead she felt only the steady hum of anger as it pulsed through her veins. Everything seemed unreal, as if she'd gone to sleep in her own life last night and awoken in someone else's. But the reality was, this was her life.

The door opened and Gareth walked in. His mouth opened in surprise, but he quickly recovered. "You're still awake," he said.

Meg spun around to see him standing in the door. "I am," was all she could say. Now it seemed utterly foolish that she'd put on the silk chemise. Humiliating that he'd believe she'd been sitting here pining away, wanting him to come in and take her into his arms. Wanting him to hold her and kiss her and touch her.

He set two bags down, then closed the door behind him. His eyes caressed her body as he took in the full sight of her. She refused to look away. Let him look. Let him see what he did not want.

"I didn't put this on for you," she said with defiance. "I know that's what you're thinking, but it's not true."

His lip quirked the tiniest amount. "If not for me, who would you put that on for? It is a garment for a lover." He closed the distance between them. She could smell the hint of rain on his skin. "Do you have a lover, Meg?"

It wasn't a legitimate question; they both knew that. "You know that I don't," she said, raising her chin a notch. "You were gone a long time."

"I went for a walk."

She hesitated a moment, but then said, "You didn't have to offer to marry me, Gareth, I would have survived the scandal."

"I have no doubt you would have survived. But I would not have been able to live with myself knowing that your act had ruined your reputation and prevented you from having marriage or children."

"Thank you for making such a sacrifice." For once she let the full force of her sarcasm drip into her voice.

His hand slid down her waist to rest on her hip. Her body reacted to his touch, despite her anger. "What is this?" he asked.

"What is what?"

"This." He fingered a piece of the silky fabric.

She felt her chest flame and it spread all the way up her neck and settled into her cheeks. "It is a night-dress."

"And you put it on. But not for me?"

"I purchased it for tonight, yes. But when you left, I didn't see any reason it should go to waste. I didn't know . . ."

"Didn't know what? If I was coming back? Meg, I would never desert you. This might not be a love match"—he met her gaze as he spoke, the heat in his eyes nearly palpable—"but I am your husband, and I will be your husband in every way."

His words washed over her. Her husband in every way. He did intend to consummate this marriage. Her heart jumped within her chest. But before she could protest or give it a second thought, he'd pulled her to him and kissed her.

Her husband in every way.

Her heart beat a rapid tempo in her chest and every nerve seemed to awaken as desire mingled with her anger. His lips tempted and taunted, and she realized she couldn't deny him even if she wanted to. But the truth was, she didn't want to. She wanted him to kiss her, to touch her, to make her his. She wanted to be his wife in every way.

"Do you have any idea what you look like in this?" Again his hand ran against the silk, leaving a trail of gooseflesh in its wake.

He didn't give her time to form an answer. His lips found her collarbone and she nearly forgot her name, let alone what she was wearing.

"It whispers across your flesh, teasing to hide it from view, but it doesn't. It simply enhances your beautiful body. I don't know where to touch you first," he said.

Meg had never felt particularly beautiful. It wasn't that she thought she was plain or unattractive; she'd simply never given it much thought. And no man had ever told her she was beautiful. But here she was, nearly naked with the man who was now her husband, and he thought she was beautiful. Beautiful. She felt herself smile.

"Touch me anywhere you wish," she heard herself say.

He again kissed her collarbone, then let his lips

move to her shoulder, then the skin right above her breast. Her breath quickened. He knelt in front of her. His hot breath warmed her flesh as he leaned closer to her. Through the fabric, she felt the moisture of his mouth as he took the tip of her breast into his mouth.

She cried out and buried her fingers in his hair. He continued his torture as he laved her breasts with kisses. He'd once before kissed her in such a way, but through this silk it felt more intense and sensual. A hungering rhythm ached between her legs, and she squirmed to try to alleviate it. But she knew only he could ease the ache.

His hands ran down her belly while his tongue teased her right nipple. Again and again he suckled and licked and kissed until she thought she would break into a million pieces. Her legs were weak and she was ready to simply lie down on the floor and let him take her right here.

"I know what you want, love," he said.

He picked her up and carried her to the bed. Before he put her down, though, he kissed her so fiercely that it almost brought tears to her eyes. She writhed on the bed, waiting for him to join her and knowing there was more, knowing he could bring her pleasure and make her cry out his name.

"Please, Gareth," she whispered.

"I know, love, soon, I promise." He finished removing his clothes, but instead of crawling in next to her, he went to the foot of the bed. He picked up her left foot and kissed her ankle, then licked his way up to her knee.

Oh, what this man did to her. Licking and nibbling

the back of her knee. She smiled at the mild tickling. Settling himself between her legs, he continued to lick her left leg, her inner thigh, to be exact.

He pushed the silk material up to her waist, then placed his hands beneath her bottom. Having his warm hands cup her bottom was so intimate, so sensual. He kneaded her flesh until she relaxed and closed her eyes. And then she felt the warmth and moisture of his mouth as he kissed the curls between her legs.

"Red hair everywhere." He made a guttural sound that tingled her ears. "I love that."

He'd done this once before. In her father's office. "Naughty kisses," she whispered.

"What?" he asked.

"Naughty kisses." Good heavens, she might not survive the night. "In my father's office." She sounded breathless. "You told me you wanted to do naughty things to me and then you kissed me there."

"Naughty kisses," he repeated. "I like that."

She liked it too. At first he simply placed sweet kisses at the triangle of hair. Harmless kisses meant to tease, but nothing more. And then he got bolder and she knew blush stained every inch of her body. His mouth opened and his tongue tortured the hidden nub and she tried to keep from screaming, but it became impossible to keep quiet.

It was also impossible to keep still, to keep her legs on the bed, and to keep her hands out of his hair. She bucked against him, using the leverage of her heel on his shoulder to lift her to his mouth. Her mouth was dry, her throat scratchy from crying out, and yet she did not care. Small waves of pleasure crashed over her and built and built until it was as if the center of her shattered.

She rocked and cried his name and clung to his shoulders until it ended.

He placed one more kiss right below her belly button before moving his body to align with hers. She could feel his hardness against her belly. And she knew she should probably be embarrassed, too shy to look him in the eyes, but no shame came. She boldly met his gaze, then let a smile slide onto her face.

His wife in every way.

"So you like naughty kisses, do you?" he asked.

She found she couldn't yet speak, but she gave him a full smile and nodded enthusiastically.

"I suspected as much. Saucy wench."

She laughed heartily at that. The laughter faded when he moved up and she felt the tip of him at her entrance. Instinctively she opened for him, pushing herself up to accept his full length. It pinched and was tight and unfamiliar, but natural at the same time, as if her body needed him to fill her.

Nuzzling her neck, he began to move. She wrapped her legs around his body and clasped her feet together.

"You're so tight. And you feel so good. So slick."

The rhythm of his movement began those tiny waves of pleasure again. She tried to meet him with every movement, but faltered a few times. He didn't seem to notice. Quicker, harder, faster he moved until he shook and spilled inside her.

He collapsed against her, kissing her throat gently.

"Now you are my wife."

Chapter 19

Meg closed the door silently behind her, then smiled at Gareth, who lounged on the bed. Still unclothed. Good heavens, but her new husband was strikingly handsome.

"What did you find us?" he asked. "I'm starved."

"Cheese, bread, and some figs." She curled up in the bed and crossed her legs.

He sat up with her and the sheet fell to his waist. His chest was sinewy and had a smattering of dark hair that tapered into a line and eventually disappeared beneath the sheet. Against the glow of the firelight, everything took on a new sheen.

It seemed her anger had disappeared beneath the seduction of his touch. She should be ashamed that she was so easily persuaded and overcome.

She handed him a slice of bread and a piece of cheese. Her stomach rumbled. It was amazing how marital activity could evoke such hunger. She chewed thoughtfully and eyed her new husband. He looked satisfied and sleepy. His hair was askew, and the normal stubble on his cheeks and chin had darkened and thickened. She reached over and ran her fingers across his right cheek.

He released a half chuckle. "No matter how often I shave, it grows back so quickly. Probably that's why my grandfather always wore a full beard. Too much trouble."

She had to admit, what looked unkempt on some looked undeniably inviting on him. "It looks good on you," she said.

He nodded but didn't meet her gaze, as if to hide his discomfort at her compliment. He grabbed a fig from the plate.

"Tell me more about your family," she said. "What was your father like?" She waited for his hesitancy, fully expecting that he would make some excuse and not answer.

But he did answer, the words rushing out of him as if they had been bottled up for years. "He was exciting. Full of dreams and adventure. We never had money, but we did have a home. A grand estate, or at least one you could imagine had been grand at some time in its past. It was in some disrepair by the time we left. I believe the Brockmore family owns it now."

Oh, it was a grand place. She wasn't certain when, but she knew it had been restored to its grandeur under the care of the Brockmore family. She'd been there only once, but it was truly lovely. And Gareth had been born there.

"He was always looking for a way to reestablish

the family fortune. He made several investments that ultimately failed. But more often than not, he tried to win either in the boxing ring or at the gaming tables. As fate would have it, one night he lost everything in a game of cards. The rest of the money, my sisters' dowries, my mother's jewelry, and our home. All of it, with one hand of cards." His voice was lined with bitterness. He shrugged and leaned against the pillows behind him. "Everything fell apart then."

She lay down beside him and rested her head on his arm. With her hand, she lightly traced her nails up and down his chest.

"My mother was furious with him. They had four children with a fifth on the way and now they had no way to care for them. The family had long since let go of all the household servants; I have no memory of ever having them. So there were no other places to retrench and we had nowhere to go."

Meg listened and continued to rub his chest. It took a lot for him to confide in her, and she didn't take it lightly. Nor did she want to break the spell of whatever spurred his disclosure.

"My father started drinking," he continued. He released a humorless laugh. "Apparently we still had enough brandy in the house for him to do that, and my mother packed us all up and took us to Ireland to live with her parents. Two months later, she gave birth to my brother. One month after that, we received notice that my father had died, in a boxing ring. Evidently he'd been trying to win back some money, but had been so drunk he'd never even landed one punch."

She rolled over and placed her chin on his chest so

she could see his eyes. "That must have been a terrible time for you. You remember it all?" she asked.

"Most of it. I was twelve, so certainly old enough to know what was going on around me. But my mother did her best to prevent us from knowing the truth of the situation. I couldn't understand why we left him. Especially after he died. I was so angry with my mother. I know now that she did what she felt she had to for us children. But she deserted my father, and ultimately that killed him." He shook his head. "They were both selfish."

He took a deep breath. "That's why I came here. To see what it was about this place that made it so difficult for him to take care of us. What had been so enthralling about London, so important, that he could gamble so frivolously with our future?"

They were questions she couldn't answer. No one could. But now it all made sense. Why he'd left Ireland and moved to London. He'd come to prove to himself that he could survive this town in a way his father hadn't been able to do. She had no words she could offer to comfort him. She knew what it was to lose a parent, but their losses had been so different. Even so, the loss had changed both of them, had led them on the paths they were on today. So in that small way, they were kindred souls.

Unable to comfort him with words, she offered the only other way she knew to console him. She kissed his chest, then got braver and kissed his collarbone, nipping and sucking gently, then she moved up to his neck, then his ear. His eyes were closed and he moaned softly. Beneath the sheets, her hand found evidence of his arousal. No matter what the past had brought, right here, right now, her husband wanted her. And, dare she hope, needed her as well.

She sat up and pulled her nightdress over her head and tossed it on the floor. Then she covered his body with her own and met his mouth for a fiery kiss. She could feel his arousal pressing against her stomach and she moved her body slightly to rub against it.

"Such a temptress," he said. "I've had the most difficult time resisting you since we met." He eyed her as if there was more he wanted to say, but nothing else came.

She smiled and gave him another kiss. "You need not deny yourself any longer. I am yours," she said.

"Stay here," he said, when she started to roll off him. "This position works as well. You need only sit up a bit more."

She did as he instructed and found that he was quite right. Straddling him put her in the right position to take in the full length of him. Tentatively at first and then more boldly, she moved on him. His hands cupped her breasts, and she realized if she leaned forward, he could take a nipple in his mouth. Feeling like the temptress he'd called her, she did so. He suckled hard while she slid up and down on him, and then her pleasure came in wild waves, catching her off guard. She tossed her head back and yelled his name as the sensations washed over her. His release wasn't too far behind hers, and when she leaned down on him, she felt his heart beating quickly beneath his chest.

Gareth could hear her even breaths and knew she finally slept. It was still dark, but the first hints of light were beginning to creep onto the horizon. He could make out the sleeping form of his bride curled next to him on the bed. It still seemed unreal that he was married now. What would his mother say? More than likely she wouldn't even believe him.

He slid out of bed and walked over to the window to watch the sun complete its journey. He had told Meg things about his family that no else had ever known. Things he never thought he'd disclose. He'd fully expected to feel panicked as he revealed these things to her, but he didn't. It seemed natural to share such things with her.

She was easy to talk to. Easy to trust. Which was good considering that despite all his protests and good intentions, he was beginning to care about her more and more. It didn't make sense. She drove him mad with her reckless behavior, and more often than not, he found he could not concentrate when she was near.

Gareth silently repeated the wedding vows they'd taken the day before. He'd meant them. No, he didn't love Meg, but he wouldn't be surprised if he did at some point. But commitment wasn't about love. It was bigger than love. Love was fleeting, selfish, and capricious. Commitment, though, was steadfast and strong. He needed only to hold on to the right one, commitment, to have a lasting marriage.

Meg stepped into her father's study to bid him good morning. Since she'd slept so late this morning, she'd missed breakfast. But her father was not in his study; instead someone else greeted her.

"Miss Piddington, how lovely to see you." Henry stood when she entered the room.

"It's actually Mrs. Mandeville now," she said with a smile. Or Her Ladyship, but she neglected to mention that one. "I was looking for my father."

"He's not yet downstairs," he said, his voice unusually tight. "I expect him any moment." He fingered the buttons on his jacket. "We have a meeting."

She nodded. "Very well. Enjoy your day, Mr. Sanders." She turned to go.

"Meg, wait."

She paused. He'd never before called her by her given name.

He took several steps toward her. "I was so sorry to hear that you had to marry that Mandeville man." He reached and clasped both of her hands. "My offer still stands."

"I beg your pardon?" she asked.

"My offer of marriage."

Was he mad? She laughed and tried to pull her hands free, but he tightened his grasp. "It's too late; we married yesterday."

He nodded. "But you could always get an annulment. I would be here for you. Would marry you and save your reputation. I do hate to watch you throw your life away with such a wastrel. I can save you, if you would only allow me to do so."

She pulled her hands away from his, then took several steps away. "Mr. Sanders, I'm afraid you have overstepped yourself."

He actually looked affronted. "I do apologize, madam, I only worry for your happiness."

"You need not concern yourself with my happiness. And may I be so bold to say that I am not in a position to have my marriage annulled, as it were." She met his gaze and hoped he understood that she fully belonged to Gareth now. "We will not speak of this again."

And with that she left the room. She could have reminded him about Gareth's title and that he outranked both of them, but that was not the reason she'd married him, and she didn't want anyone assuming that.

Chapter 20

Meg had not gone into the factory today. She wasn't quite certain why, but she hadn't been ready to put in an appearance. Gareth, on the other hand, had gone to work. Even though her father had told him it wasn't necessary, that they would rearrange his position to one more fitting for a viscount and son-in-law. Gareth could have his selection of the opening staff positions. Her father had even gone so far as to offer him Mr. Sanders's position. Not to replace him, per se, but to be an additional factory director.

But Gareth would hear none of it. According to him, there was nothing about his work that was unfit for a man in any station in life, and until those positions were available and it was evident that he was qualified, he would continue working the grinding machine.

Surely Gareth wouldn't expect her to change every-thing about her life. He'd said she could continue working, but had he meant it? She needed to speak with him and make certain he understood what she wanted.

If he wasn't too good to have a position, then he shouldn't believe anything different of her. She could continue to work at the factory, and together they could build it into the most profitable confectionery in all of England. And her father could retire a wealthy and happy man, knowing that his beloved factory would be well cared for.

She straightened the pillows on the bed one last time. Her first full day as a wife, and she had no idea how to fill her new role. What was expected of her? Was she to join Society and have tea with duchesses and the wives of earls?

How scandalous would those other wives think her if they knew she'd spent most of the day remembering all the delicious things he'd done to her body? They'd tried two positions and both had worked rather nicely. Were there more? Additional pleasures that were still to come? Could they, for instance, make love outside a bed? She looked around the room. On the floor, perhaps, in front of the fireplace?

No sooner had she eyed the plush rug than Gareth stepped into the bedroom. She felt the blush heat her cheeks. Would he know where her thoughts had been? She sat in one of the chairs facing the hearth.

"Hello," he said.

She nodded. Things were awkward; she couldn't pretend they weren't. They'd made love last night, but it hadn't really changed anything, at least not in the big sense. They weren't strangers, but the lovemaking had not created an enduring stretch of intimacy. They were still here, married not by choice, but by necessity.

She was tempted to rise from her chair and throw herself into his arms. To kiss him again as she had last night, boldly and passionately, despite the awkwardness hanging in the air. But she refrained.

"How were things today?" she asked.

His lips tweaked in a half smile. "Word spreads fast. It was different. Munden ignored me, but everyone else was a lot friendlier. They called me 'Your Royal Highness.'" He shrugged out of his jacket and hung it on the back of the chair.

He didn't seem annoyed, mostly amused by the new nickname. He sat in the other chair in front of the fireplace, facing her. The fire still lingered from the morning, casting only a soft red glow onto the floor.

"Perhaps they think you'll be taking over now that you're in the family," she said.

"No, marrying you should have no bearing on my position," he said.

"That's simply not true. You're correct that you can keep your current position, but doing so will affect the way you're treated. And there's simply no reason to keep that position."

"So you agree with your father that I should take a management role at the factory?"

"I do. It is not as if you haven't earned it, or that you wouldn't have. You're a hard worker, Gareth, and you deserve the recognition. Had Munden not accused you of the theft, you no doubt would have impressed everyone there with your intelligence and work. My father would have given you one of those staff positions. Now you need only tell him which one you want."

"I don't want to take something I don't deserve," he said.

He was living under the assumption that he was like his father, which simply wasn't the case. She knew he'd never gamble away their money or risk his life in a boxing ring. But Gareth couldn't see that. "You're not like him, you know," she said softly.

His eyebrows slanted down. "Like who?"

"Your father. I know you worry about that. But you're not like him."

He crossed his arms over his chest and gave her a sardonic smile. "I'll consider taking one of those positions." He said nothing about her comments. "What about you?" He made no secret of his desire to change the subject. "When are you going to speak to your father about your wish to work at the factory?" he asked.

He wasn't pestering or teasing; he was asking a legitimate question. Which could only mean that Gareth believed in her, and did so without reservation. He accepted the possibility that she could manage the factory and did not question her unconventional desire. Inexplicably, tears sprang to her eyes. She quickly turned away and looked into the quieting fire. "I will do that. I will speak to him soon, I promise.

"I think it's time we tell my father about Munden's extra activity," she said. She wanted to change the subject before she broke down and cried like a complete ninny. "I don't see much chance of the real thief contacting him now that we've proved you didn't take those boxes. Therefore there's no reason not to show the ledger sheets to my father."

"I suppose you're right. Remind me and I'll get them

for you later. Right now I want to talk about why we've been in the same room for several minutes and I have yet to kiss you. As I've thought of little else today."

Her pulse thumped faster. She had thought of little else today as well. Just fantasized about his hands on her body and the things she wanted to try with his. She hadn't yet had the opportunity to explore his body. Had only touched his chest and arms and back. She wanted to run her fingers up his long legs. She wanted to follow that trail of hair down his belly. Gareth moved from the chair to the floor and beckoned her with his hand. "Come here, wife," he said.

She went to him and knelt beside him.

Then he reached behind him and snatched a tiny box out of his jacket pocket. He opened the box and took out a piece of chocolate. "I nearly forgot. Here." He held it out to her.

She leaned forward and opened her mouth.

He chuckled. "So now I must feed you?"

She met his glance and nodded.

"I will have you know that this is from the first batch of the chocolate they're mixing with the condensed milk. It's supposed to be creamier. We all got a taste today. None of them are molded yet; they're just pouring it out in sheets and then breaking it apart."

"This is your piece, then?" she asked.

"Yes."

She sat back. "Then you should eat it."

"I thought you might like to taste it."

"I would. Together?" she offered.

He broke a piece off, then reached forward. She opened her mouth, and he placed the piece on her tongue. She closed her eyes and enjoyed the dark flavor.

It was creamier than the regular chocolate. When she opened her eyes, she found her husband's rich hazel eyes on her.

He bit into his piece, and she watched his lips close around the sweet morsel. It was a sensual experience and she found she was ready to touch her lips to his and see if the chocolate lingered.

She swallowed. "I think this is going to be a big seller."

"I think you're right."

Gareth kissed her mouth then. His lips met hers in a hungry dance. She could, in fact, taste the chocolate on his tongue, and it fueled her desire. He cradled her face with gentleness as his mouth teased and tantalized her. Pulling her hand to the front of his trousers, he pressed her against him.

"Do you feel how much I want you? I thought of you all day at the factory. What it was like to touch you and have you touch me. What it felt like to be inside you."

He gave her no time to answer before he kissed her again. He couldn't wait. He'd wanted her too long, and now he could have her. Completely. Anytime he liked.

Kissing her was the same as tasting a delightful treat for the first time. Addictive and tempting. He could never get his fill of his mouth on hers. His hand found her breast by merely slipping beneath the low-cut fabric of her dress. One move of the muslin and he was touching her. His skin on hers, so soft, so sweet, just as it had been last night. And she'd been so willing and passionate. Never before had he experienced a woman with such passion.

Tentatively she moved her hand against his hardness. He sucked in his breath and clenched his eyes closed. She was inexperienced and naïve, but bold. It was a heady mixture. Enough to send him over the edge, else he controlled himself. Bolder still, she slipped her hand inside his trousers and beneath his drawers.

"You're so warm," she said.

He moaned when her hand made contact, and he pushed himself against her. He could wait no longer. No man could have that much control. He quickly removed his clothes, then slowly pulled off her dress and her underclothes until she stood before him gloriously naked.

"You are so beautiful. Your legs. Your breasts." He moved his hands up the insides of her thighs and spread her legs. The dampness that met his fingers shook his constraint. It was time.

He turned to walk to the bed, but she grabbed his arm.

"Why not right here?" She motioned to the floor. "The rug is well padded."

He nodded and gently placed her on the plush blue carpet, then situated himself on top of her. He pressed against the apex of her thighs, begging for entrance.

"Please," she said.

It was all the encouragement he needed. He entered her with gentle force and she shuddered against him. She was so hot, so wet. He squeezed his eyes shut, trying to rein himself in, all the while wanting to let go and ride the sensations. Her legs wrapped around his back and she bucked up to meet him.

Sweet, delicious torture. It might be enough to kill a man, but it was worth the risk.

He leaned down and suckled her right nipple and felt the muscles inside her contract as she found her release. His name was still ringing in his ears when his own climax came. Intense, deep, powerful, it shot through him and he growled in response.

"That is a nice welcome home," he said.

She nuzzled closer to him, but said nothing. He stared at the fire for what seemed like an hour, neither of them speaking. It was nice. He and his wife. He might not have all of Meg, but he had her body. Her hand traced up his abdomen, and he shivered in response.

"I almost forgot to tell you," she said. "This morning I ran into Henry in my father's study. He seemed most urgent and offered to save me from our marriage."

Sniveling bastard. "Did he now? And how did he think to do that?"

"An annulment."

"So he has not yet given up on marrying you."

"I've never encouraged his attentions," she said.

"Has he let his attraction be known before?"

She shrugged. "He has made it known in the past that he fancied me. Until recently, though, I didn't give it much thought. I actually didn't even think it was more than him being friendly to his employer's daughter. Apparently I misread him."

"Apparently." He ran his hand down her back and cupped her bottom. "Did you tell him that our marriage can no longer be annulled? Once I claimed your body, you cannot belong to another man."

"Not in so many words, but I insinuated that our window to file for an annulment had passed."

Perhaps next time he saw Henry Sanders, Gareth would tell the man himself. Meg was his, in every way possible. He leaned over and kissed her passionately. He needed to take her again.

"Mr. Munden." Henry cleared his throat. "I would like to see you in Mr. Piddington's office at the close of today's work." He nodded to the factory workers surrounding Munden.

Henry made his way up the stairs to the office, well aware that the men he'd left in his wake were discussing him. They thought him a dandy; he knew that. But it mattered not. In the end he would win, and they would see the truth.

Apparently Munden waited not only until he'd completed his shift, but also until the factory had emptied before he knocked on the office door. Sanders knew Munden was attempting to annoy him by making him wait. But Sanders appreciated the opportunity for privacy, as the discussion was to be a sensitive and important one.

"Sit down, Mr. Munden." Henry liked how it felt to sit behind this desk, powerful and in charge. "I'm afraid I have bad news for you. It seems I have discovered your extra source of funding, and I must inform Mr. Piddington of your theft."

Munden visibly swallowed, but said nothing.

"It was quite clever, I'll grant you that. To remove the pages from the ledger. It took me a few months to piece together the information, but I found it nonetheless. You've pilfered a handsome sum. Tell me, what is it you planned to do with the money?"

Munden sat on the edge of his seat. "I bought a racing horse. He's racing this Saturday."

Henry was enjoying this. It wasn't as perfect as his original plan, but it would afford him a hefty income. "A racing horse? Interesting. Well, my knowing this bit of information will obviously unsettle your plans, but rest assured I have a plan of my own that can work to your benefit. You will continue as you've been doing. Fixing the book, taking the money, only now you'll be taking that money for me." He clapped his hands together. "A perfect plan, don't you agree, Mr. Munden?"

"I don't agree." Munden came to his feet. "I have a different plan, actually. I was telling the boys downstairs. I'm moving on from Piddington's."

No, that was not how this was supposed to happen. Henry clenched his hands. Ignorant bastard. "This is not a negotiation, Munden. You will do as told and take the money for me. Or I will ensure that your little embezzlement will not go unnoticed by the authorities. Prison. Do you think you can survive that?" He didn't wait for the man to answer. "I will make sure you are adequately compensated for your trouble. But make no mistake, you will work for me."

Munden's lip raised in a snarl. "I don't work for you. By the time you tell the authorities, I'll be long gone. You made the decision to leave here a lot easier for me."

His fingers began to twitch. Everything was unraveling. All his careful planning. His precise plans for how to make the factory his. They were dissolving right before his eyes.

"No!" he said as he came to his feet. He reached

inside his coat and pulled out the revolver hidden within. "You will not walk away from this."

Munden eyed the gun, then his head tilted back and he roared with laughter. "Is that supposed to frighten me? You? There ain't nothing frightening about you. Look at you, with your fancy suit and your clean cravat. I could snap you with my hands."

The man didn't even flinch. Made no move to either leave or protect himself. Henry felt the boiling in his head, the pounding in his ears. The rage surfaced and engulfed him as if he'd stepped into a cloud. "Not frightening," he repeated. "Not frightening?" he said again. "Not frightening!" And then he squeezed the trigger.

Munden's expression changed to one of surprise. He clasped his chest, then looked at his hand covered in blood. He opened his mouth to speak, but no words came out. His face contorted in pain and he crumpled to the floor.

"Not frightening." Henry walked to stand over Munden's sputtering body. "No, I don't suppose I am frightening. But I've always been an exceptional marksman." He waited a bit longer until Munden had taken his last breath, then he stepped over him and left the office.

It had become clear that his clever plan had ultimately failed. Meg had married that bastard and she had no intention of leaving him. And now Gareth would get the factory and all the lucrative funds from it. The thought made Henry ill. All his hard work building this factory, and he'd see none of the rewards.

Foolish Piddington. He could have set this right. He could have forced Meg to marry Henry when he'd first proposed. Henry took one last look at the factory, and it became clear what he had to do now. He couldn't allow Gareth to destroy all the work he'd put into this building. He'd made Piddington Confectionery known throughout London. He wouldn't allow a simple factory worker to come in and ruin that.

Chapter 21

The following morning, Meg and Gareth entered the factory together and the entire room stilled. It was time that everyone became accustomed to their marriage, just as they had begun to be accustomed to her presence at the factory. She was fully aware that all eyes were on her as she walked past them and into the downstairs office where Munden spent most of his days. The room was empty. Perhaps he was somewhere on the floor.

She would find him later. For now, she would go and clean up in her father's office to prepare for his return the following week. She climbed the stairs, then opened the door.

She screamed before she'd fully registered what she was seeing. And in mere seconds Gareth was at her side. Munden's body lay in a dried pool of blood on the office floor.

Gareth stepped closer to the lifeless body.

"Gunshot," he said quietly.

Meg just kept her eyes affixed. She could not look away. Not from the blood, not from the knocked-down chair, not from Munden's open but dead eyes. She felt her knees wobble, and again Gareth was at her side.

"We need to get you out of here."

"Amelia," she said.

"Who?"

She pulled her eyes away long enough to stare into Gareth's face. "Amelia, my friend. Her husband is an inspector. He'll know what to do. We need to send for them."

Gareth nodded. "Do you have their address?"

"Yes."

He retrieved a piece of paper and dipped the pen, then handed them to her. "Write your instructions here and we'll send someone for them." Footsteps sounded on the staircase. "In the meantime, I don't want anyone else up here." He stuck his head out the door while she busily wrote down Amelia's address and instructions for Amelia and Colin.

When Gareth turned back around, she handed him the note. "I can't stay in here," she said.

"I understand. Why don't you wait downstairs in the storeroom."

She held on to the railing and looked straight ahead. The factory was buzzing with talk, no doubt people wondering what all the fuss was about. And they had a right to know. But she was not the one to tell them.

They should be sent home today; the factory closed. She needed to speak with her father about how to proceed, but of that much she was certain. After she gathered herself, she would dismiss them all.

She numbly stepped into the storeroom, then sat on a bench. How was she supposed to feel about this? Sorting through the emotions was confusing. Who would have done such a thing? Surely this wasn't a robbery, as funds were never kept in her father's office. Everyone here knew that. What had Munden been doing up there anyway? She didn't think he even had a key to that room.

Meg stood and paced the length of the storeroom. She'd been in here before—on that night with Gareth. The night someone had locked them in together, and it had started a chain of events that had ultimately led to their marriage.

They had been locked in. On purpose. And someone had known about that. She stood and ran to the door and out onto the factory floor.

"Gareth?" she yelled.

It didn't take him long to run down the stairs and meet her.

"What's the matter?"

"I know."

He shook his head in confusion. "You know what?"

"I know who did this. I know who locked us in the storeroom. And I know who shot Munden."

He closed the door and shut out the prying ears of the workers.

"What are you talking about?"

"That night we were locked in here. It wasn't an accident. Someone locked us in here on purpose."

"Why?"

"I'm not certain."

"Then how do you know?"

She shook her head. "It didn't make sense before and I didn't even really notice. But sitting here today, I remembered. The day I came here and gave the alibi. Henry was here with Munden. I was explaining the scenario, and Henry asked me why someone would lock us in here. I didn't even recognize what he was asking; I thought it was mostly asking why it mattered that we were locked in together." She shook her head. "Don't you see? It was him all along. He's the one that shot Munden."

Gareth rubbed his temples. "Sanders asked you who locked us in, and this means he killed Munden?"

She released a short breath. "I know it doesn't make a lot of sense, but think about it. Why would he ask that question? Why would he assume that someone locked us in rather than it just being an accident with the door?"

"Unless he locked us in himself? Is that what you're saying?"

"Perhaps. I don't know if it was him who locked us in, but he knew. He's behind all of this, I know it," she said.

"But why?" Gareth asked.

"That, I haven't figured out. But the rest I'm positive about."

"Then if he did all of those things, more than likely he took the chocolate boxes," he said.

"Right. And he's the one that sent that note to Munden."

"That doesn't prove he's a murderer, Meg."

"No, but it makes sense. He was the one that was behind the theft, meaning he's the one with the most to lose. Maybe I'm wrong, but I just don't think so. His name just keeps popping up."

Gareth pulled her into his arms. "You are a rather good sleuth, you know. I am sorry you had to see all of that."

She melted against his chest. "It's all right. I don't think it did any permanent damage. Did you send for Amelia?"

"Yes, Jamie has gone to get them."

"Thank you."

It took a little over an hour for Colin and Amelia to finally arrive. By that time, Meg's nerves had settled to a calmer level, and she had already released all the employees for the rest of the day. Gareth quickly filled Colin in on all the details after brief introductions.

"How are you?" Amelia urged as the men talked.

Meg gave her a smile. "I believe I shall survive the day."

"I want to go into the office and examine the evidence," Colin said.

They all turned toward the stairs, but then Gareth stopped. "I think it would be best if you stayed down here," he said to Meg.

Colin cleared his throat. "Better to allow them now rather than fight them. They'll come up regardless."

"He speaks from experience," Amelia added.

Gareth nodded, and they continued their way to the office.

"Did either of you move or touch anything?" Colin asked. He leaned over the body.

"No," Meg said.

"He's been in here all night." Colin picked up

something with his tweezers. "Maggots have already settled in."

She tightened her shoulders to stand up straighter. There was no reason for Gareth to believe she couldn't muster the strength to handle the situation. The two of them stood out of the way while Colin and Amelia went around the room. He inspected everything and she took notes for him.

Aside from the dastardly nature of the situation, watching her friend with her husband pleased Meg. Amelia was happy. Meg knew her and Gareth's marriage would not ever be like the wedded bliss of her friend. Amelia and Colin loved each other. There would be no such love for the Viscount and Viscountess Mandeville.

"Amelia, look at this," Colin said.

Amelia leaned over him. "That is an excellent specimen, but now is not the time, love." Amelia looked up at Meg. "Fingerprints on the desk," she said with a smile.

"Well, it would be a perfect clue if Scotland Yard would but listen to my proposal," Colin said. Then he stood to his full height and took one last look at the room. "I think that's all the collecting we can do. I'll take this shell casing to James and see if they have a match on record. It's a new system, so it's unlikely."

"We know Henry did this," Meg said. "We only need to find him."

Colin nodded. "Do you have an address?"

Meg wrote it down and handed Amelia the paper.

"I'll come around tonight and let you know what I uncover. But chances are he's already left town," Colin said. "I'll need to notify Scotland Yard about the situation. I will do all I can to assist, but you'll need the officials working on this."

"Thank you for coming out to help," Meg said. "I didn't want to call anyone else, until you could assist."

Amelia embraced her, then stepped over to Gareth. "I've heard quite the stories about you, Mr. Mandeville. I do hope you will take care with my dear friend." She shook his hand. "And congratulations on your wedding. We find married life positively inspirational," she said, then looked to her husband.

"Positively," he agreed drolly.

She punched him playfully in the arm. "You are terrible."

Meg walked her friends to the front doors. It was wrong to be envious of a friend; Meg recognized that. But she couldn't help herself. She didn't want Amelia denied any of the happiness she'd found with her husband, but Meg longed for the carefree relationship the two of them shared. Despite her longing, she knew she and Gareth would never have that. She would have to learn to be happy with things as they were.

Chapter 22

Meg had said she was handling things well, but seeing a murdered body was too much for a lady to have to handle. Gareth squeezed her hand.

Colin was going to investigate further Meg's claims about Henry. In fact, he was going to visit the director at his home and then report back at the Piddington estate later that evening.

For now, Meg was eager to discuss everything with her father. She was tired, but strong. Stronger than any other woman he'd ever known. His mother had endured a lot, but in the end she'd given up. Gareth had to wonder if Meg would do the same. She'd certainly never given up trying to prove his innocence. Perhaps under the same circumstances, instead of leaving, Meg would be strong. Meg would stay.

It was on the tip of his tongue to tell her that he loved her, but he swallowed it quickly. He let the realization drift through him. He'd known it was coming; hell, he had probably loved her for a while and simply didn't want to admit it. But now was not the time to admit it to her. Not when he doubted very much that she could feel the same way. Not after the careless way in which he'd treated her.

After the day she'd had, he didn't want her feeling guilty for not being able to reciprocate his love. He'd been selfish throughout too much of their relationship; he would not ask her for her heart; she'd already sacrificed enough on his behalf. He wanted so much to comfort her, smooth her hair, and whisper of his love, but it would not bring any solace to her.

Meg immediately headed for her father's study when they entered the house. Gareth stayed close behind her.

Her father was standing at the window, leaning on his cane.

"Papa," she said.

He turned and smiled. "Hello there."

"We have much to tell you. You should sit down."

He looked at Gareth, and Gareth nodded in agreement, so he hobbled to a chair and sat.

"I'm sitting, now tell me what is the matter. You seem most agitated."

Gareth was prepared to tell him everything on the off chance that Meg could not do it. But he didn't anticipate that happening. In a situation where most women would have fainted and wept, Meg had taken control and stayed strong.

"Mr. Munden has been murdered. In your office, Papa." She turned to face Gareth, so he came and stood behind her. "Gareth and I found him this morning.

Oh, it was dreadful. Shot to death, right in the factory." She didn't wait for her father to have a reaction or to ask questions; she just kept talking.

"We sent someone for Amelia and Colin since I knew Colin would know exactly what to do with the situation. He said we did the right thing in keeping people out of the room, so he was able to look for evidence. But while we were waiting for them to arrive, I waited in the storeroom downstairs. The same one that Gareth and I were locked in." She recounted the same story she'd told Gareth earlier about Henry's question the day she compromised them.

Then abruptly she was done talking and she stared openly at her father, waiting for his response.

He said nothing for several moments. Then he took a deep breath. "Are you saying that you believe Henry killed Mr. Munden?"

"Yes, Papa, I'm certain of it."

"It doesn't make any sense. Why would he do these things?"

"We don't know," Gareth said. "But we did discover something earlier while investigating Munden. We were trying to link him to the stolen candy boxes and we broke into his residence to try to find some evidence of that."

Piddington snorted. "You and my daughter broke into the man's residence?" He shook his head. "I do believe I gave you far too much freedom, Meggie."

"Yes, we did. But it was something we really needed to do," Meg said defiantly.

"In any case, we found no evidence of him stealing the boxes. But we did find an anonymous note and we found ledger sheets. Sheets removed from your ledger book. Munden was pilfering funds and then removing the evidence. Apparently Sanders must have discovered this and used it as leverage. I'm still not certain why he wanted to put the crimes off on me though."

Piddington nodded. "I knew about those funds. I didn't know who was taking them. I assumed it was Sanders himself. I thought he might have gotten himself into some trouble since he has a fondness for expensive clothes and didn't want to ask for extra money. I gave him a raise, but the money still disappeared."

"You knew and you didn't say anything?" Meg asked.

He released a large breath. "Yes, clearly an error on my part. But I never imagined Henry would go to such lengths." He rubbed the back of his neck. "It is rather fortunate that I had a new will drawn up this morning with my solicitor. Henry would likely have destroyed my confectionery once it became a public company, but this morning I changed that and gave it to the two of you."

They were all seated in her father's study when Colin arrived.

"I do apologize for my tardiness. I waited at Mr. Sanders's residence for several hours to no avail. I'm afraid he's left town," Colin said.

"Thank you, Colin, for everything," Meg said.

"Should we expect to hear from him?" Piddington asked.

"It's hard to say for certain. If he's afraid, then he's probably left town or is hiding until this situation disappears. If he's angry, though, then you might very well hear from him. For the next few days, I would advise that you stay home and call the authorities should you suspect anything. That includes you, Meg," he added.

She nodded.

"I have posted a man outside the house, for protection. More than likely he's left town. Cowards generally do that sort of thing. I apologize I couldn't be more helpful. Meg knows how to get in touch with me if you need anything else." Colin stood to leave. "I'll check back at Mr. Sanders's residence in the morning and let you know if I discover anything new.

"I can't believe the factory is to be ours," Meg said as she snuggled into the sheets.

Gareth fell into the bed beside her. "It is a strange turn of events," he said. He still couldn't believe that the entirety of Piddington Confectionery would be his. It didn't seem right. It seemed right that it belong to Meg, she wanted it, but him, he had barely worked there for four months.

"Now you *must* stop working on the factory floor. That would simply be unheard of," she said.

He bent his arms and laid his head in his hands. "I'm not going to do that. It's your money. Your father's money."

"You are my husband. This would have happened had I been born a boy. No one would have questioned that. This is no different. I am an heiress and that makes you an equal heir. Would you not share your wealth with me?"

"I don't have any wealth, Meg."

"But you would share with me what you have," she said.

"Yes, I would."

She sat up and faced him. "You're not your father, you know."

He looked at her, but said nothing. How did she know he was worried about that? He'd never said anything to indicate he wondered how long until he had the same drives that his father had. He already knew that once the money came to them, he'd have to have a solicitor set up accounts and give them allowances. He didn't want to be in charge of it. Didn't want to risk having all that money at his fingertips.

"I know you worry about that," she continued. "Worry that if you don't labor your days away that you'll end up as he did. But it won't happen."

He licked his lips. "You don't know that."

"Of course I do. I know enough about you to know that you don't have it in you—"

"To do what? Be selfish? Wasteful? We all have that in us, Meg. We only need the right circumstances to bring it out. I'm not willing to take that risk. I might take one of those management positions at the factory, but until that time, I'm going to continue working."

"But you're a viscount," she said.

"And you're a woman, but you want to work. The title means nothing to me. Being born with a certain name or amount of money doesn't mean that I'm above laboring like the rest of the citizens in this city."

He rolled over on his side. "Look at men like Henry and my father. They probably didn't start out wanting what they hadn't earned, but at some point they began to believe that they deserved more than was justified, and it led them to make destructive decisions. I don't ever want to assume I deserve something when I don't."

Most of all, he didn't ever want to assume that he deserved her. He was a selfish bastard, he knew that, but he wanted so much for her to love him. He wanted to know what it was like to be loved by Meg.

But he'd never ask her to make such a sacrifice as to give him her heart. After all, what had he ever done to deserve it? He'd deceived her. Put her in the unenviable position of the wife of an impoverished viscount. He'd brought her nothing but trouble. As much as it would destroy him, he wouldn't blame her if she walked out. For the first time in his life he understood why his mother had left. Love simply wasn't enough, and he and Meg didn't even have that.

Chapter 23

The following morning they received word that Colin had still been unable to locate Henry. It was Sunday and Henry should have been home since work was not required that day.

"Where could he have gone?" Meg asked.

"Perhaps he is staying out of sight until he feels it is safe to make a new life for himself," her father said. "I still have a hard time believing he could kill someone. He was so mild mannered."

Gareth took a bite of his egg, and added nothing to the conversation.

"It is driving me mad. He deserves to be punished, but more than anything I wish to know why he locked us in that storeroom. I still can't put those pieces together," Meg said.

A footman entered the room and handed her father an envelope. "This just came for your, sir."

"Thank you." He cracked open the wax seal and read the note aloud. " 'If I am not to have it, then no one will.' "

"What does that mean?" Meg asked.

But Gareth was already on his feet and heading out the door.

Meg stood. "What is it?"

"The factory," her father said numbly.

"He's going to do something to it," Gareth said, then left the room.

Meg followed. "Why would he send a note?"

"To get attention," he yelled. Then he sprinted down the front steps of Piddington Hall and down the driveway toward the factory.

Meg picked up her skirts and chased after him. It didn't take long before she felt a pinch in her left side, but she ignored it and kept running. Every step, she felt twigs and pebbles press against the tender soles of her feet. It didn't seem as if she'd ever make it there. Down the hill and then to the main factory door. Gareth already stood inside.

"What do you suppose he's going to do?" Meg asked. Her breath was labored and her heart was beating so quickly, she had to put her hand to her chest to hold it in.

"I don't know."

There was no sign of Henry anywhere on the factory floor. Meg ran to the storeroom—no sign of him there either. Then they ran into the downstairs office, the room where she and Gareth had spent so much time working on the chocolate boxes.

They found Henry there pouring lamp oil all over the table and the floor. The slippery liquid lent an eerie sheen to the wood planks.

Meg became sharply aware that they had nothing with them to restrain him, no weapon of any sort to negotiate with him.

Gareth held his arm up behind him. "Meg," he said evenly. "Get out of here. Go call for the fire brigade."

"You're too late!" Henry yelled. "This oil"—he held up the bottle—"it's all over everything. Upstairs, all over your father's office. All over the storeroom, the machines, the floor, the supplies. Everything. One little flame and all of this"—he motioned around him—"will be gone."

Meg knew what they needed to do was stall him. Distract him until they could think of something else. Perhaps her papa would have enough foresight to call for the authorities.

"You won," she said.

"Meg, leave now," Gareth said.

She took a step to stand in front of Gareth. Her husband instinctively put his arm around her waist and pulled her against him.

He leaned down by her ear. "Please, Meg," he said. "I don't think I can save you from this."

She closed her eyes briefly, but said nothing to Gareth. "You won, Henry," she said. Her voice was shakier than she would have liked. She gave a false laugh. "You are far more clever than all of us. We didn't even realize you were the one until yesterday when we found Munden's body."

Henry laughed. "I am clever. More than you could even pretend to be. You were lucky." He pointed a match at them. "Both of you. I'll admit, you frustrated my efforts on more than one occasion. But I figured out a way to win nonetheless."

"One thing I'm still unclear about though," Meg said. She squeezed Gareth's hand.

"What is that?"

"Why? Why did you do all of this. Why compromise us and then try to set Gareth up as a thief?"

Henry snarled. "That was not supposed to happen. It was supposed to be us." He pointed at her. "You and I. We were supposed to be the ones locked in the storeroom. I knew your father had sent you to the factory to retrieve his ledger book. I paid someone to lock us in there so that we would have to marry. That way I knew I would get the factory." He looked around him. "And all of this would be mine. Rightfully so since I built this place."

Meg bit her tongue. He'd done nothing more than organize paperwork as far as she was concerned. This factory was a product of her father's hard work. His ingenuity.

"But you weren't here," she said. "That night in the storeroom, you were never here."

"No. The bloody carriage broke a wheel on my way here and I was stalled. But that fool that I hired saw you go in the room and slammed the door. So that foiled my plans. That's when I came up with the idea of stealing the chocolate boxes. If I could make Gareth out to be a criminal, then when you were compromised with him, you would be forced to see another way out to save your reputation. I knew the lowly Irishman wouldn't do the honorable thing. So I would be able to sweep in and gallantly offer to do so."

"But that didn't work out either, did it?" Gareth asked. "By the time you were able to do that, she turned you down."

Henry glared at him.

"Do you want to know something ironic, Sanders?" Gareth asked. "Up until yesterday, upon Piddington's death, this factory would have been yours to administer."

"What the hell are you talking about?" Sanders asked.

"Piddington's will," Gareth said. "The business was to become a company with you in charge. The factory would have been yours."

Henry looked from Gareth's face to Meg's face, searching for confirmation. Then without warning, he dropped the candle, and flames engulfed his body. He screamed and ran toward them.

"Move!" Gareth yelled at Meg.

They ran out of the office and Gareth pulled the door closed in an attempt to block the flames from the rest of the area.

She ran toward the main door, then stopped and headed for the stairs to her father's office.

"What are you doing?" Gareth asked.

"My mother's photograph. It's the only one we have of her."

"I'll get it. You go. Outside. Gather as much water as you can. Find a way to call for the fire brigade. With any luck we'll be able to save the rest of the factory, but I think we'll lose this building." Before he let her go, he pulled her tightly to him and kissed her. "Go. I'll meet you outside."

Wood cracked and fire began to climb up the walls surrounding the downstairs office.

Gareth headed for the stairs. Tears sprang to her eyes as she ran toward the front door. She had sent her husband up a flight of stairs while the room below him was engulfed in flames. He'd climbed the stairs as quickly as he could, while holding his shirt up to cover his nose and mouth.

Once outside the full impact of her foolishness hit her. The picture didn't matter. She loved her mother, but nothing was worth as much as Gareth's life. He could be killed. Her heart beat rapidly. She didn't know what she'd do without him. She wasn't ready to lose him. She wasn't finished yet. Wasn't finished learning things about him. Wasn't finished loving him.

And now she'd sent him off to his death. The sun beat down brightly and all around her seemed like any other day. She turned back to face the building, so certain she'd never see him again.

"Meggie, what has happened?" her father's voice asked from behind her.

She turned and fled into his arms. "A fire. Gareth is still in there. I sent him for Mama's picture, Papa. I sent him in there." She buried her face in her hands.

"Gareth is a strong man, do not fret. He'll be safe. Stay out here. I've already sent for the police and the fire brigade." He headed for the factory door.

"Where are you going?" she asked.

"To retrieve your husband. All will be well, Meggie. Be strong, my child."

She stood on the grass for what seemed hours. No tears, no words, merely utter certainty that both men in her life would never return. Both men that she loved. The realization hit her so quickly, she nearly cried out. Her hand flew to her mouth.

Smoke was billowing out of the windows of the factory in angry puffs. And embers were flying out of the right side of the building. She wiped her hands on her dress for what must have been the hundredth time. Wondering what she should do, what she could have done differently. One silly decision and she'd lost everything she held dear.

She almost didn't notice the factory door opening and her father coming out with Gareth's limp body slung over his shoulder. Not an easy feat no matter the size of her father.

"Is he . . . ?" She couldn't bring herself to say the words.

Her father laid her husband on the ground and she sat down and pulled Gareth to her so that his head nestled in her lap.

Her tears slid down her cheeks and landed on his forehead. She felt his neck and wrists and found a pulse, but it was faint. He was breathing, barely, but he would not wake up. She shook him, screaming his name, but no response.

Then she pounded on his chest, pleading with him to wake up, but no response. She leaned over him and cradled his face.

"Please," she whispered.

Her father stepped up to her and handed her a shirt drenched in water. "Pour some in his mouth and wipe his face with this," he said. He coughed violently. "I'll be all right," he assured her.

She squeezed the shirt over his mouth and a few drops slid in, but mostly they poured down his chin. She did that a few more times before wiping the cool, wet fabric across his smudged skin.

It was so unfair that the moment she realized she loved him he'd be taken away from her. The very thing she'd been most afraid of, and here it was, in her lap. She'd fallen in love with him, and now she was going to lose him. The pain threatened to tear her heart in half. And that wasn't even the worst part, she realized, no, the worst was that she'd never gotten to tell him. Tell him all the wonderful things about him that made her love him. And now she never would. He'd die in her arms before she could tell him anything.

"I love you," she whispered into his hair. She smoothed kisses on his head and wiped the blackness off his face. "I love you," she said again. "Oh, Gareth, don't leave me. Not now. I'm not finished with you!" she screamed.

Then he sputtered and coughed and she leaned him up. She squeezed more water onto his lips. "I'm not finished with you yet either," he said, his voice hoarse and dry.

She laughed and hugged him closely to her breast. "I'm so sorry I sent you in there. That was so selfish. So foolish. That picture, it's not worth losing you. I held on to my mama so long, so afraid to ever hurt the way I did when I lost her. And in doing so, I nearly killed you. I nearly took the life of the man I love. I love you."

"I love you too."

"Do you really?" she asked.

"Oh yes. I've known for quite some time now." He coughed. "I didn't want to ask you to love me in return. I had already taken too much of you."

Laughter and tears came together then and she held his head close to her, kissing him all over his face. "I was so afraid I'd lost you. So afraid I'd never be able to tell you how I feel. I can't believe I only realized it today. But it has been there. I don't know for how long, but it's been there awhile. Loving you, and I didn't even realize." She shook her head. "I won't waste one single day."

He sat himself up and reached into his pocket. Then he pulled out the photograph of her mother. The frame was bent and black fogged the glass, but he wiped it on his pants leg and handed it to her. "I can deny you nothing," he said.

"Then I shall be careful in what I ask of you." She vaguely noticed that the authorities had arrived and already the fire brigade had begun spraying water at the building. "My papa," she said, then turned to find him.

He stood speaking to one policeman. He wore no shirt and his face was smudged, but aside from that he seemed stable.

"He saved me," Gareth said.

"Yes, he did. Carried you out on his shoulders. I've never seen anything like it. I always knew he was strong, but you're nearly as tall as he. And his leg is not fully healed."

"Help me up," Gareth said.

She did as he instructed, and together they walked to her father's side.

"I believe this is yours, sir," Gareth said and handed the photograph to him.

Her father's eyes sparkled with tears. "You shouldn't have gone for it."

"Papa, it's my fault. I sent him back for it. I know how much you miss her and the thought of losing this last bit, I couldn't bear it. But it nearly got both of you killed. I'm so sorry."

"Meggie, you did what you thought was right. No

one can think straight under these circumstances. Loving her was the greatest thing I've ever done. And to know you have found that . . ." He put his hand over his heart. "That is the greatest gift." He shook Gareth's hand firmly, then embraced his daughter. "Enjoy every day."

Loving Gareth as she did put her heart in extreme danger, but it was worth the risk. Almost losing him today confirmed that. Loving him for even one day made the risk worth it.

As if hearing her thoughts, Gareth pulled her into his arms. "I love you," he said.

"And I you, my dear husband."

Epilogue

"**W**e solemnly swear to unravel mysteries by ferreting out secrets at all costs," they all said in unison.

"Now then, I believe we all agree that our attempts to entice the Jack of Hearts have thus far been futile. We must step up our efforts if we are to snare the thief," Willow said.

"Agreed," Meg said. It was so nice to be back to the regular aspects of life. The plans to rebuild the part of the factory lost in the fire were in full force. Gareth, her father, and she were working hand in hand on every decision. Now that the mystery of the stolen boxes had been solved, she could focus her sleuthing attention back on the Jack of Hearts.

"I must interject something first," Amelia said. "It is simply too scrumptious to keep to myself."

"Amelia, honestly, it wasn't—"

But Amelia did not let her finish. "Willow met Detective Sterling last evening. We had a dinner and invited both." She closed her eyes and a full smile appeared. "But neither Colin nor I expected quite the show those two put on."

Charlotte laughed heartily.

"You did not tell him you were the one sending him the letters, did you?" Meg asked.

Willow pursed her lips. "I could not help myself with all the boasting of his skills. He is despicable," she muttered.

"Oh, I would have paid great money to have seen that," Charlotte said.

"Indeed. It was not a night I will easily forget," Amelia said.

"Nor I," Willow said in disgust.

Meg laughed. One thing was for certain. No matter what life brought, adventure was never too far off. And the Ladies' Amateur Sleuth Society was expert at detecting it. Solving the mysteries was grand entertainment and excitement at every turn. But she never would have expected that love would be the greatest of all her adventures.

Next month, don't miss these exciting new love stories only from Avon Books

A Duke of Her Own by Lorraine Heath

An Avon Romantic Treasure

The Duke of Hawkhurst is proud—and really rather, well, poor! To save his estate, Hawkhurst finds an American heiress to marry and hires Lady Louisa Wentworth to teach his betrothed about London society. Trouble is, Louisa is in love with the duke and now Hawkhurst has to make a big decision—before it's too late.

Finding Your Mojo by Stephanie Bond

An Avon Contemporary Romance

Gloria Dalton is beginning to regret her plan to move to Mojo, Louisiana. The town's residents definitely don't want her around. And to make matters worse, she runs into her first love, Zane Riley. Zane doesn't recognize the person Gloria has become, and she's determined to keep it that way. But the best laid plans . . .

The Earl of Her Dreams by Anne Mallory

An Avon Romance

After her father's death, Kate Simon disguises herself as a boy and hides at an inn on the way to London. Of course, she hadn't anticipated sharing her room with Christian Black, Earl of Canley. When circumstances force the two to join forces to uncover a killer, they both discover more than they ever dreamed.

Too Great a Temptation by Alexandra Benedict

An Avon Romance

Damian Westmore, the "Duke of Rogues," has more than earned his nickname. But when tragedy strikes, Damian abandons his carefree lifestyle to seek vengeance. He never expected to encounter Mirabelle Hawkins, the one woman who could thwart his plans . . . and heal his heart.

Visit www.AuthorTracker.com for exclusive information on your favorite HarperCollins authors.

REL 1006

Available wherever books are sold or please call 1-800-331-3761 to order.

 **AVON TRADE...** because every great bag
deserves a great book!

0-06-113423-6
$12.95 ($16.95 Can.)

0-06-075592-X
$12.95 ($16.95 Can.)

0-06-078668-X
$14.95 ($19.50 Can.)

0-06-089930-1
$12.95 ($16.95 Can.)

0-06-077311-1
$12.95 ($16.95 Can.)

0-06-087340-X
$12.95 ($16.95 Can.)

Visit www.AuthorTracker.com for exclusive
information on your favorite HarperCollins authors.

Available wherever books are sold, or call 1-800-331-3761 to order.

ATP 1006